BEAUTIFULLY
WRECKED

TRISHA MADLEY

CONTENTS

1

HARLOW

I've been working at Rae's Bar for almost two months, and I still feel like the owner has it out for me. He barely talks to me; he won't let me work long shifts, especially night shifts alone. I'm not asking for busy nights but on a Tuesday evening, I'd like to get all the tips, not split them with Mindy.

He's so infuriatingly annoying. Jake Rae. My boss. A pain in my ass. So why the hell do I love seeing him every day even though I'm in a relationship!

Eighties rom coms have ruined me. Like that scene in *Dirty Dancing* when Baby first sees Johnny. He takes his sunglasses off and it's like the world stops at his dangerous vibes and bad boy persona. That's the feeling I got when I first saw Jake Rae. He looks nothing like Johnny Castle but his longish dark hair that sometimes hangs over his dark brown intense eyes invokes the same feeling I imagine Baby had when she saw Johnny.

Ugh. Damn eighties movie night with my mom.

It took me a few weeks to get in the groove of waitressing, but now I actually know what I'm doing. It's not my dream job, but it isn't a bad one either. I wait and clean tables, chat with the customers, and sometimes make drinks. All in a day's work at Rae's Bar.

Callie, my best friend, helped me to get hired. We had worked together at the local hair salon. Because of recent events, I needed to add a second job. My college courses will be starting soon. The class curriculum will be increasingly harder. I don't have time for two jobs in my schedule. So... I quit my receptionist and sometimes shampoo girl job yesterday. I make more money at the bar, plus it fits in with my school schedule. It's the obvious choice.

Today I need to do two things I've been avoiding. The first is to ask Jake for more hours and the second is to tell my parents that I'm working at Rae's Bar. I can't hide the truth any longer or under this sweatshirt.

My father is going to kill me. I have somehow managed to keep the news of his little princess waiting tables at the local dive bar.

My background is different from Callie and Jake. I live in a different part of town than they do. I still live with my parents in a gated community, attend the local college for early childhood education, and have been with my high school boyfriend for almost four years.

When I get the nerve to tell my parents that I'm spending my time with blue collar workers, street drag racers, and of course, the regulars who drink their weight in beer, I hope they will understand but I'm expecting the worst reaction possible from them.

Sure, there have been some handsy drinkers and inappropriate comments, but I can handle myself. I appreciate that Jake has always been quick to squash it or throw them out of the bar.

Speaking of Jake, he's staring straight at me from the back entrance door of the bar while I sit in my car contemplating my life. His dark hair falls over his dark brooding penetrating eyes. His intense stare makes me want to jump out of the car to ask him what he's thinking. Part of me wants to run away; the other part is fighting to jump into his arms.

We've had such a weird and sometimes awkward relationship. He doesn't have conversations with me. Although, it seems as if he's always watching me. Not in a creepy way, but in a way that makes every inch of my body aware of him. Maybe it's more protective or something.

The few times we've hung out outside of work, we've had Callie or some of his friends are always with us. He somehow or another got stuck with me. It's not like he ever wanted to hang out with me. I couldn't explain to my parents why a strange guy who wasn't my boyfriend, Declan, was taking me home so he usually just dropped me off at the bar parking lot. Our conversations consisted of small talk. But I know there is so much more underlying than he lets on. I'm sure of it.

I'm not quite sure what to make of it. It doesn't matter though. I've got more than enough problems to keep my brain occupied.

Jake gets easily agitated with me the few times I've called off, so by coming clean with my parents, I won't have to lie. I've had to call off several times due to my parents needing me home for certain events or I just couldn't manage to come up with a reason why I'm working when the salon is closed. It somehow has been easier to lie to Jake about Declan than to tell him the truth. Would he understand that I couldn't work because I had to go to the Lake Haven Country Club Gala with my parents?

I've also managed to keep the bar patrons from telling my parents. Although, I know that my parents would never interact with the people who visit Rae's. It's not their scene.

My time is running out. I need to get up the nerve to tell them, all of them. So, I've decided to come clean later tonight.

Maybe.

I open the car door, slinging my purse strap over my shoulder.

He exhales a puff of smoke, then he tosses his cigarette butt to the ground with a flick of his wrist.

"Why are you just sitting in your car? Everything all right?" his glare is unrelenting.

Closing my door, huffing out a breath of air. I trudge up to him.

"I'm good. Just taking a few minutes before I'm fed to the wolves. How's the new menu coming along?"

"Good. Got a few more days, then we'll be ready."

I walk past him into the bar as he holds the door to the back entrance alley for me. He's quiet, as usual. The smell of cigarette smoke mixed with leather almost halts my steps. Instead, I continue into the bar.

Rae's Bar is nothing special but at the same time, it represents everything special about this town.

It was owned by Jake's family, specifically by his grandparents. He took over for his grandmother. I've heard it hasn't changed much since he's taken it over. Well, I guess until now. He's decided to add food to the menu and update the kitchen. Rae's has only served beer and liquor but he's trying to revamp the town's only bar. He's also been building a stage and looking for a band to play regularly.

Once inside, I pass through the hallway that has bathrooms on the right and at the end is Jake's office. I walk past the closed door, straight into the kitchen. Mark gives me a smile while chopping some vegetables.

I give him a quick wave with an added hello. Jake is no longer behind me, the door shuts. He must already be locked away in his office.

I make my way out to the bar, and flip on the twinkle lights above the bar mirror accentuating the liquor bottles. I set my purse on the shelf and drape my apron around my waist, clock in on the register, and begin counting my drawer.

"I didn't think you'd make it this early. I thought you'd still be at the salon," Mindy says, tossing her long blond hair over one shoulder.

She has been working here for at least three years. Divorced and a cougar if I've ever seen one. Mindy is probably in her forties, She's gorgeous. Blond hair, on point makeup, and built like a twenty-year-old. Boobs that would make Pamela Anderson jealous. Let's just say, most guys and even the ladies aren't complaining about the view.

"I've changed my schedule around." Even though I quit, I just want to keep that to myself for now. Mindy gets territorial over her work hours. She's got two teenage boys and no husband to help support her. She likes to make sure to remind me at least twice a shift.

Last week she made the comment, "Why do I even need to work when mommy and daddy Layne pay for everything?"

She has no idea that things aren't as perfect as they appear.

I continue with my opening shift duties of cleaning tables, gathering, and rolling silverware. Quietly going about my business.

The bar is dimly lit, with original dark hardwood floors that when you first walk into the entry, before the Rae's opens, your footsteps echo throughout the space. The bar top itself is made of an oak that was used from a tree that was struck by lightning on his grandparents' property. When Callie told me that story, my heart melted.

The bar stools are dark red leather and in fairly new condition. There are high top tables and regular round tables scattered throughout the room. The newest addition was the stage. Jake and Van worked to finish it last week. Jake has three bands already lined up.

Callie walks through the front door. Her shoulder length blond hair is curly today. She smiles brightly when she sees me. "There's my girl. It sucked being at the salon without you today." She comes over and wraps me up in a hug like she hasn't seen me in years. "I missed you."

"It's only been one day and I'm right here," I toss back. Hoping Mindy didn't pay attention; I peek over my shoulder. She's nowhere to be found.

"I know, but old Mrs. Magee didn't like the color that her hair turned out even though she picked a God forsaken color that I told her would wash her features out. I mean black doesn't look good with her pale skin tone. But what do I know?" She throws up her hands for added drama.

Callie is unlike anyone I've ever known. She's feisty, opinionated, loyal, funny— I could go on and on. We almost lost her in a car accident and then she was almost kidnapped. It was a crazy chain of events but thankfully she is healthy and happy. Her boyfriend, Ben and his daughter, have a lot to do with her happiness now.

She is also the only person besides Declan who knows my secret. She has ordered me on several occasions that I need to come clean with everyone.

Easier said than done.

"I think Mindy hates me. She keeps rolling her eyes or shooting me death glares," I tell Callie, while casually trying to peak over my shoulder to make sure she doesn't hear.

"You're doing fine. It's because you're new, she has to give you a hard time. Plus, you're cute and a threat to her tips. It's like shampooing Mildred's hair. She has a special way she likes it to be washed, and since you were new, she had to complain every time you touched her head. Now, she loves it when you shampoo her. Either way Mindy will love you with time."

It's like she's judging every step I take. I know she's thinking that I don't belong here. Her side eye glances, and her snide comments make her opinion of me clear. I just have to save some money. I don't really have a plan, but I know I can't live at my parent's house forever. I know they would support me financially, but it shouldn't be that way. I'm getting my teaching degree and living on my own.

Callie breaks into my thoughts. "It's about to get busy. I'm not in the mood for drunk frat boys tonight. They're like this thong that's riding up my ass. Seriously, why do we torture ourselves with these apparatuses?"

I laughed. She does it for Ben. The love of her life. They had a rough road, but they made it through. I hope that Declan and I can do the same.

I pick up the rack of glasses. Callie gives me a knowing look, "How about I do that right now?"

A pang of annoyance sets in. "I'm not disabled," I say it a little too harshly.

Callie rolls her eyes, "I know that, but you are six, almost seven months pregnant," she says in a whisper, so no one will hear her.

At least, she won't spill my secret.

"You can't wear that sweatshirt forever. Jake will expect you to wear the new t-shirts he ordered. And let me just say, it won't cover that baby bump you got going on."

"I know. I've got to tell Jake," I huff out a breath. "And then the world."

She pats my shoulder, giving me the silent support I need. It's nice having her unwavering love and support.

Thankfully, my first table of the night are my friends; Van, Emerson, and Ben. Everyone welcomed me into their friend group with open arms. I don't hang out with them often, but when I do – I feel like I belong.

"Working with Callie at two jobs must be torture? How do you stand it?" Van asks. His dark hair falls over his deep blue eyes. Between Van's gorgeous face and Ben who is equally handsome but blond, these are some lucky ladies.

"Careful, she's my girl. Only I can say stuff like that." Ben chimes in, while Callie joins us, taking a seat on Ben's lap.

"Stop it," I tap Van's shoulder. "Callie has been a life saver in so many ways," I tell them. I honestly don't know what I'd do without her. She seems to be the only person I can count on right now.

"I know you're still in school, but are you looking into any preschools or daycares?" The stunning brunette asks. I freeze. How did she find out?

"Excuse me?" It's all I can muster. Did she find out?

"For a job so when you graduate, you'll need experience. That'll be a great place to gain experience," she explains.

A huge puff of air escapes my lips. For a job, not childcare for the baby. Finding my voice, I answer, "Of course." I swallowed my heart that was just in my throat. "The daylight hours won't work with my schedule. I've had to quit the salon recently. So," I shrug, "this is going to be it for me for a little while."

Emerson is literally the prettiest woman I've ever seen. Dark hair and dressed to kill. She makes me want to put on a suit and heels and kick some corporate ass.

"That's great, you've got a plan. Once you have your degree, you can do anything." Van leans down, kissing her on the top of the head. As if she's said the most important thing in the world.

Hopefully, my plan isn't to raise a child on my own. Declan isn't exactly excited or supportive. Unfortunately, I don't think our child will be his first priority. And that scares the shit out of me.

Jake comes from the kitchen doors that are behind Van. He doesn't even look at me, and sits down next to Ben as if I don't exist.

"Go ahead and wait on the table I just seated. I think these guys will be good for a while." He tells me, while Emerson gives me a reassuring smile.

I restrain myself from saluting him. It would be nice to let him know what an asshole he was being.

As I walk away, I hear Van saying, "Dude, be a little nicer to her."

I don't think he was mean; he's just avoiding me. Every time I get near him, he leaves or decides I need to do something else other than what I'm doing.

2

HARLOW

Table nine sucks.

They are rude and rowdy college boys. Mindy fills up some shot glasses for me. Once I carry them over on my tray, I lean over to serve them the shots.

A hand covers my arm as I set down the glass. I immediately jolt back, removing my arm from his grasp.

"Sorry. I didn't mean to make you upset." His boyish grin makes me pause. "I hate that my friends are so drunk and are trying to rile you up. They are just trying to get me a date with you." He seems as if he's around my age and has a friendly smile.

Showing his bright white teeth. He seems sincere enough. He isn't the typical customer who frequents Rae's with his polo shirt and khakis. His light hair, parted to the side and his sun-tanned skin tone seem more like he belongs at the country club. Regardless, there is no way I'm going out with anyone. There is also the small fact that there is a tiny human growing inside me. There is no way I am willing to have that conversation with a complete stranger who wants in my pants.

"You can tell them to leave you alone; I have a boyfriend. He's the quarterback for Poland University."

His eyes widen. Oh shit. Why did I just tell him that?

"Wait! You're dating Declan Mercer. He's awesome! Why the hell are you working in a shithole like this? You should be at the big frat party tonight."

"We've all got to make a living, don't we?" I shrug, trying to act casually. "If you'll excuse me, I will take your food order now."

"Just keep the whiskey flowing." The guy with light brown hair says from beside him.

When I make my way back over to Jake's table, he looks pissed. Eyes are narrowed in on the table of jerks. "Did they say something to you?"

"No, they just asked if I was dating anyone?"

"Aren't you?" His voice is tense and takes me by surprise. Is he mad at me?

"Yes, Declan and I are still together. He'll be home next weekend if you'd like to meet him." I say sweetly, trying to defuse his weird attitude. But even after the words leave the air, I don't like how they sound. I don't like discussing Declan with him.

"I don't want to meet him," he grumbles. "In fact, the way you call off to be with him all the time, you'd think he didn't want you working here." His attitude is off the charts.

For the life of me, I can't figure out why he thinks it's any of his business. I'd like to tell him I haven't seen Declan for weeks. I've lied about the reasons I've called off so much. It won't do anyone any good. He might think less of me. Although, I'm not sure if that's possible.

"I'm working here because I need a job. You happen to have hired me, so here I am." I want to courtesy for extra emphasis but instead nod. No need to poke the bear.

He rolls his eyes at me as if he can't contain his emotion then abruptly gets up and leaves. I don't watch where he goes.

"I wonder what his problem is?" Emerson adds.

Van kisses the top of her head lovingly. "I can relate," he whispers to her, but I don't think anyone heard him but me.

I excuse myself, feeling very uncomfortable and confused.

The frat boys have now doubled, and I've been running back and forth to the bar like a crazy person. These jackasses better leave me a good tip.

Jake has been helping Mindy behind the bar but hasn't offered to help me deliver to the other tables. Fine. He's ignoring me, again.

As he makes the drinks for the ladies at table one, I try not to watch the way his hands work like he's making art. The ice falls from his hands into the glass; he pours the perfect amount of alcohol. Whiskey. Then he shoots some cola into the glass from the soda gun. His masculine fingers twist the delicate lemon, sliding it along the rim of the glass. I'm getting hot. Like really flushed. How can watching his hands turn me on?

Damn pregnancy hormones. I've been a horny mess for the last few weeks. Declan hasn't been around to relieve my tension. Not that he ever has. Naive me didn't think you could get pregnant without having an orgasm. I'm so stupid.

My phone vibrates in my pocket. Declan's name flashes on the screen. "Hey." I answer. Speaking of the non-orgasm giver. See, this is not like me.

I wouldn't normally have taken the call, but we've been playing phone tag for two days.

"Babe! God is it good to hear your voice. We just finished practicing. I was a monster on the field. We are definitely going to win next week's game against the Tigers. What are you up to?" he barely takes a breath in between words.

"Working at the bar." He would have known this if he had called me last night.

"I thought we discussed this; I don't want you to work there. All I need is for one of my friends to see you." he says, his voice growing angry.

"So, what if they do?" It's not like his friends care about what I do. They are too busy following him around.

"You have more class than to work at a job like that. Do you realize a bunch of race car junkies own that bar? They're losers. Your dad's going to sue the shit out of them for making their debutant use her dainty hands." he chuckles.

My stomach drops at his gross comment.

"Quit being such an ass," I snap.

"Fine. I was just joking," he scoffs. "You're not as much fun pregnant. Seriously, they are not going to make this easy on you."

"I can make a lot of money here. It's not bad at all. Callie is working tonight, and her brother is working. I'm good. You don't have to worry. He's treating me...fine." He's tolerable and odd, but so far has been a good boss.

He doesn't make me carry anything heavy, makes sure I eat on my break, and tells me to keep a drink behind the bar if I need it. See, he's following all my doctor's orders without knowing my situation.

"We're talking about Jake Rae, right?" he asks, as if he has no idea what I'm talking about.

"Yeah. Why?" He never pays attention to what I'm saying. Frustrated, I listen as he rambles.

"I've told you about his reputation. He does illegal street racing. He's been arrested a few times. He's the race master for most of the races and gets all the hoodlums together for some underground racing." He growls, "How many fucking times do I need to tell you this is a bad idea?"

What the heck is underground racing? And why is he being so forceful toward me? He didn't even get upset when I told him we were pregnant. That wasn't a good conversation either, but he seems more passionate about this whole Rae's Bar issue than us having a baby.

"I'm not quitting. I have to save up some money before..." I pause, not wanting to say the words out loud. "And besides this is the only place that can work with my schedule. You know this."

"I told you we'd figure this out. I wish you would have done what I wanted." He huffs. "I'm all for your body, your choice, but what about me? I'm going to the NFL. Sometimes I wish you would have listened to me early in this pregnancy."

My stomach drops. We've had this conversation many times. The day I told him I was pregnant was the worst.

"Declan, the test is positive."

"No. It can't be. Aren't you on the pill?"

"I am but my period is late, and this says I'm pregnant." I shoved the test at him.

"Take it again. This can't be right."

"I took five of them. It's right. They all said we are pregnant."

He yanks it from my hand, throwing it to the ground. Stepping on it. Like that is going to make it disappear or something.

"I'm not doing anything other than carrying this baby. We can do this together. I know we can." I pleaded with him, my heart breaking knowing that he doesn't want this baby.

"If you keep it, you have to take care of it. I'm not doing anything. Do you hear me? Nothing."

The memory is as clear as if it happened yesterday. I love Declan, but can I still love him if his first reaction was to not have the baby?

After many arguments, he has now assured me he wants to be a father to this baby. He wants to marry me someday when he gets in to the NFL. Sometimes he'll talk of how great being a dad to a boy will be, other times he doesn't even want to talk about the baby at all. It shouldn't have to be this hard to convince the person you love to become part of your life.

Declan pulls me from my thoughts, "Did you hear me? I don't want you to work there. I'll have my dad send you some money every month. He can foot the bill for a while. He's on your side with all of this. You know, my dad thinks this can help his image."

"How will this help; it can only make him look bad. His son knocked up his high school sweetheart," I realize what I just said. Glancing at the closest table next to me of ladies who seem to be engrossed in their own conversation, no one seems to be paying any attention to me.

He huffs, "You know nothing about publicity. He'll look like a hero. Swooping in to take care of his precious grandchild because his son is pursuing his dreams and the girl can't afford the baby all by herself. Damn, people will eat that shit up."

Nausea takes over my body. Not because I've got a tiny human growing inside me, but because its father is being a hateful jerk.

"I have to go. My order just came up." I don't give him a chance to say anything. I don't know what to say. How could I have gotten myself into this mess? How could I have ever thought he would be ready to be a father? Every time we talk about this baby, it becomes more and more clear, I should be on my own.

Callie comes over, touching my shoulder. "You good?"

"Yeah, just Declan calling to say hi." I lie, trying to sound happy to hear from him. Glancing to see the jacket in her hand, I ask, "are you leaving already?" I smile, trying to reassure her and maybe me too.

"Yeah. Ben and I have some things to do." She gives me a wink as Ben comes over to kiss her cheek.

"Don't let Jake get to you. He just doesn't want to see the customers treat you inappropriately," he reassures.

"Thanks, Ben. But I can handle myself."

Callie and Ben head for the door while I head to another new table full of college-age boys taking a seat in my section.

Great.

"You did good tonight." Mindy says as she counts the tip money. "We made at least two hundred dollars more because of you. Your cute little ass shaking around this bar might be a good thing." Mindy wiggles her shoulder in a playful manner.

This has to be the nicest compliment she's ever given me. I think.

I can hear Jake clanging bottles around. Probably emphasizing his annoyance with me.

"Thanks. I don't think it has anything to do with me. We all did great."

"Those guys at table eight were here for three hours and kept ordering different drinks just to keep you at the table and watch you shake your ass. How many times did someone ask to put their number in your phone or ask for your digits?" She obviously knows more about this game than I do. And do I shake my ass?

I giggle uncomfortably, knowing that I did get more attention than I'm used to. "I'm already in a relationship," I tell her for the millionth time hoping she'll stop her comments.

Jake slams the door behind him, walking into the kitchen.

"It doesn't matter. You're young. Unless you're married or knocked up, you are fair game. Hell, even that doesn't matter to some guys," she says as she hands me a stack of cash.

"I guess as long as this keeps happening, I'll put up with whatever I have to." I count mostly twenties, totaling two hundred and twenty dollars. I still have a pile of smaller bills to count through.

"Wrap it up girls. I have shit to do. I'll walk you guys out." Jake says as he appears pushing a broom across the room. Mark has already gone for the night.

"Where are you headed, it's like two thirty in the morning?" Mindy asks in a sweet voice, but with a wink in my direction.

"The only place there is to go after a night of work. The shop."

"Ah, of course you are. I thought maybe Kelly or Amber were going to keep you busy tonight." She suggests.

He tilts his head. "Maybe they will." he smirks, aggravating me. I don't even know why.

Mindy yells, "Good for you. Just don't knock them up!" As Jake steps back into the kitchen.

Blushing at her comment. This is the second time she mentioned being knocked up. It's got to be some sort of coincidence. There is no way she could possibly know my secret.

Another invading thought enters my mind. I bite the inside of my lip to stop me from asking Mindy a million questions about Jake's comment. Who are these girls? Does he see two of them at a time? What do they do at the shop? Are they pretty? Oh my God, I need to stop this.

Harlow this is none of your business, I repeat to myself over and over until it's time to go.

3

HARLOW

Jake grabs his leather jacket while I snag my bag. Mindy left a little while ago, murmuring something about her bratty kids. I helped move some chairs around and wiped down the counters before Jake said it was time to quit for the night.

"I'll put on the alarm," he murmurs. When I first started, he warned me that we won't ever be allowed to walk out of here by ourselves. He wants at least two of us to leave together in case something happens. Everyone on closing usually walks out together but not tonight. Now, I'll have to endure the torture of agonizing silence.

For the first time he looks me dead in the eyes. His deep dark eyes feel as if they are trying to see through me. He stares for a moment. It's like he wants to say more, but he turns away. His bizarre behavior is difficult to figure out.

The outside air is cooler than when I started my shift. I wait as Jake sets the alarm. I'm unsure if I should wait or just head over to my car.

The alarm beeps. Jake walks past me without a word.

Okay... I guess I'll see him tomorrow night. My car and a motorcycle are the only vehicles left under the parking lot lights.

Where is his car?

He answers my unspoken question when his leg lifts over the bike, takes the helmet off the seat, and puts it on his head. His slim, strong body straddles the bike as he stands with the machine between his legs. His helmet is angled down as if he's studying something on his motorcycle.

It's as if I'm watching a motorcycle commercial. He's wearing a black leather jacket, black boots that sit on the ground. He unexpectedly makes the bike look small, but somehow, he looks perfect straddling it.

Pulling my eyes away, I stop staring like a crazy person. Open my car door to a Jake-free zone. As I climb in, I throw my purse on the passenger seat. With my keys in hand, I start up my small SUV, only nothing happens.

Absolutely nothing.

It doesn't turn over or light up or anything at all. "Ugh!"

"You've got to be kidding me." I yell, hitting the steering wheel. Hoping by some miracle it will help the car start. "No, no, no!"

Any other time, I'd just call my dad to come help me, but obviously I cannot do that without him finding out I'm working at Rae's. My parents think that I'm babysitting for a family, in one town over, who work the late shift at the hospital. I'd give myself away for sure.

I could try my mom's phone, I'd rather explain the situation to her first, but there is no way my father would let her leave without him. I'm not ready to have him find out about my life and career choices at almost three in the morning.

Shit, what am I going to do?

I look over at the motorcycle that hasn't moved yet. I can't see his face with his helmet on, but his head is angled in my direction. I'm sure he's wearing a what the fuck expression under his it.

I put my head down, concentrating on starting this vehicle by osmosis. I step on the brakes, the gas pedal, hit the steering wheel with the palm of my hand, again. Nothing works.

A knock on my window scares the shit out of me. Damn it! I know who it is.

I press the button to open my window, but nothing happens.

Crap.

I crack my door open so that he can torture me a little longer tonight. The lights glisten off his beautiful dark eyes. His hair is everywhere from pulling off his helmet that he has cradled at his side. A few dark strands hang over his eye.

"You okay?" he asks, in the softest tone I've heard him ever use with me since the day I met him.

"No... I mean yes. Technically. But my car won't start."

"Let me take a look. Pop your hood," he says before I can give him an answer.

It takes me a moment to find that damn button. Pushing the stubborn button a few times before finally the red hood pops open. I really have to learn how to fix a problem like this on my own. Especially now that I'm responsible for another person. I would have had to call my dad no matter what the outcome was.

I get out of my car, while Jake's head is deep under the hood. Once I reach him, he's jiggling all kinds of wires, even has a small wrench in his hand. Where did that come from? I know it didn't magically appear from the engine.

"Sorry to bother you. I know you had plans," I try to sound sincere. A part of me is a little happy I've delayed his visit with Katie or Amber or whatever their names are.

"I think it's the battery, but it could also be the alternator. I won't know until we change the battery. Do you want to call a tow truck or your boyfriend or something?" he stands up, swiping his hand down his jean covered leg. "I'll wait with you until they come," he utters in a soft voice. I didn't know he could talk that way. It made his voice so much… I don't know. Hotter?

It takes me an embarrassingly long time to find my voice. "Umm… I'm not sure. I hate to bug my parents this late at night."

"And the boyfriend?" His expression turns dark, and that usual snarky tone is back.

"The boyfriend is probably into the bottom of a keg of beer by now plus he's over an hour away." I say, giving him too much information.

He grunts. I'm unsure of what that means.

"I'll give you a ride or I can even run to the shop and get you a new battery. I'm sure we have one there." He crosses his arms over his chest.

"Umm… ok, I'll just wait here until you get back."

"No." He states.

"What do you mean, no?"

"I mean. I'm not leaving you here by yourself. You either get on the back of my bike, or we sit here until the tow truck shows up, which if you don't want to pay an arm and a leg for, I suggest you take a ride with me."

"Can't you just let me in to the bar. I can wait in there until you get back."

"No. I'm not leaving you alone in the middle of the night. God knows what you'll get yourself into. I'm not dealing with that tonight." He closes my hood, then leans like a supermodel against my car. Arms crossed across his chest, his sharp jaw pulsing, the lights emphasizing his sparkling eyes.

I suppose he's waiting for some kind of answer.

"I've never ridden on a motorcycle before. I have no idea how to do it."

"I'm not asking you to drive the thing. Just sit still and hold on to my waist," his tone is snarky, annoying and I'm over his attitude toward me.

"I don't know. What if I fall off?" I counter, my tone matching his.

"What do you mean, fall off? You aren't five, you can hold on, can't you?" he says abrasively. "Just sit there like a sack of potatoes. Literally, don't do anything but relax and hold on." He walks over to the ground, picking up his helmet. "Here," he shoves his helmet toward me.

I rip it away from him, placing it on my head. Only, it's huge and covers my eyes.

He laughs. I mean a guttural laugh directed at me.

"You look like one of those dudes with the helmets from the movie Spaceballs." He chuckles. "Let me fix this for you."

He comes dangerously close, so close that I can smell his cologne and cigarette smoke wafting toward me. Normally I would be repulsed by the smell of cigarettes, but coming from him, it awakens something inside of me. Excitement stirs and I can't help but lean closer.

Instead of saying something sexy or smart, I awkwardly say, "You know you shouldn't smoke, it's not healthy?" I can't believe those words stupidly left my mouth. My brain to mouth filter clearly is not working. I sound like his mother. It's surely not the cool and casual personality I'm trying to portray.

He finishes buckling the helmet. "I'm trying to quit. Plus, it depends on my mood. And the night."

Jake climbs on, swinging a long leg over the bike, then tilting the bike straight and upright. Then he kicks the stand back with his foot. "I won't bite. Just climb on. Put your foot on the peg and throw a leg over."

Nerves wreck my stomach. Should I be doing this? There is nothing holding me on this thing. No doors or windows, or seat belts. Is a pregnant woman allowed to ride a motorcycle?

What choice do I have?

I do what he tells me. Following his example, I stand on the foot peg, grab his shoulder, and swing my leg over in the most ungraceful manner. Almost catching my shoe on the leather seat, I squeezed his shoulder, trying to keep myself upright. I manage to find the other foot peg, but not before I feel the bike wobble.

"Christ, it's not a jungle gym," he gripes.

I scoot my butt a little down the seat to adjust myself. I'm very close to him. I don't know how I should hold on. I probably should hold onto his waist, but it might be weird. His presence is doing odd things to me. Like making me unsure of myself. He's hot and cold. Serious then protective.

As the bike rumbles to life, I can feel it in my bones along with something new.

Excitement, danger, and freedom.

"Hands around my waist. Don't fucking let go. And don't fucking adjust yourself like that again. Find a comfortable spot on the seat and stay there. If you do that while we're riding, I'll wreck."

I don't say anything. He scolded me like a child; he doesn't deserve a response.

"It makes the bike move while in motion. If you're moving against the bike, it makes it harder to control. Got it?"

I nodded.

"Harlow? Do you understand?" He asks louder. I grasp he couldn't see me nod. I'm a mess. I don't know if it's being this close to him or that I'm trusting this guy with my life.

Wrapping my arms around his waist is uncomfortable and exhilarating at the same time. The smell of leather invades my nose. I want to move closer and inhale but instead I awkwardly wrap my hand until they meet. His jacket is open, allowing me to feel his hard stomach against my hands.

He starts out slowly, and I hold my breath. As he gains speed, I can't help but let out a scream as we take off down the street.

This is exhilarating. It seems like we pick up speed down the road I've only driven on a million times, but this time it's like I'm seeing it for the first time. Even in the dark night, the trees come alive. The air is cool, crisp, and alive with a cacophony of different smells.

At first, it's the scent of dew-covered grass then moments later, as we pass a farm, cow manure permeates my nostrils. Surprisingly, I don't find it appalling. Houses that I've passed thousands of times seem different. They all seem full of life. The road is magical.

What seems like an entirely too short ride, we pull up to the Bradley Restoration garage. I've been here with Callie before, but I mostly sat in the corner. It's a small town; these guys are older than me and graduated a few years ahead of me. I never had to interact with them until Callie.

It's a huge garage. It's nicer than I originally thought. I pictured a tiny garage full of old cars, rusted car parts, and tools. It's actually clean, spacious, and a newer race car takes center stage. Even though I know it's well past three in the morning, the lights are all on and the party has just started.

We pull up to garage doors. Van and Emerson are here along with some other people I don't recognize.

The bike turns off. Jake says, "Time to get off."

I try to slide off, but it doesn't work. My foot gets caught on something. I can't even imagine what I must look like. Jake yells, "Wait."

He grumbles something while he gets off the bike first. "You're going to kill yourself getting off that way."

Once he's off, the bike tilts and I feel like I'm going to fall again. He tells me to use the pegs to stand up, then put a leg over. It's easier now that he isn't in the way.

"Sorry. I told you I never did this before," I snap back at him. "You should have just left me at the bar. I would have been fine."

"Come on." That is all he says. *Wow, he's one moody bastard.*

"Wait, can you help me get this off?" I point to my head.

He lets out another grunt. This must be his language. He steps close, brushing my chin. He leaves a trail of heat. My body responds in a way I've never felt and can't name. Again—it must be those damn pregnancy hormones.

He pauses, his blue eyes staring into mine almost as if we can't tear our eyes away from each other. Is he feeling something too?

I barely notice that the helmet is removed, but once it is, the current is dissolved.

"There. Come on, we'll get that battery." He heads toward the group.

Emerson greets me first. "What are you doing here? I mean, not that I'm not happy to see you but...you worked all night. "

I smile. "No. It's all right. My car won't start." I point to Jake, "He's going to fix it."

"Oh. You've definitely come to the right place. These boys live and breathe cars."

Being around them at the bar, the conversation usually is about the latest car tune, whatever that means. None of the guys are focused on me. They are too busy looking for a battery in the parts room.

"Oh yes. I'm surprised you don't hang out with us more often," Ems says. Her smile is friendly. I really like her. I'm usually there in the background, staying to myself. Callie is much closer to Emerson than I am. She moved here after she and Van became a couple. Her ex-husband made her life a living hell.

I've only seen the good that my friends have to offer, apparently there is far worse that goes with this group. According to most people in the community, I've heard more bad than good about them. The illegal races. The cops. The drinking. The fights. The groupies. The girls. Ugh.

Emerson smiles. "I'm glad you are now. Let me introduce you to the exciting world of watching men fix cars."

4

JAKE

I can't focus on what the hell I'm supposed to be doing. Harlow is standing to my right, talking to Ems.

Since the moment she walked into the bar, my brain hasn't worked right. Not that it fucking ever has but at least I could function.

I knew it was a horrible idea to hire her. She's going to be the death of me with those green eyes that literally fucking sparkle. She is nothing like the girls I run around with. I am not an honorable guy. I take them out, show them a good time, fuck them, then leave. I'm great at one-night stands.

There have been times when I'd do a few weeks with a girl but then they want the whole boyfriend/girlfriend bullshit and I'm not about to play that game. But something about Harlow having a boyfriend is bugging the shit out of me. No. Bugging is such a stupid word for what I'm really feeling. It's more like I want to take my fist and shove it through this dickhead's face.

I crank on the bolt a little harder than I need to and damn if it doesn't break. Now I'll have to heat up the bolt in order to get the damn thing off.

"Shit." I jump up, taking the wrench with me, slamming it on the workbench. I take deep breath. My nerves are shot. I need a fucking drink. Whiskey is the only thing that can stop these fucking feelings oozing up my throat.

"Umm... do you have any idea what's wrong? I'd like to get home soon." Harlow says quietly behind me.

"No." I snap. Not meaning to, but I'm really frustrated with myself for reacting to her this way.

I'm supposed to be getting a battery for her car but, the one I thought I had isn't worth a shit. So, here I am trying to steal one from Van off his junk of a car, a 1998 Dodge. The battery is so fucking old I doubt it'll work. There is also the little problem that I busted the bolt.

Van must sense me losing my mind because he sets his keys on the bench.

"Take my car. You can drive her home," Van suggests. "I can't believe we don't have the right one here. I kept everything in stock, but somehow, we went through batteries like water."

"I have my bike. I'll just take her home." Seems like the only solution to get me away from her as quickly as possible.

"Have you been drinking? You seem off, man."

"What? No. Just frustrated. I had plans, but now I'm stuck babysitting." As soon as the words are out of my mouth, I see Harlow's eyes drop to her feet.

I'm an asshole. I know it. I'm tired of everyone thinking I have some sort of drinking problem. I stupidly had an incident. No one was hurt and I didn't get arrested. But since then, everyone is on my case. Having to take Harlow home isn't helping my mood. I shouldn't care that I hurt her feelings, right?

"I can just call for a ride. I'm sure I can get someone to pick me up," she says, but somehow, I don't think it's going to be that easy at three in the morning.

"I can take you." Ems offers.

"That'll be great," Harlow says with the most excitement I've heard from her all night. I can't help but notice the tension melting from her expression. "I don't think my parents will appreciate a loud motorcycle pulling up in their driveway."

It doesn't sit right. I don't like how she'd rather have Ems take her home than me. And how the word motorcycle sounds like it's offensive to her.

"I'll take you in Van's old Dodge. I promise it's quiet. You can even say I'm an Uber if it'll make you feel better." I know my tone is shitty. Her face reddens. She's probably pissed she has to ride with me. "I'm sure Van doesn't want Ems to be out this late by herself."

"You're right. I would have taken Harlow, but now you can." Van wraps an arm around Emerson's shoulders.

After we say our goodbyes, I open the car door to the car. It creaks so damn loud. I wonder when he last drove this thing.

Harlow's feet rustle the gravel. I can't help but look up. The lights from the garage cast a shadow over her. I can't see her features clearly and somehow; she looks more beautiful than I've ever seen her before.

Harlow tugs at the door but it won't open. I hit the unlock switch from inside, as she yanks again—nothing happens. A frustrated sigh escapes.

I walk around to help her. I'm met with the fucking smell of cupcakes and coconuts. You have got to be kidding me. Does she want me to take a bite out of her? Because I'm fucking ready to. How did I not notice the way she smells? The only thing I can think of is the motorcycle exhaust overpowered her delicious scent.

"Sorry. It seems stuck." She says quietly, pulling me from my cupcake induced haze.

After tugging hard, taking my frustration out on the older than dirt door, it opens.

"Get in. I don't want your family to worry more than they already have."

Once inside and driving down the road it occurs to me that her family treats her like a baby. She is twenty-two and I swear she is giving off the vibes of a teenager who is about to get grounded.

"What's the address?" I ask, knowing exactly where she lives. The big house is on Halfacre Road.

"Halfacre Road". We're the only house," she says. I play along. I want to ask her a million questions, instead I remain silent that it is almost deafening.

It's about ten more minutes until she speaks again. "Thanks for bringing me home."

"Sure," I tell her in a not a big deal kind of way.

"My parents don't know I'm working for you. So maybe the Uber idea isn't a bad one?"

So, Rae's Bar is her secret? It pisses me off. I hate to be her secret.

"Okay. Yeah, I'll be an Uber driver. Your car broke down, and you didn't want to wake them up. Got it." I can't help the annoyance in my voice. I know she hears it too, because she looks away.

I'm agitated at the way she needs to lie to her parents. She is a grown ass woman. Believe me, there is nothing childish about the beautiful girl in the car with me.

"I really like working at the bar, but my parents are overprotective." I can't look at her without wanting to explode with frustration. I keep my eyes trained on the road. Her soft voice will derail my anger, and I need it right now.

"I've noticed. Are you ever going to tell them? I don't think anyone is going to keep your secret. Mr. Blair is a regular and he works at the post office. He can't keep a secret to save his life. One friendly conversation and your secret is out."

Secret? I'm nobody's fucking secret. The word leaves a taste of poison in my mouth.

"I'm going to tell them. I just want to tell them at the right time."

"Right," I say. Done with this conversation.

We pull up the driveway to her house. It sits on top of a steep hill and overlooks the small town. I wouldn't say it's a mansion; however, it isn't the average house in the area.

The porch lights are on along with at least the entire main floor lit up like they were expecting guests.

"Thanks. I'll see you tomorrow night." She says quietly.

"I'll have a battery for you. I can change it in the morning, and I'll drive it over once it's finished."

"No. I mean you don't need to do that. I'll ask Callie for a ride over. Callie works with me from the salon to the bar. It's nice to have such a similar schedule with her."

Part of me wants to argue because I know Harlow just quit the salon and she's lying to me for some reason. I keep my mouth shut. I don't need to be running around for this chick anyway.

I nod.

She thanks me again and leaves the car. A tall, gray-haired man is waiting at the door. My window is down, and I hear her say, "Uber driver."

He takes a step around her, heading my way. Thankfully, he isn't paying much attention to my face, and I grab a dusty baseball hat from the dash before he reaches the car.

"Here's a tip for your services." I dip my head further down, so he doesn't recognize me. I'm not sure if he knows who I am, but I don't want to cause problems for her.

I nodded. Mr. Layne quickly hands me the money. He doesn't linger or say anything else. I watch him walk toward Harlow who must have been waiting for me to tell her dad her naughty secret.

She is watching me, biting her bottom lip. She says something to her dad as he passes by her into the house. He nods and she mouths to me. "I'm sorry."

I keep my eyes trained on her and when she turns away, with my hand hanging out my window, I let go of the bills in my hand and drive away.

5

HARLOW

Thankfully, my dad bought Jake's suggested story. I can't stop thinking of how shitty it must have made him feel to have five bucks handed to him from my dad.

He didn't seem offended, at least not from what I could tell. I expected to see him flying down the driveway, screeching tires or something to that effect. Jake owns his own bar, my dad handing him a few bucks is insulting to say the least. I'll have to apologize to him tomorrow but right now my parents are interrogating me.

"Instead of calling an Uber, I could have picked you up," Dad offers.

"It's okay. Thanks for waiting for me, but I'm going to head to bed." I give both my parents a kiss goodnight and head up to my room. Thankfully, I'm unscathed for the moment. I'm going to have to come clean because three hundred dollars in tips is a heck of a lot more than I make at the salon and fake babysitting.

As I lay down, the baby moves inside me. Little waves in my stomach. The little flutters are a constant reminder that it's not just me anymore.

This is not how I imagined my pregnancy. I even stupidly thought Declan would be here sharing the nights with me, rubbing my belly, kissing and cuddling with me, talking about what names or color we want to paint the baby's room. At this point, I'm not even sure we'll be living in the same place when the baby is born.

A tear falls down my cheek as I fall asleep.

***

"Good morning, dear." Mom greets me with a kiss on my cheek. Inwardly, I smile at her motherly love. She is an amazing mom, yet sometimes she lives in a dream world—everything will work as it should. She doesn't see the obstacles that are in my path when it comes to Declan or this baby.

She places a plate of waffles and bacon in front of me. I take a seat at the kitchen island. Our kitchen is spacious with a farm chic decor—as my mom likes to call it. White cabinets, cobalt blue tile backsplash, and marble countertops. My mom dabbles in interior design. She has been a schoolteacher forever. She prides herself for a trendy and pristine house. At least that's what she always tells me.

"How is the baby this morning? You had such a late night. I'm glad the Uber driver got you home safe. I worry about something bad happening to you in your condition."

I take a bite of food to control myself from rolling my eyes at her comment. Changing the subject, she asks, "What are your plans for today?"

Contemplating telling her the truth. I hate lying to her. The guilt is eating at me. I owe her the truth. She held me in her arms the day I found out I was pregnant. Reassuring me everything would be all right. Even though that is her usual response to every situation, her words were comforting.

She's owed the truth. I take a deep breath and say, "I got a new job." I release the words like I've blown out a hundred birthday candles.

Her face lights up at my news. Her reddish hair is styled in her short curly bob. Not a hair out of place even though it's the weekend and her routinely scheduled Saturday cleaning day. She's even wearing a nice blouse and leggings just to clean. Her green eyes that match mine are excited at my news.

"Where? I didn't know you were looking."

"Yeah, since the baby is coming soon. I thought another job would help me save some extra cash for when the baby comes. The babysitting for the Millers isn't paying well."

She places her hand over mine on the counter. "Oh honey, you don't need to worry about money. Declan has assured us he's handling the finances. You'll be able to finish school and take care of the baby."

I love her, I really do, but she isn't thinking clearly or maybe she's right, but I just don't feel it in my soul that Declan is ready for this responsibility.

"Mom, I know he'll help, but I want to be able to take care of the baby too. I made three hundred dollars last night."

"At the salon?"

"No. At Rae's Bar. My new job." My voice is shaking more than I want it to, but at least the words are out.

"You are not going to work there another second. Do you hear me?"

Oh, I hear him all right. How could I not hear my dad's voice booming loudly behind me?

"Now Howard, calm down." Her shook expression has now taken on a calm, fake reassuring smile.

"The work schedule will be better for me with school. I only have a few more months left to finish school and stock away some money. I blurt out the words as fast as possible before he can cut me off or yell.

"No daughter of mine is going to work at a bar let alone a bar with the hoodlums that frequent there and don't get me started on *that* Rae boy. You are not safe to be within a foot of him."

I can't help but roll my eyes at him. "I think you're overreacting. He has been nothing but nice to me. He is even fixing my car and brought me home last night."

"He what? Was he an Uber driver I gave money to?" he scoffs rubbing his forehead, almost as if he's trying to get rid of a headache.

"Yes, you gave my boss money for driving me home. Which was embarrassing in itself." Now I'm the one who is frustrated.

"And what's wrong with your car?" I will give him the details. The veins in his forehead have yet to relax. After ten more minutes of convincing him to let Jake replace the battery. He takes a much-needed trip down to his basement man cave.

Once he's gone, it's mom's turn. "You need to go easy on your dad. He's just worried about you. You are going to be a mother soon. You'll understand."

I got up from my chair. Even more aware of my belly than yesterday. Did it grow a ton overnight? Just another thing to add to an already spectacular day.

"Please don't remind me."

Mom frowns, disappointment all over her face. Guilt nagging its ugly head, I try again.

"It's just Declan and I haven't really discussed the financial aspect. I just want to be prepared if things don't work out between us."

"Are you two having problems?" The concern in her voice is evident.

"He is an hour away. He has a lot on his plate. I'm just worried he'll change his mind when the baby comes." She steps in front of me, then wraps her arms around me.

"Darling, I know you didn't plan this, but whether he is here or not, we are. You don't have to do this alone. We can support the both of you just fine."

I step away. "I don't want you to. I mean, I'm sure I'll need some help, but I want to do this on my own. I feel like you've done so much for me, and I've disappointed you and dad by getting myself into a bad situation."

She wraps me in her arms again and kisses the top of my head. "Oh honey. You have not disappointed us. We didn't plan on being grandparents so soon, but we are excited about it. If working at the bar is going to make you feel more prepared, then I'll talk to your dad."

I don't talk to my dad. Mom takes me to campus. I only had one class today, psychology. On my way out of the education building, a familiar red car is glistening in the sunshine in a prime parking spot.

"It can't be." I shake my head, trying to decide whether I'm dreaming or if my car is actually there. Would Jake have driven my car here? How did he know I'd be here?

I step slowly toward my usually trusty SUV. She let me down last night, but she's good as new. Or so it seems.

There is a piece of paper stuck under the wiper blade. Did I get a ticket? Great, he parked it in a professor's spot or with my luck it's probably the deans.

Taking the ripped notebook paper sliver from the wiper, I gently tug it as if it's a bomb ready to explode.

Grumpy Bossman:

New battery.

> **Shift starts at 6.**

> **Don't be late.**

It didn't explode but it sure as hell caused something to stir inside me. Anger. Gratefulness. Annoyance. How dare he order me like that? How dare he be so sweet as to deliver my car to me?

I punch in my door code and climb inside. As soon as I close the door my phone chimes with a text. It's from Jake who I have affectionately labeled Grumpy Bossman in my contacts.

Grumpy Bossman:

> **Key is under seat in the center console in the gum container. Don't be late for work. We will start the full menu tonight.**

Sure enough, the key is sitting in my gum container ruining the three last pieces. I need to concentrate on that and not the fact he brought my car to me and fixed it.

Declan would have told me to call for a tow truck and then went to bed even if he was home from college.

Even though he has now told me twice not to be late in the bossiest text tone, I can't help but feel relieved. He's nothing more than my boss. He knows it just as much as I do. So why can't I wipe the smile off my face?

I pull into the driveway of my house. My dad's Porche Macan is sparkling in front of the garage door. He stands straight up startling me.

I guess we're going to have a conversation.

"Hi Dad," I say in an innocent tone.

"I see your car has been fixed. How much do I owe that Rae boy?" he says, while vigorously drying off the hood of the car with his special drying towel.

Here we go. I'll just play this casually.

"I'm not sure. He delivered it to school. I'm going to head in and grab a bite to eat before my shift," I say it so fast, hoping to not give him time to answer.

"I thought you were going to quit that ridiculous job," he says tersely.

"No. I have to work, and I said before it works best with my school schedule." I let out a breath. "I don't want to fight with you about this. I only have a few months left before this baby comes. I do not want to be broke. After the baby comes, I can get a position at a daycare and then I'll get free childcare."

"You can work at a daycare now." He argues back.

"We've been over this. My schedule doesn't allow it right now. Next semester I won't have to take as many classes. Plus, I need to intern at the local preschool. I have it all under control."

His eyes crinkle but remain trained on me. His glare has yet to falter.

"I don't approve of this. You are an adult even though you are putting yourself in an unnecessary position. Go on inside." He waves with a towel in hand to the direction of the door.

I don't respond. At this point, there is no point. How is he more upset over this job than the fact I'm growing a tiny human inside my body right now?

Once upstairs, I change into my new work shorts. This one has an elastic band. My stomach has popped for sure. My mom picked these up for me when she found out I was pregnant. I've kept them in my drawer, and they've mocked me every day, waiting for me to get the courage or the right amount of discomfort to wear them.

Here I am staring at myself in an oversized Rae's sweatshirt and maternity shorts. I hope and pray those damn new shirts don't come in for another few weeks.

I know I need to tell my boss and coworkers, but I know I can't do it today. Just a few more weeks. I'm worried if Jake finds out he'll fire me. It wouldn't be the worst thing to ever happen, but it would just prove to everyone I can't provide for myself and this baby.

It is brutal tonight. Busy. Hot. And damn hot.

Did I say hot?

I swipe my sweatshirt covered arm over my face. Hoping the sweat doesn't fall into the basket of French fries I'm carrying over to table six.

Mindy has already told me to get rid of the sweatshirt not because she thinks I'm over heating but according to her I'm messing with her tips.

"How are the boys supposed to see the girls through that ugly thing?" she said about five minutes ago.

I wish I could rip this off. I'll go outside and cool down on my break.

"Here you go," I say to Mr. Cobalt.

"Thank you, dear," The sweet gray-haired man tells me. He's a little on the thin and frail side. I'm glad to see he ordered a large portion of fries and a cheeseburger.

"Anything else?"

"Are you all right, honey? You are as bright as this," he says while holding up a ketchup bottle."

"Just a little hot in here." I turn away before he tries to order me to take off this sweatshirt.

Walking back over to the bar, Mindy has a brown box full of black shirts she's rummaging through. She holds one up against her chest. As I get close, I see they say Rae's Bar on them. I can't help noticing how a certain bottom half of the shirts are missing.

Shit. Shit. Shit. It's worse than I thought. At least with the old t-shirts, I could cover up a little, these new one's are a crop top nightmare.

"Harlow, look here. Our tips are going through the roof tonight." She doesn't even care to hide the obvious. The T-shirts might as well say, "Look at my boobs and leave me a big tip."

Thanks a lot, Jake, I mutter to myself. Immediately a mad face emoji enters my mind.

"You're definitely going to rake it in," she shouts, again but then scowls. "You're going to wear them too. You can't tell me the giant sweatshirt isn't hot as hell? Why do you wear them every shift? I know it's getting chillier out but not here."

"I'm fine. Besides I know you fill out the T-shirt better."

"Damn right I do." She tosses the shirt at me. "New uniform. Change in Jake's office."

"Let me finish up. I'll change in a few." I'm one hundred percent lying. I have no intention of showing off this growing baby bump.

After another twenty minutes, I am on fire. I can't take it anymore. Sweat is dripping down my forehead and down my back. I have to step outside.

Not telling Mindy, I walk out the back door to the alley. Cool air encompasses me. Sweet relief washes over me.

I let out a breath. Then inhale. My head swims, dizziness sweeps over me. The dumpster in my line of sight starts to narrow. Jake calls my name. My head spins.

"Harlow!" Jake calls.

"I'm okay. Just hot." I yell at him. My vision blurred. Hoping he'll turn in the other direction. He doesn't.

6

JAKE

She left table nine's order on the line. Their order was there for over ten minutes.

After checking the storage closet, I checked the alley. She only takes a break when I tell her. I didn't tell her to.

There she is hunched over. Starting off into space. I've seen this look before but not on her.

"Harlow!" I call; she wobbles. I react. Stepping into her personal space.

She tells me she's fine. She's pale. Almost grayish.

"Sit down." I hook an empty milk crate that's been used as a stool for as long as I can remember with my foot, sliding it under her.

She lowers, holding her head in her hands. "I'm okay. Give me a minute." Her voice is low, almost a whisper.

"You're overheated. Take off that ridiculous sweatshirt."

She tugs at it, but she doesn't have enough strength. In normal situations there is no way in hell I'd pull a girl's sweatshirt off her without her verbal permission, but I'm pretty sure she'll pass out if I don't.

"Let me help." I tug, luckily, she doesn't fight back.

She leans back against the wall in relief. I trail my eyes over her face and see some color returning. Her red hair is plastered to her face. My fingers itch to brush the strands away but I hold back. Now is not the time to do what I've been wanting to do since the moment I met her.

Her eyes stay closed as she takes some deep breaths. I can't help but notice her plump pink lips or the freckles dotting the bridge of her nose, flashing my eyes closed to reset my brain from concentrating on her beauty.

When they open, they land on the sliver of skin between her shirt and her stomach. Only I know her figure. I've memorized her figure. Slim frame, hourglass hips, round ass. I haven't looked at her closely lately- only because she's been covered up, but I know she wasn't as round as she appears now.

Her belly is... different. Swollen.

She must notice my eyes roaming over her body. Harlow rushes to cover her stomach with her shirt. Looking away, my focus goes to my boots.

She sits up, laying her sweatshirt across her lap. "Thanks. I feel better." Her voice is stronger. Mad even.

"Don't hurry. Wait a few minutes before you try to get up."

"Okay." She thankfully doesn't argue. The brief blink of fire is gone.

Unable to get the picture of her swollen stomach out of my mind, I wonder if she's just gained some weight or is something seriously wrong with her? Does she have a stomach issue and needs medical attention? Is that why she almost passed out?

People usually gain weight quickly when they are pregnant, and she isn't... she can't be. She would have said something. She's too responsible to let this happen. She has plans. Even though we haven't spent a ton of time together, the little bit we have she's told me about school, about teaching, about her boyfriend.

Boyfriend. I take a step away, giving her some space, but also allowing me a moment to get my shit together.

"Do you want me to get you a drink? You still don't look like yourself." It's true, although some of her color has returned, she still looks pale.

She shakes her head no. "I just need to cool down. I thought I was going to pass out for a moment there." She brushes a few strands of hair off her face.

"That's what I thought was going to happen. Do you think maybe you're sick or something?" I want to ask more, but it's none of my business; she's none of my business.

Her forehead wrinkles. "No. I overheated. Just give me a few minutes. I'll be good as new to finish my table."

I huff. "Nice try, but you're done for the night." Bracing myself for what I know is going to be a fire breathing red head.

"Jake. I. Am. Fine. Okay?" She doesn't disappoint. She is a fire breathing red head for sure, living up to her reputation. She's acting like I'm the crazy person for insinuating she should go home and rest.

I pull another crate up beside her and take a seat.

"I get it. But I am still your employer. I don't need an employee to pass out and bash her head on my freshly mopped floor or your blood to stain my floor." Knocking my knee against hers, she smiles a genuine smile for the first time and for the first time since I've stepped outside, I feel... okay.

We are quiet for a moment. Both lost in our own thoughts or at least I am. Anxiety is rushing through every inch of my body. I want to ask her what is really wrong? Is she pregnant or am I a complete moron for even thinking about it? Isn't asking any girl if they're pregnant the worst thing a guy could ask?

Pulling me from my thoughts, she says, "I'm sorry about my dad. It was amazing you fixed my car, brought it to school for me, and the only thing I did was make you an Uber driver." She picks up a small rock from the ground. Playing with it between her fingers.

"I'm sure he didn't realize it was me. It's not like I've got a great rep in this town. Some of my labels are town drunk, drag races those loud cars on our peaceful streets, and revs my motorcycle all hours of the night waking up the whole neighborhood." I stand up, needing to do something other than word vomit every bad thing anyone has ever said about me. If I did that; I'd be stuck in the same spot for a while.

Her green eyes shine under the alley light. "You nailed it." She smiles.

"That must mean you're feeling better. Agreeing with my bad reputation."

"I just have heard it all, but I don't believe you're bad at all. I actually think you're...nice." Her voice squeaks.

God she's cute. She's hot as hell but also just so innocent and pure. Naive even. She has no idea about me. About my past or even what I'm into now. Street racing is in my blood; I live and breathe it. If only she knew about me. I need to step away from this girl now. She has a good life, a happy family, and a decent boyfriend.

"Looks like you're feeling better. If you want to finish your shift, you can. But I suggest you don't wear a sweatshirt. You don't need to get overheated again."

Leaving her alone in the alley, I head back into the bar to cool off.

Once back inside, I head straight for my office. My sanctuary. I slam the door behind me and take the bottle of whiskey out of my drawer. Studying the bottle for a moment, I slip it back into my drawer.

Everything in my body is telling me to take a drink, to quench my anxiety, but the last few times I tried, it didn't end well.

I don't know why this girl gets to me. Bonfire parties at the lake have been my refuge. The only place where I can have fun, not worry about the bar or racing or money. My sister brought that girl into my space.

I've given her rides back to the bar or to the salon. We barely talked. Only small talk. I'm really good at not saying too much. I don't ask questions. I hate questions. I only gave her a ride because Callie asked me to or Callie rode home with Ben. Now my best friend and sister are together, I guess they planned it that way so they could spend some time together. I never planned to spend time with Harlow. But it seems that's all I do. And all I think about.

There's a knock on the door.

"Yeah." Even I know how agitated I sound.

Mark slips his head through the door. "We need you out here, boss. Harlow passed out," he says, rushed.

As I jump out of my chair, panic rises in my throat. I can't get there quickly enough. There is a crowd huddling around her while she's on the cold, hard wooden floor. I push Mindy aside as she stands in the way. "What happened? She was fine a few minutes ago."

"She was fine one moment and the next fell into Mr. Smith's lap. Thank God the old goat was there to catch her," Mindy says with a slight chuckle, clapping her hands together making the motion of her falling.

When I reach Harlow, she's the same pale color as before. Thankfully, her eyes are starting to open. Someone has a cool towel on her forehead.

Mindy says from beside me, "We called an ambulance. They'll be here in a few."

Harlow moans. "I'll be fine."

Her voice is shaky and low. Not believable at all.

Callie is holding her hand. "You need to get checked out. Something could be wrong. It could be..."

Harlow halts her words by trying to get up. But she doesn't get far; she squints, then her eyes close, and moans again.

"I just need a few seconds," Harlow mumbles.

She slings her arm over her face, as if she's trying to hide from us. Her color is even grayer than it was outside. Callie caresses her arm.

My fingers itch to touch her, but I shove them deep into my pockets. I take a few steps back.

"Where is the ambulance? I'll make sure they can get in here easily." I need to get away from here.

"I got it, boss," Mark tells me. Already moving toward the door. Damn it.

Turning back, I scan the scene before me. Searching for her features, but before I even make it to her face, I see a small amount of dark red mixed in with her strawberry blond hair. There is blood in her hair.

I crouch down beside her. My fingers sift through the strands; a hiss escapes her lips. "You must have hit your head."

She nods and grimaces.

Taking the towel, I try to gently pat the blood while inspecting the cut. Thankfully, it doesn't seem too deep. Releasing the towel, more blood seeps through the cut. I place the towel over the cut and apply some pressure to stop the blood.

"I need to call your parents." Callie takes out her phone from her back pocket.

Harlow groans. "Please don't."

Her eyes still don't open. A pang of worry nags at me. Where the fuck is the ambulance? I can't just sit here holding her head.

As if they heard my silent plea, Mindy yells, "Paramedics. Incoming!"

I move back, giving them the space they need, so does Callie letting her go.

They asked what happened and asked for her name. What day is it? Her address? Her phone number? All answered correctly by Harlow. She finally opens her eyes when they shine a light on them.

Good. She's okay. A rush of air releases from inside me knowing she's alert. She looks better. Her green eyes focus on the paramedic. I take another step back, letting them do their thing. But I'll stay until she's safely tucked away in the ambulance and on her way to get checked out.

"Is there a chance you could be pregnant?" The paramedic asks.

Harlow moans and Callie answers, "She's seven months pregnant."

It's like a cement brick falls from the sky and swings into my chest. The wind is knocked out of me at the realization that Harlow is pregnant with Declan's baby.

7

HARLOW

A familiar high-pitched voice can be heard first, followed by a deep rumbling voice. Even though I'm unable to see them, I know exactly who's here to see me, and I'd rather disappear under the covers.

My parents.

"I knew she shouldn't work there. I knew this would happen." His voice vibrates off the cement hospital walls. Dad.

"Would you quit griping? Our baby is in the hospital." My mom responds while her heels clack down the hallway.

Mom appears first; her hand covers her mouth in shock.

"Oh, honey. Are you all right?" She rushes towards my bed. "They said you banged your head." She turns to my father. "Look. Her head is all wrapped up, Harold." She rushes to my side, taking my hand in hers. Then reaches up, tracing over the bandage covering the gash on the top of my head.

"I'm fine, Mom. The doctor said I got overheated and a little bit dehydrated."

"Harlow, that is it! You are not working until after the baby comes. I forbid it! And don't you roll your eyes at me. This is ridiculous. There is no need for you to work and go to school. Your job is this baby and being available for Declan."

Honestly, I don't have the energy for this conversation. My parents are reacting over the top right now. I know they are worried, but so am I. Not because I fainted, but because they expect me to have everyone take care of me. I'm not a damsel in distress or a dainty southern bell.

"Please. I have a headache. I don't want to talk about it. I overheated and didn't drink enough. I'll be better once I finish this bag of liquids. Okay?" Pointing to the bags of fluid above my head on the pole and then tugging on the tubing for emphasis.

"We are just so worried. The baby is fine?" Mom asks. Her voice softens.

"Yes. They checked the heartbeat and did a sonogram. Everything is fine." I set my hand onto hers. A swell of emotion settles over me at the doctor's reassurance from ten minutes before my parents walked in.

"What a relief." She lets out a puff of air.

My nurse comes in and must see the exhaustion on my face. She hasn't been pleasant, in fact, she seems rather irritated, which might be to my advantage. She is wearing Minnie Mouse scrubs which are the complete opposite of her personality. Nurse Joan doesn't exactly radiate the happiest place on earth.

Her dark eyes assess the lines from my IV to my fluid bags. "You need to rest. Are these your parents?"

"Yes. Mr. and Mrs. Harold Layne." My father holds out his hand for her to shake.

She ignores his hand and keeps fiddling with my IV. "Time to go. She needs her rest and for these fluids to hydrate her." Nurse Joan actually shoos my parents out of the room.

And they listen.

Lying back, relief calms my nerves at the notion that Nurse Joan is on my side. At least for a moment.

A few minutes later, the calm and quiet take over and just when I close my eyes, there's a light knocking at my door.

As I open them, a familiar certain leather jacket is visible first, then those damn dark beautiful eyes. Watching me before he says a word, he takes a few steps in without asking.

The small brown bear with a yellow bow around its neck in Jake's hand takes me by surprise. Did the grumpiest person I ever met bring me a teddy bear?

"How are you feeling?" he finally finds his voice. How can it sound so perfect?

"Better." My voice sounds as if I've swallowed a bag of gravel.

"I waited for your parents to leave. I knew they wouldn't recognize me, but I thought I'd give you some privacy with them. I wanted to check on you. I felt bad that you hit your head and all. I wish I had made you go home. Then you wouldn't be here right now. And I should've..."

Raising my hand, which isn't easy since it's attached to an IV, his rambling thankfully stops. "It's fine, Jake. I'm a big girl. It wasn't your fault. It just happened. I'll be more careful next time.

"Next time?" His voice rises. "You are not coming back to work."

"Are you firing me?" I shot back.

"No. But you can't come back to work in your condition. You're pregnant." His voice cracks.

He's standing far enough away from me; he looks as if he comes any closer, he'll catch my pregnancy. His hair is a mess. Maybe from his helmet? He's wearing Rae's T-shirt under his leather jacket, jeans and boots which means he came straight from work. I wonder how long he's been here.

"Yes. I am. I'll be fine by tomorrow. I can still work my next scheduled shift."

His eyes go wide. I can't recall anytime he's looked as shocked as he does now.

"You absolutely are not working your shift tomorrow. You're still in a hospital bed if you haven't noticed. I don't think there is any chance they're releasing you tonight. Are you going to wheel yourself in through the front or back entrance?"

He's as serious as I've ever seen him. No smirk or smile. Poker face.

A smile breaks across my face. "I think the back entrance. I wouldn't want to bring attention or anything."

"You're off the schedule." He grits his teeth together.

Frustrated, I sit up, ready to argue my case when Nurse Joan trots in. "I don't want to kick out the father of the baby, but if he's going to keep arguing with you, he'll have to go. You can give her the bear but then you have to stop the overbearing male crap and let her sleep."

I think both of our mouths fall open.

"I'm not..." He doesn't finish.

"He's not the father." I add. "Just a..." A what? Friend? Boss? "He's just checking on me." Finds its way out of my mouth.

He nods. "I'll let you sleep." As he walks over to me, he places the cutest stuffed teddy bear I've ever seen at the end of my bed. He turns toward the door but turns back to me. "Please take care of yourself and the baby. We'll talk another time about work."

The knots in my stomach ease as he leaves. Maybe he won't fire me after all. Leaning over is not as easy as it used to be, but I still manage to pluck the cutest teddy bear and curl around it as I close my eyes, too tired to think any more.

***

I slept awfully through the night. Between the nurses in and out checking my vitals, worrying about the baby's health because I was so stupid for not taking care of myself, supporting the baby, losing my job, but most of all, thinking about Jake. About that stupid teddy bear I clung to all night. Declan only crossed my mind after I realized he hadn't called to check on me. Even after I had texted him that was in the hospital. He never answered mine or my parents phone call.

Ugh.

Now that I'm home and resting, things are better. Mom and Dad haven't barged in to give me another speech on how careless I was. How things are going to change around here. They are making me feel like a child. I hate it. But maybe they are right. How am I going to support a child on a server wage?

A knock on the door reluctantly gets me out of bed.

"There's my girl." Callie pulls me at arm's length away from her, examining me. "You look much healthier than the last time I saw you. You need to take care of yourself." Yanking me in for another hug. "I do not want to ride in an ambulance with you ever again" Callie's voice is stern, but she still wraps me tightly in her arms. My best friend's hug is like a warm blanket to my nerves.

"I am so glad to see you too." I'm thrilled in fact. It feels as if she's my only ally in this mess I've gotten myself into. She holds up a bag.

"I brought you some donuts and cookies. I know you're supposed to eat healthy for the baby and all that crap, but you need some sugar to keep you vertical not horizontal." She holds up the bag of goodies, giving it a good shake.

"Thank you. You have no idea how much I'm craving donuts right now. How did you know?" Peeking in the bag, my mouth waters. Glazed donuts. A flutter in my belly takes me by surprise.

"You'd talked about glazed donuts at least five times last week. Plus, I love them too. So, you better share at least one of those with me."

She sits at the foot of my bed, and we dig into the bag.

With a mouth full of donuts, she asks, "Where's Declan? I thought he'd be here watching over you."

"I haven't really told him what happened. It's no big deal. I'm fine." Trying to sound like I don't care about Declan supporting me or worrying about me and the baby. My hand finds my belly.

Her blue, perfectly lined eyes widen, and abruptly she stands up, her arms flailing through the air. "Why the hell isn't he here? You passed out cold yesterday, spent the night in the hospital, and he doesn't think it's a good idea to check up on you? To make sure you and the baby are all right. To make sure you didn't break your head open or the precious baby decided to enter the world too soon?" She spins, looking at me.

"Calm down. Nothing bad happened. He hasn't had a minute to call and check in on me... us."

"Excuse me? Her arms flail. "He hasn't had a minute to find out how you're doing. He needs to get his ass here and look after you and the baby." Callie points her finger down to the floor to emphasize her point.

"I appreciate your concern, but everything is fine. Here, see for yourself." Grabbing her hand, I place it over the spot where the baby is now giving me some good kicks. The baby is almost as wound up as Callie is.

Her face softens, lips curling into an o shape. "It's kicking me!" She squeals.

"Yes. It is. It seems to be matching your crazy energy."

"You know you can't name the baby it, right?"

Rubbing my hand over my belly, the hope of knowing the gender of the baby is exciting yet scares me at the same time. It makes the baby real. It makes the responsibility all too real.

"I haven't come up with the perfect name yet." I'm not lying, I have no clue what to name this baby.

"I want to ask you something, but I don't want you pissed at me?"

Wringing my hand together, I brace myself for her question and swallow, "You can ask me anything."

"Why do you stay with Declan? He isn't making you a priority. If I was carrying Ben's child, he'd move heaven and earth to spend every second with me."

Closing my eyes and taking an honest breath, I say, "I don't know."

***

Callie left a few minutes ago. We laid around and watched two rom coms. I grabbed my phone, wondering if there will be a text from Declan anytime soon, but hoping to see one from Jake instead.

Why am I wanting to hear from my boss instead of the love of my life, the father of my unborn child?

A little voice inside me knows the answer – Declan isn't the love of my life.

8

HARLOW

This morning, I wake up feeling refreshed and ready for class. I grab my laptop and backpack from my desk and head downstairs to the firing range where I know my parents are waiting to lock me up in the house, so I can't go to school or work.

Mom is at her usual spot behind the island in our spacious kitchen. She hasn't heard me because she's busy humming along to some tune. Dad is at the table reading the newspaper. They look straight out of some 1950s sitcom. I never really paid attention to how picture perfect we look. I guess I ruined that when I got knocked up.

Might as well keep the facade going. "Good morning."

The corner of dad's paper drops down, and he peers over it. "Heading to class without breakfast?"

"I'm going to grab something there."

I didn't realize my mother is armed with a plate full of pancakes and syrup and oh my word does it smell delicious. I swear she just waved the plate under my nose, and I responded like a dog sniffing it. This baby is hungry.

"Eat and we'll talk about work later. You're just lucky the doctors gave you the okay to go to school today."

Placing my bag on the other chair, ignoring his comment, the plate of pancakes is calling my name. I take a seat and taste the most delicious syrupy buttery goodness I've ever tasted.

Distracted by my taste buds, I barely notice my dad staring at me.

"I hope you don't eat like that in front of Declan. He may find it uncomfortable."

I stop chewing and wipe my mouth. Not interested in his opinion, I keep eating like a Neanderthal. This baby is starting to turn me into a food monster.

"Sorry." I say while swallowing.

"Look, we need to discuss this whole situation at length. Let's discuss it over dinner tomorrow night. Declan will be coming as well, along with his parents. We need to coordinate this situation before it gets completely out of control." My father says, direct as always.

"You talked with Declan?" I ask while swallowing another bite.

"Of course I did. He was very concerned for you and the baby's health."

The baby and my health? He hasn't had the decency to call me, but he's checking in with my father. Why wouldn't he have called me? I left several messages for him. When he called back early this morning, I was in the shower. He left a quick message that said, "Glad you're good. I'll call later. I've got practice."

Doesn't sound like he's interested in me at all?

"Nice of him to check in with you." I idly move my fork around the syrup with a piece of pancake.

"Now stop acting sorry for yourself. The boy has a lot on his mind. It would help if you didn't put yourself into ridiculous situations such as a bar that has you running around like a chicken with your head cut off. That Rae boy is nothing but trouble. A drunk. He can't support himself, let alone anyone else. God knows how that hole in the wall stays open." Silence fills the air as he goes back to looking at his paper.

I can't believe what my father has just said. He sees Declan as some sort of hero and Jake as some kind of loser. When did he become so conceited? When did he become better than a man who owns his own business even if it is a bar?

"I'm not acting sorry for myself. Jake has been nothing but a good boss. It wasn't his fault that I wasn't watching my food intake. Sometimes I forget to eat. I have a lot on my mind. Maybe if Declan wasn't so damn busy with football, I wouldn't have to support this baby all by myself." I shoved the plate away from me, with a sudden loss of appetite, and push myself away from the table. "I'm heading to class. I'll talk to you later."

"Harlow. Please finish your breakfast. Your father just wants what's best for you. Don't leave mad." My mom chimes in and of course, she's backing dad.

"It's fine. I have to go." Pushing my anger down deep, I kiss my mom on the cheek. Not wanting to leave with her upset. She takes my father's side in most situations. I know she means well, but I'm not in the mood to fight with either of them. I'll need all my strength for whatever fight is coming my way tonight with Declan and his parents.

***

I just finished a class where the professor showed us how to manage a child who was not wanting to listen in the classroom. Maybe I could use the newfound knowledge on my father. His listening skills could use some help.

My phone rings as I'm heading to my car. For the first time in days, Declan's name appears.

"How are you feeling?" He asks.

"I'm fine. I wasn't expecting you to call me, since you seem to only communicate with my father."

"Harlow, what's with the attitude?"

"Because you haven't spoken with me and I'm the one who was in the hospital."

"I called you this morning and you didn't answer. You are the one who has to work that stupid job. I told you to quit. And now I'm ordering you to quit. I can't be worried about you while it's football season. This is my big year. Now stop being like this and I'll see you tomorrow night at dinner. I'll be there around seven."

Declan doesn't even let me respond before he hangs up on me.

My stomach churns. He doesn't care about me or my feelings. Declan dismisses every thought I have. And I'm going to be connected to him for the rest of my life.

Just as dread fills my heart, a subtle movement from the inside startles me. My baby. The baby I've been trying to pretend isn't there. The baby that I know is coming but have no idea what to do with it.

I can't even give it to a good father who wants to be a part of its life. How is Declan going to be when it's here, when he can't even be bothered to call me when I'm in the hospital?

His parents are a whole new problem. They're even more wealthy and snobbier than my parents. His father is a Corporate Lawyer, and his mother is in advertising. They work outside of Lake Haven and travel into the city for their jobs.

I could never understand why they chose to raise their family in our small town if they looked down on so many people who live here. Declan said they like it here, but I don't believe it for a minute unless they get some sort of power trip being richer than every other family living here. They've always been nice to me, but as soon as they found out I was pregnant, they haven't been as friendly. Matter of fact, tonight will be the first time in months they have seen me, let alone ask how I'm doing.

I have a shift at the bar in about a half an hour. Callie called this morning and told me not to come in. To rest up. But I've got a baby to save for, so it's time I had a talk with Jake about my job.

9

JAKE

An alarm blasts in my ear. Reaching my arm across the bed, I feel for my phone. By some miracle I find it, the alarm ceases.

Rolling over, I scrub my hands down my face. It's time to get my shit together and open the bar for the night. My phone says it's about five thirty p.m. I slept most of the day away. Which is fine with me.

My body aches and my head throbs from the alcohol consumption last night. I kept telling myself not to drink, but by the end of the night, I couldn't help it. Between the stress of opening the kitchen and hiring a new band, I get caught up in all that needs to be done. The alcohol helps me manage. Plus, the fact Harlow has been on my mind, doesn't help. The good news was I stayed at the bar, away from people.

"Hey, babe." A startling groggy voice comes from beside me.

Shit. Sophie?

Her hand snakes over my chest; remnants of our night together come flashing back. The dancing, the drinking, her clothes falling off and me giving into her viciously seductive curves. As the night went on, all I could think of was that the girl I really wanted is with someone else.

"Do you want me to stick around and help tonight? I make delicious Sangria." She purrs, laying a kiss on my chest. Her long light pink hair tangled in a ball on top of her head tickles my nose. Practically inhaling it.

Yep, she's got to go.

I've known Sophie forever. She races cars too. She's been a friend with benefits for years. I haven't slept with her for a year or so. I hope she isn't going to make this difficult.

Getting out from under her might be like ripping a thorn off a rose. I slowly rolled in the opposite direction of her, easing myself out of bed causing her to flop over.

"Christ, Jake. You really know how to make a girl feel wanted." She shrugs the covers off her, slipping a shirt over her perky tits. "You can really be an asshole."

Easier than I thought.

"Sorry, I'm already running late." Leaning over I place a kiss on her cheek to appease her. Without waiting for a response from her, I head into the shower. It's a dick move leaving her like this, but I'm not in any position for a relationship and she wants one.

Once showered and dressed, the coast is clear. Sophie isn't anywhere to be found. I head down the stairs to my office. Opening the door, there are piles of paper and boxes lying around. Someday I should hire someone to organize it all or maybe it's something I should do.

My head aches and my stomach churns. I'm pissed at myself for giving into the drinking last night. I want to be a better person; this is not how I want to live my life. I have a bar to run. I can't race forever. This is my backup plan.

Racing is more of an adrenaline rush for me. I don't need the acknowledgment or praise I'm the best driver or have the fastest car. The high I get from the rush of being a split second away from losing control of the wheel is why racing is my lifeline. But if the day comes where I find someone, maybe if things don't work between Declan and Harlow, could I be good enough for her?

Trying to tame my thoughts, the papers on my desk become a distraction. After what felt like hours but it was probably ten minutes. A knock on the door takes me away from the piles of paperwork growing on my desk.

Mindy pokes her head in. "Anything I need to know about for tonight? Specials... shit like that?"

Mindy is my favorite employee. She is no nonsense and makes killer drinks. Plus, she looks fucking hot for her age. I mean, she is the definition of MILF. Gorgeous blond hair, bright blue eyes, but she tends to wear a face full of makeup makes her look like a Barbie Doll's mom, but her best feature is what keeps the customers coming back, her tits. It's the truth, and she flaunts them.

Her sons on the other hand, are a pain in my ass. Somedays they fuck with her schedule and leave me hanging. Harlow isn't any better.

Fuck... I'm not even outside my office and her tight little ass creeps in my head. Scrubbing my hands down my face, I let Mindy know I'll be out in a few to explain what I've got planned. She nods but lets me know Sophie is sitting out by the bar looking like she's planning on patronizing Rae's Bar. Double fuck!

"Oh yeah. Looks like you're in for another sleepover," Mindy teases.

No thanks. I don't want her to get attached; however, I could use her help to pour some drinks. Contemplating the thought for a second—nah, not worth the fallout.

After confirming the menu with Mark, I make my way out of the kitchen. Our food supplier came through on time, and the liquor is fully stocked. We're ready to get the night rolling. All that is left to do to get Rae's Bar out of the medieval times is to hire the perfect band.

The DJ works for now, but what we really need is a live band that can engage the crowd and make them not ever want to leave or at the very least return night after night for more.

Once my checklist of daily tasks is complete, the neon red Rae's Bar sign is lit up and ready to serve Lake Haven patrons.

"Hey there." A familiar voice stops me from lifting the last case of beer off the shelf and onto the counter. It doesn't make it. How can it when the voice belongs to Harlow Layne? What the hell is she doing here?

As I rise up to meet her gorgeous green eyes with literal gold flecks sprinkled like God knew exactly where to place them to make her shine brighter than any other person's eyes in the whole world.

She says, "Jake?" she says, bringing me back from whatever stupid thoughts ran through my head.

Shaking my head, I respond, "What the hell are you doing here?"

She frowns, a crinkle in her forehead narrows the shape of her eyes. I feel like shit for putting it there.

"When someone says hello, the proper response is, hi, back to them."

"When that someone just got out of the hospital and who should be at home resting, which is the response she's going to get?" Finally, the box is lifted to where it belongs. "What are you doing here? Last time we talked, I thought I made it clear you needed to stay home." As I speak, my words come out harsher than I mean. The only way to keep her at a distance is being straight with her.

Harlow straightens her shoulders. "And I told you; I'm coming back to work." She shoves a piece of paper in my face, scraping it against my nose. "This is called a medical excuse along with medical approval to continue my duties without limitations." She can barely hide the victory written all over her face.

Is she serious right now? What in the hell makes her think waiting on drunks or carrying heavy trays is healthy for the baby? More importantly, how can I keep her away from me? I already know I can't stop thinking about her when she's gone. How am I going to stay away from her when she's always around?

"I'm about to wipe that smile off your face. You're not working here. Go find yourself another place to work."

"You said we'd talk about this another time, well, the time is now. I'm coming to work. There is absolutely no reason I can't work."

"Except for the fact you can't take the time to keep yourself hydrated. If you can't get yourself a drink, how do you expect to keep my customers hydrated?"

"You're a prick, do you know that?" Her arms cross, and she takes a step toward me. "Now... give me my job back and then I'll apologize for calling you names." The smell of pure innocence and perfection radiates off of her. My eyes close for a split-second savoring the moment. "So?" she prods.

Her words jerk them open.

"No." I cross my arms and walk away to get some control over myself. If she keeps this shit up, I'm going to lock her in my office and not let her out.

Her footsteps sound behind me. She's fucking relentless. A frustrating brat is what she is.

I head for the office and close the door behind me. Before I make it to my chair, the door opens. And she's standing in the door frame looking even madder than before.

"I start my shift in ten minutes. Either you let me work or I'll..."

"You'll what?"

"I don't know. Okay." She deflates, dropping her head down to her chest, then her innocent eyes trap mine. "Jake, I need this job, okay?

My parents want me to stay home day after day, planning the baby's room and the shower. Waiting for Declan to come save me and this baby. But what if he doesn't help me? What if I'm on my own? Maybe I won't be, but I need to prepare myself in case I am all alone." Her eyes swim with unshed tears, ripping at something deep inside me I can't even begin to admit.

"I'm sure you're overreacting. I'm sure he's a decent guy; he'll take care of you both."

"But what if he doesn't? I can't depend on my parents forever. I have to finish school. I'm so close to graduating."

Those words wake something up inside me... hope. Maybe she doesn't want to be with Declan. Squashing it deep down. I don't want the drama of competing for her against someone I'm sure is far better for her than I could ever be. But maybe he isn't as great as I think he is. I really need to find out for myself.

No I don't. I need to stop this. I need to stop caring. Why am I fighting this so badly? It's none of my business if she doesn't get enough rest or water or whatever else she needs. No... she needs to stay Declan's problem, not mine. I'll let her work here. And I'll stay clear of her as much as possible.

"Fine. Come back tomorrow night to work. I have your shift covered for tonight. But if you end up at the hospital, you're done."

Her lips quirk up in a smile but quickly fade into a frown. "What?" My tone is accusatory even though it's the last thing she probably needs to hear from me.

"I have an important dinner meeting tomorrow evening. I'll work now instead."

This might be my only opportunity to win this fight.

"No. I have help tonight. You can come in after or not at all."

"Jake, that's not fair!" she yells at my back as I retreat away from her. Harlow's tone is demanding and loud coming from someone who normally speaks so softly. "I have to be at this dinner. My parents will kill me if I'm not there. Please."

Damn it. She did it again.

Please.

Who says please in a way that makes you want to give them whatever they demand and wrecks something inside of you that you can't even put a name to?

Everything in me doesn't want to look her in the eyes because if I do, I'll cave. But it doesn't matter, this weird pull she has on me overpowers any self-control I possess. When my eyes meet her worried ones, I cave.

"Fine." I point to her "You *will* be on light duty. I'm not budging on that. Just not tonight. We're not busy." My firm tone is rewarded with her bright smile.

Fuck me!

10

HARLOW

"Did you start the grill? They'll be here in about ten minutes," Mom asks Dad as he shuts the glass door out to the patio behind him.

"It's a beautiful evening. The temperature has cooled down to manageable conditions instead of the arm pit of hell that it usually is here in the south," Dad lets us know.

I giggle, but Mom regards him with her usual scolding tone, "Harold!"

"What? It's the truth." He shrugs. "And yes, everything is on schedule."

Mom shakes her head at him. From the outside we look like the perfect family. But I'm the one who ruined the picture. Becoming grandparents at their age was definitely not on their bingo card.

I remember a time when seeing Declan was the highlight of my day, now I'm dreading it. This dinner is going to be miserable. I'm mad at him. The last time we spoke, he wasn't concerned about my health or the baby. I'm not sure what's going on, but something is off between us.

I'm about to start mashing the potatoes, as Declan arrives with his parents. Mr. and Mrs. Mercer walk into the kitchen, the air in the room changes from fun and breezy to rigid and cold, just like their personalities. Declan used to be carefree and funny, but now he's so serious and disconnected.

"Good evening, Mr. and Mrs. Layne," Declan says, as he shakes my dad's hand.

My dad covers his hand over Declan's. "Now, Son, please call me Harold. I bet you're hungry with football practice starting up."

"He is eating us out of the house and home," Mrs. Mercer chirps. "We love when he's at college, we don't have to run to the store as often."

"We have plenty to fill him up." My mom's tone is as bright as the smile on her face.

Mr. Mercer has his eyes on his phone and doesn't seem the least bit interested in my parents or what his wife is saying. He's dressed in a dark suit and matching black tie. His glasses are sliding down his nose as he types away on his phone.

Mrs. Mercer is just as neat with her tailored raspberry suit and white blouse. Her heels click on the tile floor as they enter the dining room.

"Please take a seat. We are so happy to have you over. We are all going to be family now that we have a new baby on the way." My mom says happily, as if this is the best news in the world.

Mr. Mercer, on the other hand, sets down his glasses and phone, bringing everyone's attention to him. "In regard to the child, we need to discuss some items with you. I'll wait once everyone has their plates filled to proceed."

"Oh. All right," Mom nods, then hurries off to bring the rest of the food to the table. Declan obediently helps her along with my father. It's crazy how everyone fell into line at his demand. On the other hand, I'm just standing behind my chair holding on to it so I don't fall over with astonishment. What is he going to say? His son and I are going to be parents. We need good advice, but I'm not sure he's going to say what I want to hear. I'm pretty sure they aren't going to push a watermelon out of their vagina's.

Once the bowls of potatoes, corn, peppers, onions and steak are emptied onto our plates, I wait patiently for Mr. Mercer to speak.

He takes his good, old time. Taking a few bites, the rest of us sit silently chewing. Declan is to my right. He has my hand in his on the table. Mine is excessively sweaty; I have no idea how it isn't slipping free from him.

Declan looks at me with his blue eyes and smiles in reassurance. At least, that's what I am telling myself. I really need his support right now. The baby must feel how tense I am, because it chooses this moment to swim around like a fish in a bowl. My goodness, the flutters in my belly are constant. Placing my hand on my stomach and taking a deep breath seems to calm my anxiety.

Mr. Mercer has salt and pepper hair, slicked back with some type of gel or mousse, and a perfectly shaped mustache. He wipes the corner of his mouth with one of my mother's midnight blue flowered napkins. He places his elbows on the matching tablecloth, commanding the room.

"I want to thank you for having us over for a lovely meal. It is wonderful to know there are still decent families in the world. With that being said, we have found ourselves in a very precarious situation. Our children are no longer children and are in fact going to have a child." He pauses, and I wonder why he's giving a speech to us like we are the press and not two families who are now attached to each other for life.

When his voice registers, he says, "They need to be married before this child comes. They will live with us. When he finishes school at the end of this school year, they will continue to live with us until he is drafted in the NFL, then he should be able to provide a home for them." He pauses while I'm still trying to process his nonsense. "When Declan is at school, Harlow will have the baby in her possession. She can decide to stay at our house or may come home during the day, but we would rather the nights be spent at our house." He pauses, looking directly at me. "I'd rather have my eyes on the baby at all times. Of course, we will have to make sure she can parent by herself before we will release the baby into her care."

Have I entered another dimension or some weird portal? Why is he talking like this?

My gaze finds my father—why is he allowing Mr. Mercer to talk to me this way? Doesn't he want to stop this spectacle? Mr. Mercer spews words, but I'm not comprehending them.

Dad's face starts to redden, just like it did when I mentioned working at the bar.

Turning my attention back to Mr. Mercer, I now know my father is feeling the same rage as I am, and my brain understands his words. "Declan is going to be a professional athlete. A star in the NFL. This child will either show he is an impeccable human being by beating the odds of a young father or it will ruin his reputation and mark him as a loser who got his high school girlfriend knocked up and made the biggest mistake of his life for some..."Harold Layne's chair scrapes against the wooden floor while his hand slams down on our mahogany dining room table. "She needs to stay here with the baby. And I will not have you speaking about my daughter like this or referring to my grandchild as some sort of mistake."

The air escapes my lungs. This is the first time he's referred to this baby as his grandchild. Making this baby seem... *real*.

Sitting up straighter as pride rises in my chest for the man, I've known all my life. His hard shell must be cracking, showing he is human after all.

"I am just speaking the truth," Mr. Mercer says, his tone as cold as ice.

"There is not one ounce of truth to the nonsense you just spoke of. Your son is just as responsible for putting himself in this position as my daughter. We can't change what happened, but we can support these two as they raise our grandchild."

I risk a glance at my mother who has her napkin covering her mouth, frozen in astonishment.

"Please don't raise your voice to me. I'm only looking out for my child's future. We have to make sure they're responsible enough not to leave the child in a car on their way into a store or remember to feed it."

Declan squeezes my hand reminding me he's beside me. I almost forgot about him. He had better say something soon to help this situation before I tug him off his chair.

Declan clears his throat, but it ends there because he puts his head down, looking at the table instead of standing up for us. "Are you serious," I hiss in his direction.

"What?" he shrugs his shoulders, pretty much telling me he wasn't sticking up for any of us. "Say something... please." I whisper; my teeth are practically grinding the enamel off each other.

"There is nothing to say, Harlow." Mr. Mercer points to me. "You two have no idea what you're doing. You've certainly proven that by trapping my son."

My mother gasps from across the table.

This is getting out of hand. Finding my voice, I say, "We don't need your help. I'm perfectly capable of taking care of my own child and so is your son. Right?" I glance directly at Declan who puts his head down.

Up until this moment, I've never realized how much of a coward he is toward his father. And what a pussy he is, he hasn't even once stood up for our child.

"I think we should all take a seat and change the subject," Mrs. Mercer interjects.

"No. We shouldn't. There is nothing to discuss. I am fully capable of taking care of this... child." The word gets caught in my throat. This baby is coming whether I like it or not, so I better start accepting it. "I will not be staying at your house. It is not my home. This is and will be our child's home. Declan can stay with us."

Maybe it's my hormones but something has broken loose inside me and I'm ready to fight for this child. For myself.

"I'm not living here." Declan finally speaks, and of course he only sticks up for himself.

"That's fine. I don't need you to live here. I've got it handled." I spit back at him.

"You surely can't support this baby by yourself." Mr. Mercer's voice is even and stern. He's not going to budge on his plan, but neither am I. I'll figure this out myself. There are millions of single mothers out there and it's not like my parents won't help. But I want to do it on my own too, as much as possible.

"Whether you like it or not, this child is Mercer blood. I will not have you tarnish our reputation. We will all get along for all intents and purposes." He turns to my father. "Harold, please. I know I may not have spoken in the best manner this evening. Forgive me." Mr. Mercer's voice softens. "We all have one goal and it's what's best for this child. My emotions have gotten the best of me—of all of us. Please let's just finish our meal and iron out the living arrangements at a later time. If Harlow would like to live here, I am sure you are fully capable of keeping everything in line."

My dad scrubs his hand down his face, taking a moment to respond. "I think you're right. Everyone's emotions are heightened on this topic. We will make sure Harlow, and this baby remain safe and healthy."

"Mr. Mercer is right. We've all said some things maybe we regret." My mother chooses this moment to chime in. Not when I really needed her to stand up for me.

"Like I said, I've got it handled," I say as I throw my napkin on the table. "Declan, can I speak with you in private?"

He groans and reluctantly stands but not before he noisily drops his fork, and it clatters to his plate.

Once we're out in the foyer, and away from prying eyes and ears, I start. "What was all that crap about and why didn't you stick up for us and the baby?"

"What did you want me to say? My dad is an asshole. Okay?" He shrugs. "He isn't going to listen to my opinion. It's all about his reputation and football." He reaches for my hand. "You don't understand. I have to do this. I need to make it to the NFL. I'm so fucking close." He lowers his voice even softer, "I can't fuck up my chance. We'll figure it out. Okay? Just relax. We still have a lot of time to figure this out."

I can see I'm not getting anywhere with anyone tonight. "I'm heading up to rest. Tell everyone goodnight for me?"

Am I a coward for leaving? Yes.

Am I in shock from how everyone reacted this evening? Absolutely.

What am I going to do about it? I have no idea.

11

JAKE

It's almost midnight. The car is tuned and ready to run. I've got the timing perfect, and all the kinks worked out of the motor. It's race time.

I've been working on this motor for two weeks. My little garage behind the bar is filled to the brim with parts. My car barely fits but it gets the job done. Racing is in my blood. I fucking live for it. My friend's race but they race on different streets than I do. Mine are all back roads, windy and very illegal. And I still make a fucking great pay day.

Where Ben and Van adhere to rules, I break them or don't follow them at all. Things have been so crazy, between the bar and Callie's accident, I can finally get back to racing. Word from some of the guys is that fucking douche bag, Trent, just got released from jail. He didn't serve much time and now he thinks he's going to race on my streets. He's afraid of Ben and Van but hasn't had much experience with me. I do things very differently. More than he could even imagine.

Weston James is on my pit crew; he also happens to be the lead singer in a band who's going to be a regular at my bar. He knows a ton about racing and music but like me, our funds are minimal.

Wes has been my ride or die since we were kids. He helps out with Van and Ben's cars when he can, but he prefers to race on the back roads, rolling up on a car and challenging them to a race and winning a boat load of cash from kicking their ass.

"We race soon. I got you lined up with some dude from Sun Valley. He's got a Corvette with a souped-up engine and some nitrous. I think we'll kick his ass," Wes explains.

"Fucking right, we will. I got mine loaded too. Where are we lining up?"

"Down on 8th street. The cops never cruise on that road until about two A.M. As long as we get going soon, we won't have to race them too."

Where the police leave the Carmichael races alone because they draw a crowd and money. The cops do not like our crew. We make our own rules. They make it their mission to look for us and fine us or impound our cars. I've even spent a few nights in jail when my ass was caught.

I jump in my 1998 red Mustang with a white stripe down the middle. God, I love her. We've been through some crazy shit together. I even banged her up pretty good last year, but I finally got her straightened around and tonight she's ready to go.

Wes jumps in the passenger seat, and we take off for 8th street.

"Do you know the guy we're racing?"

"No, some punk from Sun Valley. Just south of here. He has a Corvette. Nothing this old girl can't handle." Wes taps on the dash.

When we reach the 8th street mini mart, we're introduced to Nate and his friend, Zane, who are waiting for us.

"Let's go. One thousand," Nate speaks up. His eyes are glossy, and he looks like he climbed straight out of bed. Fuck, he looks drunk.

"No. Five hundred," I counter. If this fucker is really drunk, I'm not losing my ass to his stupidity.

"Fine. Five it is. I'll take the left lane. Zane's girl, Lana, is going to flag. She'll count to ten and off we fucking go. Are you good with that?" he asks.

"Yep." Nodding. It's not as complicated as some other races. This is the first one to the next stop sign wins. "Wes will manage the stop sign." By managing, I mean, recording the finish line with his phone to make sure the winner doesn't cheat. Zane is on lookout for any random cars that could get in the way. We don't need any wrecks before we get started.

Nate gets in his green piece of shit Corvette. It looks like it's been sitting in some old junk yard for years. Rust sprinkles the dented machine. I hate it when people don't take care of their shit. You have to take care of your equipment. It's the only thing standing between you and eating the road.

We line up. Him in the right lane. Me on the left. His girl is a cute little thing. Wearing nothing but a bathing suit top with small tits, skintight jean shorts, and black knee-high heeled boots. Before I met Harlow, I'd have been thinking about convincing her to ride home with me, but Harlow is the only girl on my mind. I'd give anything for her to see me race tonight. It's not her thing. It's not even in the realm of things she's interested in. She's gone to races with my sister, but I don't even think Harlow knows *this kind* of street racing exists.

The kind that if I tap the side of the other car, I won't get disqualified. Instead, it'll be a punch in the face. There is no such thing as disqualification in this race. If someone cheats, whoever is standing wins. I've been in several fights with someone who is too aggressive or tries to run me off the road. I've even had someone try to run over my flagger to win. All ended with an ass beating from me.

I spot Wes up at the stop sign, phone in hand. Lana steps in between our cars then practically leans her tits into my window. "If you win, I'll go home with you. I'm getting bored with him losing all the time. He has no idea how to shift the car." She drops a little piece of paper on my lap, not before swiping her hand over my pants.

Not wanting her to affect my thoughts, I pull the visor of my helmet down and strangle the steering wheel with my hands. Instead of my mind going to this gorgeous girl, it drifts to what it would be like for Harlow to be sliding her hands over my jeans.

Lana takes her spot between the cars. She raises her arms. My foot hovers over the gas, ready to release the brake, and speed down the slim road that leads to the main highway. My car takes flight; the sound of my engine overrides any other sound on earth. Focusing on the stop sign ahead and the five hundred dollars yearning to jump in my pocket.

The race takes seconds and when it's over, the car next to me is gone. "Fuck!" Did he win? Glancing in my rearview mirror, his green machine is still at the starting line. Lana is right, the fucker can't shift worth a damn.

Wes comes over, handing me the five hundred dollars he kept from Nate as collateral and then handing me my five hundred back. "Nice, man. Although he made it easy for you. Stalled his car."

Wes hops in and we don't stick around for Nate to make excuses or ask for a retry.

***

Back at the bar, Callie and Mindy are cleaning up for the night.

"You know, I should just call this place Callie Rae's. I'm here all the damn time while you're out there playing race car driver. You do have some things you have to do here. I bet if Harlow was working tonight, you would have never left." Callie swoops her hair over her shoulder for emphasis of her smartass remark.

We've talked about Harlow before. When shit went down with Ben, she asked what I would do if Harlow had feelings for me and dumped Declan. I told her I'd do everything in my power to make her happy. I never thought she'd be knocked up by a selfish prick. Now the likelihood of her ever being mine is slim to none.

Raising my hand up to her, I say, "Not tonight, Calle. I just finished a race and made some extra cash. You're not being a buzzkill."

"Well, I'm just calling it like I see it. Now, I'm going home. You can take out the trash."

Once everyone has left, I lock the door, head into my office, but not before I grab a cold beer. Sitting at my desk, the receipts from tonight look good. We were busy. Part of me feels bad about leaving my sister to deal with the chaos of tonight, but she can handle it. After everything she went through with Trent and Jackie, she's the toughest person I know.

Sometimes I wish I could be more like her. She goes after what she wants. I need to make this bar into something this town and my grandma could be proud of. The only plan I've started so far is the menu. It still has a long way to go. My dream is to expand the bar. Double its size. Add huge TV's, state of the art sound systems, and a stage that holds the best damn house band to ever grace this town.

A stage where people from other states come to see. Wes is the guy to make it happen. His talent is beyond anything the small town of Lake Haven has ever seen. He can pick up any instrument, play any song challenge you throw at him. But even more extraordinary are his own songs. The songs he writes and plays for the crowd makes him the key to my big plan becoming reality.

I take a drink from my bottle; a sense of loneliness washes over me. Maybe I should have taken Lana up on her offer. No, that's not true and not what I want at all.

Harlow.

She's what I want.

I worry about her more than I should. Thoughts of our earlier conversation replay. She wants to work and support her kid. It's just like her to not want her parents or Declan to take care of her. She wants to do this on her own, which makes me more attracted to her. Most of the women I've dated are looking for a free ride. They hear I own a bar and are only looking for free drinks and a good time.

I'm nowhere near wealthy or on my way there. Whatever I have goes into the bar or my car. I could never be what Harlow needs. I can barely take care of myself. There is no way I could be there for her, a baby, and give them the life they deserve.

12

HARLOW

"Did you decide on a color for the baby's room? I know you don't want to find out what the gender is, but you can at least look through the color samples I set on your dresser." She pauses, "Also, Declan should be at home in your room, so I was thinking of buying some new furniture to make it a little more masculine. You know, so he'll feel more comfortable."

I don't know why my mom's voice this morning is like a knife scraping across a plate. All she talks about is Declan moving in. My only concern is the baby is healthy and happy. I'm worried about how we can afford this baby and give it every opportunity to thrive. I'm worried I'm going to mess everything up.

"Harlow, are you paying attention to me?" Mom questions.

"Yes. Sorry. I'm a little distracted. Declan will be fine with the room decor." I'm not sure if she can see my eyes roll but there is nothing I can do to stop it. "Just leave the room like it is. He's going to be busy with football anyway."

Mom swipes a towel over the counter. "He is going to have to stay here. The baby will be here, and he can't miss him or her growing up." For the first time, her voice has an edge to it. I can only hope she is starting to get frustrated with his lack of priorities.

"I'm hoping he can juggle football and a baby. I really do need his help." My throat tightens at the thought of doing this alone. We're going to have to depend on each other to get through, and I can't help but shake the feeling he isn't going to be here for us like he keeps reassuring me he is.

Mom pats my shoulder. "Everything will be fine. He'll be able to figure it out. And we will be here for you too." She kisses the top of my head.

***

After her reassurance it doesn't seem to reassure me of anything, I get ready for work. Jake is letting me work, but I bet he'll be on Harlow watch. He already told me I wasn't lifting any trays over one pound. How am I supposed to make any money like that?

When I get to work, Callie hands me an older, bigger sized Rae's T-shirt.

"Here take this. You can hide that bump under this for a little while."

"Gee. Thanks." I can't hide my sarcasm but I am one hundred percent grateful.

"You look good by the way. Are you rested and ready to be fed to the wolves?" Callie teases.

"You know it. Is your brother here? I want to lay down some ground rules about this whole light duty thing."

"I have a feeling you're in for a fight. He's already suggested encasing you in bubble wrap," she quips.

"Oh great, just what I need. Last night was a disaster so he might as well make my week."

Before stopping in his office, I head to the ladies room. This baby is pushing on my bladder like nobody's business. Once I finish and wash my hands, I glance up and notice my hair. My strawberry blond locks are falling out of my ponytail. While putting the strands back in place, the baby kicks. I've felt it move and kick like crazy, but this is the first time it's kicked me hard enough to hurt. My hands fly to my stomach, rubbing against what almost feels like an actual foot.

"Jeez, kiddo. Cut me a break." I plead "It's okay. I still love you." It seems like every day, I'm experiencing something new and starting to be closer to this little human inside me. This little butter ball is growing on me. It takes me a moment to realize the words out of my mouth are actually the truth. This little butter ball is growing inside of me, pulling at my heartstrings. Minute by minute, day by day.

Shaking off my amazement and popping myself back into reality, I open the door – straight into Jake.

"Wow. Where are you going so fast?" His hands wrap around my biceps. His scent washes over me. Soap, mint, and a hint of cigarette smoke. Without warning, he tugs me closer. "You okay?" he asks, and it takes me a moment too long to find my voice.

Stupidly, I glance into his dark brown eyes. They are always so intense as if they are searching for something deep inside my soul or even some type of secret I don't even know exists.

Then he brushes a wisp of hair from my cheek. The tingle from his touch electrifies my pulse.

Looking away or stepping out of his grasp is the only way to break this spell, but I can't make myself move.

He repeats, "Are you okay?"

"Yes," my voice is low but thankfully it worked followed by my limbs as I step out of his grasp. "Umm... yes, the baby is jumping around in there and I had to pee."

I had to pee. *Really?*

He smirks. "I guess you're in the right place."

That makes me smile. Maybe he does have a little bit of a sense of humor.

"I'm glad I ran into you before your shift started. I hired a new server. You'll be training her, and she'll be doing all the heavy lifting." He crosses his arms then frowns.

"Don't give me that look?"

I huff, "What look?" Tilting my head waiting for whatever ridiculous thing he's going to accuse me of.

"You're ready to tell me no with the squinty eye thing you do. That I can't hire someone when I own this damn bar?" His voice rises. I haven't even started giving my opinion yet.

"I wasn't going to say that." It's exactly what I was going to say, but because the last thing I want is for him is to be right, I change direction. Plus, he doesn't get to guess my facial expressions. "I'd love to train her."

His eyes squint, as if he can't comprehend my words. His mouth opens then shuts. He turns away from me, heading toward the bar.

Oh no, he doesn't just get to walk away. My baby must not like it either because it kicks me hard. "Ouch." My hand jumps to my stomach.

His eyes fly to mine. "Harlow?" His voice is laced with worry.

"I'm fine. This little bugger is active today." It bothers me the way he's always noticing my every move. How he's watching me and seems to be dissecting everything I do or say. And yet it makes me feel noticed in a way no one ever has.

"Jake," I start, hands on my hips grounding myself before I lose my temper. Did he just hire someone to carry my trays? "Are you serious right now?"

"Yes. We need help anyway. With the new menu and you not being able to run your ass off, like a normal server. Callie is starting her own salon. We need extra help."

Noticing a movement behind Jake, a cute redhead, sort of my color only a few shades darker and shorter, stands behind him. Wearing more makeup than I could ever have imagined wearing, but she makes it work somehow. And too well. And she's wearing a Rae's T-shirt. The cropped tight T-shirt I can no longer squeeze in to.

She snakes her arm around his neck, her hand landing on his chest right in front of me. Nausea hits my stomach and it's not from the baby. The red head gives me an exaggerated wave and a bubbly, "Hey."

She's tall because her head peaks around his shoulder. Looking down, I need to see if her height is real, and it is. She must be six feet tall. Her hand drops from his chest, and she slides beside him. Jutting out her hand to me. "Hey. I'm Sasha. I just started today. J said you'll be training me. It's amazing to meet you."

J? Is she for real?

"Can I talk to you for a minute?" An unwavering annoyance washes over me. I want answers.

"In my office." He spins, telling her, "Go ahead and find Mindy, she will point you in the right direction."

Sasha kisses his cheek then gives me a wave. My body temperature must rise one hundred degrees. Does she really think she should be kissing her boss on the cheek on her first day of work?

"What?" Jake's raises a brow.

"Huh?" I reply caught off guard. Was I making a face of annoyance or disgust? Probably because I am.

He doesn't answer me, instead he heads into his office without another word. Of course, it irritates the hell out of me. And there is no plausible explanation why? Before I can stop myself, my feet march to their own accord straight into his office.

His back is to me, for some odd reason he slips his shirt over his head and tosses it on his desk. My shoes are glued to the floor. My eyes are locked on his perfectly sculpted shoulders. They are wide and strong and never noticed by me before. All that strength under his basic T-shirts. Those muscles trail down the perfect frame of his back.

Jake quickly slips a red shirt over his head and becomes the meanest person I've ever met by covering the art form of his body. He also left me no time to study the ink on his shoulders.

"What do you need? You can't possibly still want to argue with me." He turns to face me, running his fingers through his dark hair as those stupid loose strands haphazardly fall into perfect position.

"Umm... Yes, I do. I don't need an assistant."

He huffs, "I got you an assistant? You think way too much of yourself. Sasha asked to work tonight. I thought it was a good idea. We have the food menu, and the band is here to set up some of their equipment. If you haven't noticed I've got a lot of shit going on and my world is not consumed by you and your work schedule."

I almost feel like he slapped me in the face. Why did his comments sting so much? It doesn't matter; I'm not going to let his asshole attitude affect me in the slightest.

"Oh, don't worry. Your opinion of me doesn't matter. You don't matter to me." I snap back at him, knowing every word I said was a lie.

He steps into my personal space. Almost nose to nose. He says in a husky voice, "Oh really?"

I swallow. "No." Lies all lies. "Since when do you let your employees kiss you?" I grumble.

He moves closer, igniting flames in my chest. "Jealous?"

Swallowing down the heat, I become mute, no words come to mind.

His jaw ticks, he bites his bottom lip. "That's what I thought."

***

The last half an hour has been so aggravating. Sasha has been by my side all night. Annoying is an understatement. I mean how much can someone flutter their eyelashes or laugh at stupid jokes and say, "Oh cutie, you're just so adorable."

Thankfully, she wanted a potty break, her words not mine. I'm all too happy to comply. Mindy is at the helm of the bar tonight. Callie has already left, and Wes and Jake are setting up some equipment on the stage. It really is starting to look great. They were hanging up a black curtain, and I may have noticed the way Jake's red Rae's T-shirt rode up to reveal his six pack.

"How's Sasha doing?" Mindy asks while filling up a glass with beer from the tap.

"Good." She's a little touchy for my taste but I'll keep that to myself.

"So, let me guess, she's annoying as hell and trying to impress every dick in the room?" Mindy hits the nail on the head with that one all while giving the beer to Jack, a local post office clerk.

"Well, when you put it that way... yeah."

Mindy tosses a rag on the bar and leans over, her iconic boobs almost spilling over her shirt. "Let me tell you a secret, I think he's really worried about you. I think you should take Sasha as a compliment and let her run her ass off and you put your feet up."

I laugh. "You know you are right. I shouldn't see this as a bad thing." I take my water from my hiding spot off the side of the bar. It looks like

Mindy has refilled it and even added more ice. "Thanks for the water. This baby is thirsty."

"Oh, I didn't do that. Jake did. He's been keeping an eye on your water. Haven't you noticed, it's never got less than half full?"

She's right, I guess I've been too busy to pay attention. "I'm guessing he doesn't want me passing out again, causing a fuss, and interrupting his busy night."

Mindy shakes her head, "I don't think it's the reason."

"I'm telling you, he's only worried about his bar and me causing him to lose a night of bar patrons."

But is it true? He hasn't given me any reason to believe that.

13

JAKE

Sasha has single-handedly become the worst employee I've ever hired. How could she have done this? Harlow was on a break for fifteen minutes and in those fifteen minutes, Sasha dumped a tray of beers on Jack's head, spilled ranch dressing on Phil's lap, and worst of all; slipped and bashed her chin on the railing of the bar while she was trying to get water for herself.

"I think you need stitches. You don't want to have a scar on your chin," Harlow says to Sasha. Harlow is holding the towel because Sasha is too busy being a blubbering mess. Mascara is leaking down her cheeks. "Shh... it's okay. I'll take you to get stitches."

"No. I'll take her." No way in hell am I going to let these two go to the hospital together. I haven't been to the hospital in years and between them, I've become a frequent flier.

"Please let Harlow come with us. She's so nice and she kind of reminds me of a big sister. You should really think about making her a manager or something," she says through her whimpers.

"No. She can stay here and close." The last thing that needs to happen is being stuck at the hospital. All I need is for Harlow to pick up the flu or some strange disease.

"I can't. But I'm sure Jake will take good care of you." She narrows her eyes at me. "Won't you Jay?" Her tone laced with annoyance. Oh... she caught that from earlier?

She scoots off the stool, handing the cloth over to Sasha. "I've got a lot of customers to catch up on. Good luck."

I can't help but watch her ass as Harlow struts away from me. My eyes instantly found her. God, I can't stop looking at it. Perfection in every way. Not too small, not too big, just... perfect.

"Jake, are you listening to me? I can't have a scar. Do you think it'll be bad or oh my gosh, will they stick me with needles?"

After three hours of enduring whining, tears, and screaming like a baby, I drive up to the sidewalk paralleling Sasha's apartment. "Thank you for tonight. Do you want to come in? I can thank you for taking care of me tonight."

Absolutely no way in hell do I want to spend another second with her. I thought she was fun and hot, which is great for business, but after tonight – I don't care if I ever talk to her again. "Sash, I don't think waitressing is for you."

"Everyone has an off night."

"Yeah, but you're a hazard to my bar." As the words fly out of my mouth, a slap to my face follows.

Damn. She hits better than she carries a tray.

***

"How's Sasha?" Harlow asks, as she wipes down the bar. Looking down at my watch, it's ten minutes past closing time.

"Fired. I think or maybe she quit by slapping me in the face. Either way, she probably won't be back, and you spent all night worrying about me hiring a sidekick for you for no reason. You want full time, you got it. I'm done fighting with you and my sister."

Turning away from her, I don't wait for an answer. Grabbing the empty beer case, I start filling it with the scattered bottles on the table in front of me.

Harlow moves to my side. The scent of vanilla and maybe something fruity fills the air beside me then she giggles. "I'd say it was a shock, but I'd be lying. She was terrible. I was trying to ignore her mistakes, but when I went on break, all bets were off."

I can't help but smile. "Yeah, it definitely got worse when you weren't covering for her."

"My favorite was the way she called you J. No one calls you J."

"Okay. I get it. She's annoying."

She bumps my shoulder with hers. "Annoying doesn't even cover it. Oh Jay, what was the table number again?" Her hand falls to her chest, emphasizing her ridiculous southern belle accent.

"It was literally table number one, and it was hard to mess up because it is literally the first table." I laugh, setting the box back down and turning my full attention to her. I haven't had such a good laugh in such a long time. It's fucking great to laugh and not be so fucking serious.

"Oh, and my favorite was teaching her the POS system. You've honestly made it so easy for us. There are actual pictures of each item, and she still asked which button to press." She tosses her beautiful long hair over her shoulder. It shines under the bar lights. I want to wrap it around my fist and pull her close to me, press my lips against hers. Feel her mouth on mine.

"Jake, did you hear me?"

"No, sorry. I zoned out." *Fuck me.*

"I was thanking you for filling up my water. I know you wanted to make sure I didn't pass out again and cause your workers' compensation premium to increase."

Oh, far from that. Does she not know I don't want her passing out, bashing her head on the table or floor while she's pregnant because I'd do anything to keep her from feeling an ounce of pain? *Where did that come from?*

I run my hands through my hair. Trying to untangle these crazy thoughts warping my brain.

"You know I have to look out for those premiums; they can be hell to pay."

"Seriously, thanks. I was thirsty and I do have a problem with remembering to eat and drink." She frowns. "I probably shouldn't have admitted that to you." She scoffs, wiping down the table.

Did she not eat tonight? Come to think of it, I didn't see her eat before I left with Sasha. Without asking her, I head to the kitchen. This woman is going to eat and drink and be healthy if it's the last thing I do. Why can't she put herself first? Am I such an asshole boss because she thinks she can't eat or drink at my bar?

Maybe I'll fry her some chicken fingers. Or make her a big fat juicy burger. Would she want cheese on it? Moving around the kitchen, I grab all the makings for a cheeseburger. I toss the meat on the grill. At this moment, I'm really glad I decided to add more items to our menu.

The swinging door opens. Harlow stands in the doorway, arms crossed over her chest, and a spark of confusion on her gorgeous face. "Hey, why did you leave?" she pauses, and I know she's watching me. "You do know we're closed?"

"What do you like on your burger? Ketchup, mustard, please don't tell me mayonnaise. That's just disgusting." Flipping the meat over at this moment will give it the best taste. And I want this to be the best burger she's ever eaten.

"Why are you making me a burger? I never asked for one."

"Did you eat today?"

Her face drops. Guilty as charged.

She uncrosses her arms in defeat. "You don't have to do that. I'll eat when I get home."

"No, you're going to eat right now. Tell me how you want your cheeseburger, or I'll make it the way I like it."

"Go ahead. I want to see what you think a good burger is. Because I happen to know there is only one thing that makes a hamburger perfect." There's a twinkle in her eyes. A spark of fire and wit she doesn't show often.

Harlow leans on the counter with her elbows, testing me.

"There is only one thing that would make this burger better and it is." Opening the refrigerator door, I pull out the metal pan heaped full of my favorite ingredients.

Placing the strips of bacon on the grill beside the burger patty, I glance over to see her reaction. A huge knowing smile spreads across her perfect plump lips. "Bacon. Makes a cheeseburger perfect."

"I knew you didn't eat. You practically are drooling over there. Grab some lettuce and tomato out of the fridge for me, please." For the first time in a long time, she doesn't argue with me when I ask her to do something.

"I think the nausea is finally going away. The doctors said it would only last a few months but I'm almost eight months in."

"That's got to be tough. All of it, not just being sick." I probably shouldn't bring it up, but I can't help wanting to know more... everything. Like does her prick boyfriend care about what she's been going through? She never takes a break to call him and never talks about him.

From my experience with girlfriends, they always check to see what I'm up to at the very least. Maybe she does when she gets home or before she comes to work?

"It is tough. Everyone thinks because my parents are wealthy that everything is a breeze or I should let them pay for everything for the baby but..." She looks up at me, her hazel eyes a mixture of brown, golds, and greens all intermix in the most mesmerizing way to almost send me into a hazed trance.

"Working your ass off until you faint is not going to pay the bills in the end. If I was Declan, I'd be busting my ass so *you* could sit on yours." I tear my eyes off hers and continue opening the package of French fries. "You want cheese on these too?"

"No," she simply states.

Her silence tells me I've overstepped the line.

She moves beside me and opens the fridge door. She rummages around, appearing with vegetables and ranch dressing. Setting them down and grabbing a knife, we prepare a meal side by side in silence. Something about this is almost perfect. The perfect burger. The perfect moment. Maybe a perfect night with her. Except for the awkward silence.

14

HARLOW

He sets the plate in front of me. My taste bud's water. Has Declan ever cooked a meal for me? I've always fixed him a plate or made him dinner but never has anyone other than my mother taken such care to feed me like this. It's so... sweet and even a little... hot. Heat creeps up my skin, and my hormones go on high again. Is my face red?

We haven't said much since his comment about what he'd do if he was my boyfriend. I really don't know how to respond to him. Instead of coming up with conversation, we both eat in silence. Glancing around the kitchen, looking for some inspiration for a topic, I take in the changes he's made.

Jake upgraded the grill and fryer. Spices and oils are lined up by size, and I can't help but notice how he put everything back in its spot. He's a neat and orderly chef, which for some reason surprises me. The kitchen has a modern, clean vibe. Metal counters and sink but I absolutely love the black and white checkered floor.

"What made you want to change the bar?"

He finishes chewing and swipes a paper napkin over his lips. A spot of ketchup is left behind. His tan skin has a shadow of stubble. Some days it's more noticeable than others. I guess it depends on how often he shaves. I have a strong urge to wipe my thumb over it and...

"I know this place can be more than just the local dive bar. My Gran and I talked about it over the years. She had some great ideas and advice. So, I just decided to make some changes for both of us. I don't make any changes without her input, though," he smiles.

He and Callie love their Gran. It's written all over their faces and in their actions. She is a loving and kind person. She makes me wish I had someone in my life inspiring and supportive.

My parents love me, but they treat me like a child. Gran seems to let Callie and Jake be themselves. Which I'm starting to realize I've never been. I've always seemed to do what others expected of me. Trying to live up to the expectations of who they think I should be.

"Well, I think the changes are great. I can't wait to see the band live on stage."

"You and about a hundred other girls. Everyone loves Wes and his bandmates." He rolls his eyes, tossing a fry on the plate in disgust.

"I don't care about that, obviously." Gesturing my head down at my stomach.

"Come on just cause you're pregnant doesn't mean you can't look."

"Are you kidding me, I can't even manage my boyfriend of four years, do you really think I'm looking for another relationship?" But he's not completely off the mark, because every time I'm with Jake, I'm more concerned with what he thinks of me rather than Declan.

"Can I ask you a question?" Jake asks softly.

"Sure, I guess." Shrugging my shoulder purposely so I don't look like I'm bracing myself for impact.

"You just said you've been with Declan for four years, where the fuck is he? I know he's at school but Christ, you're pregnant with his kid." His tone is harsh.

"He's busy with school and football. It's a lot on his plate." I've already told him this.

"The fuck he is. He can't show up for you when you're in the hospital. Nothing, not even a big game is more important than the mother of your child."

"It's really, I don't know. Refreshing? To hear you say that. Everyone including my parents act like his football career is the most important thing in his life, not me or this baby." My hand moves to my stomach.

"I hope you don't get pissed at me for saying this, but Declan is an asshole. In every sense of the word. He doesn't deserve you and your parents are being pretentious jerks worrying about their status instead of their daughter." He doesn't take a breath and in turn eviscerates mine.

"They just want what's best for me." It doesn't seem like it though.

"Do they? Because they shouldn't give two shits about Declan. He can go to hell as far as they should be concerned. You don't need a man to take care of you or the baby." He points to my stomach. "You can do this all on your own."

A tear starts to slide down my cheek. I swipe it away and apologize. I'm not sure why either is happening. Is it because he's telling the truth I so desperately don't want to believe? Because I know Jake is right?

"Oh shit, I didn't mean to make you cry. Forget what I just said. Sometimes I can be too honest." He starts ripping napkins from the dispenser.

I swipe away the tears. "No. It's just that I'm like... I'm the only one in this situation. And to know someone else sees how I feel is just... overwhelming."

He reaches out his hand and quickly retracts it. "I just call it like I see it."

Jake's honesty is more than my hormones can handle at the moment. The baby also is choosing my mental breakdown to do somersaults in my stomach causing my stomach to wave which in turn causes Jake to almost jump out of his chair. His eyebrows shoot up.

"Holy shit, does that hurt? It moved your entire stomach to the other side."

I giggle. "No, it's kind of weird but amazing. Plus, you kind of have no other choice than to get used to it."

"Can I touch it?" I almost fall over.

"You want to touch my stomach?"

"Yeah. It looks pretty cool." His earnest expression takes me by surprise.

I hesitate. Is it odd that he wants to touch my stomach? Declan doesn't even want to touch any part of me, let alone the baby.

"I guess." Jake reaches his hand over, setting it gingerly over my stomach. The baby chooses that very second to kick him, and my body chooses his touch as magic. Tingles race along my stomach. Every inch of my body is aware of his nearness.

"Wow. Did you feel that?" he asks, amazement laced in his words.

"Of course, it's kind of... it was intense."

We both fall silent. Lost in our own thoughts, mine wondering why this man has so much of my attention. Him... I have no idea but he's staring down at my stomach.

"Do you have a name picked out yet?"

"No... honestly, I kind of just call it an... it."

"It?" His eyebrows raise.

"Can you tell I'm in denial? I need to accept that the baby is coming whether I'm ready or not. I could find out the gender but I kind of want to be surprised."

"You should give the baby a nickname instead of calling it.. . it. Maybe..." he glances around the room, for inspiration, maybe?

"French fry or sweet potato." His hand leaves my stomach and immediately I wish he would have left it there a little longer.

"You want to name my baby after food?"

"It's better than *it*." He emphasizes it with air quotes.

"Okay, but can we name it after candy or junk food?"

"I got it, how about jellybean?"

"Jellybean, really?"

"Okay, how about we shorten it to Beanie?"

"Beanie?"

"Yeah, you know it's cute and explains the size. You've got to start off right, even if it's just a nickname. This kid could be the next Einstein."

"You seem to have put a lot of thought into this." I say the name out loud. This baby is going to be smart. I'm going to make sure of it. It'll never need to depend on anyone because it will be, I mean they will be self-sufficient.

"Okay, thanks for feeding me and Beanie tonight."

We fall silent again, but my brain is working overtime. I'm really enjoying my time with him. I've spent time with him, but he's never been this nice to me, or I guess acknowledged me before.

He starts to clean up after his mess. "Are you finished?" I swipe the paper napkin along my mouth. "Yes, it was the best burger I've ever had. Of course, I probably would have eaten a whole cow as hungry as I was."

He leans his elbows on the counter, which in turn makes him especially close to me. So, close I can smell his body wash or cologne or whatever makes him smell delicious. "Promise me, you'll eat. If you don't trust yourself, I'll make sure I feed you every shift."

Why does that sound hot?

"I promise to eat," I say, while biting my lips.

"Good." He nods, turning away from me, giving his attention back to the sink.

Okay, I need a break. Why am I reacting to him like this? Why do I have to keep reminding myself I'm carrying another man's baby? A man who's almost never made my body react this way or in any way to be exact.

Sleep, I need sleep. That has to be the explanation.

"I'm going to head out. Is there anything else I should finish before I go."

He drops the towel on the counter and faces me. "No. But I'm glad we had a little time to talk about you and Beanie."

I can't help but smile. "Yeah. Me too. It's a shame we never really talked much before. I mean, we've been around each other plenty, but we've never really..."

"Talked, I mean really talked." His eyes widened at his confession, clearing his throat. "I mean, I'm not much of a conversationalist."

"Oh, you can talk, you've just never been very nice to me."

"That isn't true," he hesitates. "Okay, it is. You're not as bad as I thought you were."

"Bad?"

"Yeah, you know, judgy. You live on the rich side of town, go to college and belong to the country club. Then there's me, this street racer who runs a bar. Two very different worlds."

"I hope you changed your mind on the theory. I'm a total mess. I got knocked up by my high school boyfriend. I don't know if I can graduate from college, get a job, raise a kid and I'll probably have to live with my parents for the rest of my life because there is no way I can support a child all by myself." The tears come out of nowhere. Like a damn just broke.

"Woah, hold on. Calm down. Me and my big mouth. I'm sorry. See this is why I don't talk to you or anyone for that matter."

He hands me another stack of napkins.

"It's okay. I don't normally act like such a lunatic, but you seem to bring it out in me. I notice that I can talk to you honestly. I only word vomit when I talk to Callie, so it must be because you're related or something." I wipe away the tears from my cheek. "I'm sorry. This is so embarrassing." No, this is mortifying. He's literally got a front row seat to this hot mess express.

"Look, it's not going to be easy but you're stubborn enough, you'll pull it off. You don't want anything handed to you. It's far from what I thought you were like. I admire you for wanting to do this on your own, but it's okay to get some help, especially from Declan. You need to lean on him."

"I wish it were that easy. I don't know if I can trust him to be there for us. He's so wrapped up in his own life. Do you think I should stay with him?"

The question is out of my mouth before I can stop it. But now I've said it, I really want to hear his answer.

15

JAKE

Hell yes, she needs to dump his ass and never look back. But I can't tell her that. Not with those greenish gray eyes wide and scared at what my answer will be. Like whatever I say is straight from the Bible.

"It's your decision."

"What would you do if you were me?"

"I don't know what I'd do if I were you because I'm not ready to pop out a baby, but I can tell you what I'd do if my girl was ready to have my baby. I'd be there for both of them. Plain and simple whether it's for a movie night because her feet hurt from a long day at school or I have to pick up dinner because she deserves a nutritious meal because she's growing a human inside of her. If he doesn't perceive you that way, it's on him. Maybe I'm wrong but it's what I'd do if it was my girl and kid."

Her eyes widen and damn it tears start to trail down her face again. I know pregnancy can make women emotional, but it's worse than I ever thought.

I can't help it now. The urge to pull her into my arms is not because I want to hold her like I've wanted to do since the moment I met her, but because she's hurting and it's the only thing I can think of doing.

She doesn't resist as my arms wrap around her shoulders, bringing her face into my chest. Her scent washes over me. Wrapping me in vanilla and a sweet berry scent I can't name but will never forget.

Vaguely, a warm wet spot registers in my brain. Her tears. She tugs on my shirt, bringing it close to her face as if she's holding onto me for dear life. I hush her, rubbing her back.

"I'm sorry I upset you. I really need to keep my opinions to myself," I say to soothe her.

She sniffles. I hug a little tighter. I know I shouldn't. She's taken. She's not mine, but at this moment I don't care.

She mumbles something into my chest.

"What?" pulling away from her but not letting go.

She releases my shirt, and her touch falls away. "No. No. I'm sorry. I really need to go before I embarrass myself further." She rips herself away from me.

"Wait," I beg.

"No, I've got to go." She grabs her bag, rushing toward the exit.

Harlow is gone before I can say another word.

***

Gran is still awake when I get home, sitting at the kitchen table with her flower covered nightgown and curlers in her hair to complete the nighttime look.

"Awe... did you want to make sure I got home safely?" I ask as sarcastically and sweetly as I can muster.

"No, you ass, I have more important things to do then worry if my adult grandson makes it home. And if you didn't, I'd be worried sick." She smiles and I kiss her cheek. "I'm starting on Callie's wedding favors. You're more than welcome to help."

"Damn, are you already starting that?"

I keep forgetting Callie and Ben are getting married in a few weeks. I'm Ben's best man. And told there are some duties I'm in charge of; the first and most important, a bachelor party.

"Dear, I'm running behind so much. Callie's not worried about anything that has to do with the wedding. She says as long as she and Ben end the day married, it's all she cares about."

"I'd thought she'd be a bridezilla. Surprisingly Callie has been re-laxed about the whole thing."

Gran continues to concentrate, her tongue sticking out as she wrangles the ribbon together, wrapping the ribbon around the mason jar. There have to be at least fifty lined up.

She looks over her glasses. "It's not the big day yet. I'm waiting for Ben to push her buttons. We all know he's the only one who has the *GO* button."

"Yes, he does," I chuckle. "I can't wait to see Anna in her cute dress. It's going to match Callie's dress. I bet she'll be a doll."

"You know who else is a doll?"

"Me?"

She slaps my arm. "No. Harlow. How is that baby of hers growing? Is she feeling better?"

"She's working. Although it's pretty much the last thing she should be doing. If she wasn't so worried about supporting the baby, she could be taking care of herself."

"That's surprising. I know both of those families are more than capable to help her financially."

"She wants to do it on her own. Mercer is a real piece of shit." Gran slaps my arm, probably for the hundredth time in ten minutes. "Sorry. Piece of work."

"It says a lot about her character."

"It says a lot about the people who are supposed to support her too. Everyone seems to have their own opinion of what's best for her, except what she actually wants."

"It's good she's got you on her side, then."

She taps my hand.

"Gran, she's just my employee."

"And Callie and Ben were just friends. I've been around the block or two. I know you like that girl. She seems to know how to press buttons too."

16

HARLOW

"Callie, I look like an elephant. You should just nickname me Dumbo. I'm huge!"

Callie comes up from behind me. With a smile, she says, "You look beautiful and you're about to have a baby in a month. You have to bake a little longer." She leans her face toward my belly and pats it. "Don't you sweet little one?" she coos.

She chose a strapless light pink full-length dress for both Emerson and I. Emerson looks amazing and isn't doing anything to help my confidence. Being pregnant is much harder than I thought. It affects every aspect of my body. From my engorged boobs to my extra wide ankles. It's going to be impossible for me to walk in these shoes.

"Yeah, well it's going to be a beautiful day for you. I can't believe you didn't have the bachelorette party. I was really bummed out, but I understand. Plus, it's not like I can have any fun nowadays."

"We just couldn't squeeze it in between races. After the honeymoon, we're off to Las Vegas for a few months."

"I can't believe he decided to race again. But I guess it's a little different now with a new race team." Ben planned on giving up racing until he was contacted by a prominent team owner. He's a professional racer now, and we couldn't be prouder of him.

"It definitely pays more money and gives us a chance to travel as a family. It's been so much fun. Just like tonight is going to be."

"I'm so happy for you. Ben and Anna are lucky to have you in their life and so am I." Emerson chimes in and pulls us both in for a hug. Tears prick my eyes. I am so emotional that I can barely stand myself. This is going to be a long day.

Callie does look gorgeous. Her long, light blond hair is draped in natural spiral curls. Her makeup is natural perfection with long eyelashes outlining her stunning blue eyes. I can't help but toy with a pang of jealousy. Shouldn't I be thinking of my wedding to Declan? Planning a wedding? I am having a baby after all, but Declan and I don't even discuss it. He hasn't asked, I haven't mentioned it. I keep thinking maybe after the baby is here, we'll have the big conversation, but the more time comes and goes the less it seems to be in the future.

"You, okay?" Callie breaks into my thoughts.

"Of course, just getting a little emotional. Happy for you two. You both found the love of your lives."

"You did too. Declan and now a baby on the way. It doesn't get more exciting than that." Emerson says smiling while my eyes are fighting back tears.

Thankfully Emerson glances down at her phone; she lets us know we have exactly twenty minutes before we need to be at the lake for the wedding.

Emerson and I helped Gran decorate this morning. We didn't do much but followed her directions. Callie wanted everyone to do as little as possible, so she hired a wedding planner who had a whole staff to handle Gran's orders.

Gran barked at them like a Rottweiler. It was entertaining to say the least. The flowers, cake, and food weren't there when we left to get ready, so I can't wait to see what it looks like.

We're in a small tent off to the left of where the ceremony is going to take place. The guy's tent is similar to ours, but on the other side of the aisle. There's also a larger tent to the right where the reception is going to take place. Thankfully, the weather prediction for today is nothing but blue skies.

"Oh, Gran. It's breathtaking. Everything I could ever dream of." The amazement in Callie's voice is unmistakable.

It is the most beautiful scene I could have ever imagined. It's straight out of a movie. I haven't seen it yet so I'm going to try to sneak out and get a peak as soon as I can. I want to give Callie and her Gran some time alone.

Waddling my way over to the aisle, the flowers radiate throughout the air. They're made of every shade of pink you can imagine light to dark and bright to dark. Guests are making their way to the seats.

Chancing a glance over to the guy's tent, I notice Jake and Ben talking. They're outside of the tent, and I can't take my eyes off Jake. He's never worn a tux in my presence and God; does he look incredible. My eyes roam from his dark hair which normally is dangling close to his eyes but is now slicked back and neatly parted into a heart stopping style. Every strand of hair looks as if it were strategically placed. His dark eyes are bright and sparkling in the sun. His lean build handles the black suit like he's ready to walk down the runway. He straightens his bow tie, somewhere my insides melt at his gesture. How can he drive me to be so mad and frustrated, but yet seeing him ready to walk his sister down the aisle has me ready to run into his arms?

He must catch me staring because he smirks and nods in my direction. He mouths something to Ben, and heads in my direction. I want the ground to open me up and swallow me whole.

"Hey. How's the crazy bride doing?" he asks, while adjusting the cuff of his sleeve.

"She's ready to run into Ben's arms and marry him as fast as she can."

"I think he's ready to do the same." His eyes roam over my dress, making me very aware of the fact that I'm as big as a house. His hand rises to his mouth as he clears his throat. Then he surprises me by saying, "You look beautiful."

I can't find my voice, but I can't hide the smile his words invoke. Before I can come up with a response, he walks over to Callie and embraces her in a hug.

Stunned into silence and frozen in place, I watch from a distance as they exchange words. He gives her a dazzling smile, her eyes water in response. From what Callie has told me of their childhood; their mother has put them through so much. From having different part-ners, to Callie losing her biological father in a race accident, to Gran having to raise them. My parents are a bit controlling, but they do love me and want the best for me.

Tears prick at my eyes as Jake and Callie embrace. I don't have any siblings, if I did, I imagine I would want our relationship to be like theirs.

A few moments later, Gran starts to yell for us to get into place. Lining up and shushing us at the same time. "Jake, get over here and escort me to a seat like a proper gentleman."

Ben and Van are standing at the altar as Emerson walks toward them. Everyone is quiet as an instrumental melody plays. It's my turn, I take a deep breath, taking a step toward the guests.

Ben, Emerson, and Van are all glowing as I approach. Ready for the two most important people to follow me. Annabella has been quiet. Hugging onto Callie's dress while they await their turn. Once I'm in place, Jake, Callie, and Anna all walk down the aisle together.

Anna is holding a white basket filled with flowers, but she's too shy to toss them. She's holding onto Callie's hand, half hiding behind her arm. Jake's arm is looped through Callie's other arm. He's wearing a bright wide smile causing me a sense of pride for him being such a supportive, loving brother to Callie. Even though he seems tough and serious, he definitely has a softer side to him.

Anna runs into her dad's arms as Ben kisses her cheek, whispering something to her. He smiles with pride and only a caring father can give.

Ben lets go of Anna who stands beside Callie, taking her hand. Jake moves to his place beside Ben.

This is what a wedding should be like. Everyone can sense these two people belong together and deserve their little family.

I can't help but wonder what my little family will be like. Will Declan and I be happy? Will we want to live the rest of our lives together? He's been avoiding my calls using football as an excuse. But I try to concentrate on the beautiful words Callie and Ben are exchanging. Professing their love and commitment to each other. Promising to love and cherish each other forever.

The ceremony lasts only a few minutes. Short and sweet. When the minister pronounces them husband and wife, in true Callie fashion, somehow, she manages to jump up in her skintight white organza gown and into the arms of Ben. Kissing each other passionately while the rest of us hoot and holler for them.

Ben lets Callie down while he picks up Anna. He encases his arms around both of his girls. In their own safe world while the rest of us watch. Tears prick my eyes. Part of me is so happy for them while the other, if I'm honest with myself, is jealous of their special bond. I know deep in my heart I'll never experience this with Declan.

An arm wraps around my waist. The heat from Jake's breath brushes against my cheek. "Are you ready?"

He takes my hand and threads it through his arm. As if he knows I need his strength right now. Strength at my best friend's wedding? To walk me down the aisle to a party? Yes, it's ridiculous on my part, but how did he know that I needed him?

He pulls me close to his side. "Come on, let's party."

Jake has a way of knowing what I need even when I don't know myself.

As we walk arm and arm over to the reception tent, Jake says, "Whatever nonsense is spinning around in that pretty head of yours, turn it off for tonight. Have some fun and enjoy your best friend's wedding."

"I am."

"Not yet, but you will. I'm going to grab a beer. Do you want water or soda? You haven't hydrated in a while, and you've been on your feet."

"I've had plenty to drink." I can't help the eye roll that escapes. "I'll grab a glass in a few. I'm going to use the restroom. This little bug is dancing around my bladder." All of it is true, but I need to get away from him. He's so sweet when he worries over me even if it's because he doesn't want me to pass out and ruin his sister's wedding. I'm enjoying his attention.

After Ben and Callie's first dance, which included Anna spinning around them. Clearly embracing being a princess because she is. The wedding reception has turned out to be better than what Callie planned.

The reception tent is decorated with tons of purple and pink flowers. The table and chairs are covered in white linens. The table centerpieces of mason jars and intricate tied bows are lit with candles, illuminating the tent in a natural glow. The ground beneath us is made of grass, the perfect texture to walk on without sinking in heels. The dance floor has to be the most beautiful set up I've ever witnessed at a wedding. Wooden planks form the glossy floor. Tiki torches light up our view. Sand surrounds us opening up to the sparkling lake dancing off the stars.

After eating a delicious meal and two pieces of double chocolate cake, this girl needs to take a seat for a bit. Guests are having a good time. Everyone is smiling, talking, and dancing. It's a beautiful wedding for two wonderful people.

17

— • —

HARLOW

There is one person who has my attention but hasn't said much to me since dinner started. I probably shouldn't care. He's got a lot of people to talk to; this is his sister's wedding after all. He's got friends and family; he doesn't need to waste his time with an employee.

It doesn't help Declan is getting more distant the closer I get to my due date.

So, jealousy and nausea are the only things I'm comprehending right now. These Braxton Hicks contractions are no joke. My last visit to the doctors went well, but the doctor did explain some symptoms might seem concerning. It doesn't necessarily mean I'm in labor. It sometimes feels like I need to go to the hospital, but it's perfectly normal. It's all part of pregnancy. I'm guessing this tightening and pulling I've got dancing around in my stomach is perfectly normal—although it's pretty aggressive.

Somewhere between the ceremony and the couple's first dance, the fake contractions are becoming kind of ridiculous. For that reason and for that reason alone, I've found myself looking for a distraction—a distraction in the form of a dark-haired, seriously intense grumpy boss.

I'm overwhelmingly frustrated because he's nowhere in my line of vision. Glancing down at my phone to see if anyone has called. It's weird that it's mocking me since my mom or Declan haven't called to see how I'm doing. No one seems to care that I've been gone all day.

Finding myself a little irritated and dare I say grumpy, I lean back in my chair, arms crossed, ready for a fight. Jeez, these hormones. One second, I'm all in love and the next, ready to murder someone—anyone.

Ems quietly takes the seat beside me. "Are you okay?"

Relaxing, I say, "Yeah, I think this pregnancy is getting to me. It's a pain, literally, and it has my emotions on a trampoline. One minute I'm up and the next I'm flailing on my back." Adjusting my position, "And no position I try is comfortable. I'm like a whale trying to fit in a kayak."

Ems pats my hand but laughs. "Only one month left and you'll have a beautiful baby to love and care for. Truly a blessing."

"Or torture," I huff, then rub my belly to soothe the tightening. "I'll believe you more when this little beanie is out of me."

"Are you sure you're, okay? Your face is doing a scrunching thing every so often. Can I get you a drink or do you need to rest?"

"I got her one. I guessed she wasn't drinking like she should," Jake butts in with his annoying, but accurate opinion. He scoops up my empty glass, that held ginger ale and switches it for an ice filled glass of water.

Being slightly annoyed and relieved to see him, I say, "Aren't you the best boss ever." Unable to hide my sarcastic tone and speak to Ems, "He just wants to make sure I don't faint and ruin Carmichael's wedding."

"It's the Rae-Carmichael wedding," Jake says with sarcasm matching my own.

"Ooh, I like how that sounds." Emerson agrees as Van comes from behind her and wraps his arms around her.

A twinge of jealousy washes over me for a brief half of a second. Declan was supposed to bring me tonight. In true Declan fashion, he had to stay at school for a fraternity fundraiser.

Does he expect me to believe he's at a fundraiser, not a party? Does he think I'm stupid? He can spin the situation any way he wants, but I'm not convinced he's going to be here for me and the baby. As the days get closer, he becomes more distant. He has more responsibilities at school or football than with a life coming into the world in a month.

"What's that look for?" he asks, with raised eyebrows.

"Huh?"

Jake points to my forehead. "The crinkle line on your forehead, plus the scrunch of your nose." He boops my nose, literally boops my nose. It's the silliest thing that has happened to me in a long time and a chuckle tries to escape, but I stop myself. It's ridiculous to think it's cute, but it seems any attention he gives to me throws my emotions into that of a thirteen-year-old girl.

Turning serious because this whole thing is getting out of control. "I'm not making any type of look. You just surprised me by coming over here and being nice. Plus... I haven't seen much of you all day."

"Worried about me?" He can't hide the cockiness from his voice or the arch of his brow.

"No. I was just wondering if you've given your sister any attention. It is her big day, not yours."

"This pregnancy has made you crabby. Even crabbier than before. And I barely talked to you then."

"I'm not crabby, you're the grumpy one." Arguing with him is easier than admitting he's right, I am crabby. But he would be too, if he had another human being living inside him.

"You really don't think much of me, do you?" he asks.

"I think you are a good boss." If he really knew all I did was think of him.

He dives in, "You always have something negative to say about me. I get you a drink and you give me shit for it. I leave to make sure the food and alcohol are fully stocked, check on the caterers to make sure my sister's wedding goes off perfectly – and all I get is shit for it. Not all of us guys are neglectful assholes, so don't compare me to your precious footballer. Because from where I'm sitting – he's not worthy of you either."

Insert guilt or a mic drop; both seem appropriate.

"I don't mean it like that, Jake." Way to make me feel like shit. "Declan would be here tonight if he could. He's at a fundraiser. He's important to his school and team."

Why am I defending Declan? Jake is absolutely right, but I won't admit it to him. He has the launch sequence to pissing me off and making my blood boil.

"Take a drink, you're all flushed." Jake pushes the glass closer to me.

"I don't need one." Crossing my arms seems childish, but I do it anyway.

His strong jaw ticks to accentuate his annoyance.

"Fine." I only agree because all this arguing has made my mouth dry like a desert. I let the bubbles dance in my mouth, quenching my thirst. It's starting to get stifling in this tent even though there's a breeze blowing through.

Jake sits closer to me. "I can see I'm upsetting you, how about a peace offering or a fresh start? I'll leave you alone about hydrating, if you dance with me?" He extends his hand for mine, raising a brow, seemingly challenging me.

"Have you seen me lately?" I gesture to my large stomach. "I don't think dancing is what I'll do, more like waddle."

He stands, "Waddling it is."

"No. I'll stay here, and we can start over. You're right, I have been grumpy."

"Come on." He stands with his arm still out for me to take it. "Have some fun. You've been pouting. I know you wish Declan was here. I get it even though I'm giving him shit for it. Come on and dance with me," he says in a soft pleading tone then adds, "Please?"

A hint of a smile dances on his face. The pain I encountered seconds ago has been melted away by his voice and the tingles he sends through my body.

"Do you even know how to dance? I mean, you can pour a mean drink and race cars but dancing... that's a whole new talent."

"There are a few things you have no idea about me. I am a man of many talents."

He takes my hand, somehow managing to gracefully pull me to my feet. Then I find myself in his arms, against his hard chest.

Jake moves us to the dance floor. He positions a hand on my waist, and the other holds my hand. Before I realize it, we're swaying to the slow song. Somehow a deep calmness washes over me. It's as if we should have been dancing all night instead of arguing. I'm not used to the calm he brings; chaos has been the norm.

The music changes, it's a touch slower which causes him to move closer. I find myself at peace in his strong arms. I can't help but appreciate the muscles under my hand. His masculine scent mixed with the fragrant floral scent radiating from the dainty blue flower on his lapel.

Jake abruptly releases me all too soon only to twirl me around and spins me back to the same spot we started in.

It startles me or maybe it's the baby because immense pressure builds and a gush of water falls down my legs.

"What the hell?" Jake jumps back but doesn't let go. "Your water just broke."

I'm unable to answer him. I thought it only happened in movies, not in real life. At a doctor's appointment, I made sure to ask them if it really happened, of course they said yes, but they also said it was very unlikely.

My breathing intensifies. I'm finding it hard to breathe. Panic overtakes my senses.

"What should I do?" I say as I glance down at my dress, unable to see what kind of condition it's in. However, there's no mistaking the fact my legs and dress are soaked and sticking to my skin.

"Don't you know what to do? Aren't you trained for this?" Jake counters.

"No. I mean, yes but... not really. I still thought I had a whole month to go. This is too early."

"Call Declan and your parents. I'll take you to the hospital." Jake directs me to the table, grabbing my purse, digging around until he encounters my phone. He shoves it at me.

Fear and embarrassment wash over me. The last person in the world I want to take me to the hospital is my boss. I'm already going to have to bear it all to the nurses and doctors; I don't need him to see anything by accident.

Thankfully, Emerson takes this very second to ask if I'm okay. "Did you spill..." She doesn't finish, but her eyes widen in understanding. "Oh, Harlow. We need to get you to the hospital."

"I'm taking her, let me just pull the car up so she doesn't have to walk far."

"Van and I can take her. You stay here and finish the wedding for your sister."

"Yes! That would be great. You need to stay here." *Please don't take me.*

"They don't need me. I got her." He practically growls at us, not giving Emerson a second to argue. He moves toward the exit. Leaving Emerson and I confused.

Van comes up beside us, casually asking if I've spilled my drink. Emerson backhands his chest. "No. She's having a baby. Her water just broke."

"What? Woah." His mouth drops open. "Oh shit, we better get you to the hospital."

This is all so overwhelming. Everyone's in a rush, but I can barely move. It's like I'm frozen or something. Shouldn't I know exactly what to do? When does the maternal instinct kick in?

Finding some of my voice, "It's okay. I'm sure we still have plenty of time. The baby isn't going to come out for a while. Labor can take hours." I say, trying to convince myself more than them.

I call my mom. It goes straight to voicemail. They must have gone out of town, like she said. They don't have great cell phone service at the cabin. I text her instead, hoping she can at least get my text and come home. I try my dad too, but with the same outcome.

Jake appears, "Ready to go?"

"Yeah, I can't get a hold of my parents. They always answer except when they go up to the cabin. There isn't good service. My mom mentioned they might head up there, but she never gave me a definitive answer. Biting at the end of my fingernail, a greater sense of panic decides to surface. Am I going to have this baby all alone? Maybe Emerson can come or maybe Callie will leave her wedding a little early and hold my hand? Mentally, I'm losing it. Of course, I can't ask her to do that.

"How about Declan? I'm sure he'll be here soon." Emerson says.

Of course, Declan. He caused this mess. He should be here for it. He should have been my first call.

Emerson grabs my hand away from my face. "Harlow, honey breathe. You need to take in the air. Deep breaths. Breathe with me. Let's count together – one, two, three. Everything is going to be okay." She looks at Jake. "I should probably go with you."

I do as she says, and Jake touches my cheek. "Do you want Emerson to come with us?"

His touch calms the panic. The air reaches my lungs, and everything is clearer. My heart rate seems to comes down. Is it weird he somehow makes it better? As soon as he is near, all is right in the world.

Emerson and Van reluctantly agree to meet us at the hospital. Jake asked them to do a few tasks for him here, and then they were free to follow us there. Ben and Callie were ready to send everyone home, but neither Jake nor I would let it happen. This is their day.

On the way to the hospital, the nerves really kick in. Thankfully, the pain is not as bad as earlier. The hospital is a thirty-minute drive, since it's well past nine. There shouldn't be any traffic to hold us up.

"Did your parents text back yet?" Jake asks from the driver's seat, but doesn't look at me, concentrating on the road.

"No. They still must not have service." I answer, letting out a breath.

"And Declan?"

"No answer." To my phone call or text. How hard is it for him to answer me back? He left me on *read*. Who does that to their pregnant girlfriend? If we stay together, it's going to be a miracle at this point.

Glancing over at Jake, with his hands on ten and two, white knuckles and a tight grasp. He's concentrating on the road ahead of him. I can't see the expression on his face, but the tension in the air is thick. The baby also takes this moment to move in a way that shoots a pain throughout my stomach area. "Can you talk about something, anything to keep my mind off the fact I'm going to be a mother in a matter of hours."

"What's the baby's name?" He asks without a second between me screaming at him like the exorcist.

"I don't have a name. I don't know if it's a boy or a girl. I've been in denial if you haven't noticed." He tilts his head, looking at me but quickly directs it back to the road.

"Oh, I've noticed. But I get it."

"In my defense, I thought I'd have more time to figure it out. Do you think they'll let me wait or maybe my water didn't break, and it was just something unrelated to the birth?"

He chuckles. "I'm pretty sure it only happens when a baby is ready to enter the world."

"Ahh... this is painful. Are we close yet?"

"We'll be there before you know it. Let's go over some potential options. We'll start with a boy's name. You have to have at least one you like."

"This is going to sound awful, but I really haven't even thought of it – on purpose. Do you think I'm a horrible mom?

"Of course not. It's a big decision. Look at me – I'm named after a movie character in a chick flick."

"Jake Rae, which movie? I can't think of which one it is."

"First off, Jake Rae isn't my full name. It's actually Jake Rae Ryan. When my dad left and Callie's dad died, my mom wanted us all to go by the same last name. So, she just pretended like Ryan wasn't my last name. I just went with it."

A sharp pain spurs along with the recognition of the movie. Sixteen Candles, Jake Ryan. I had such a huge crush on Jake Ryan and I'm beginning to have a huge crush on the real Jake Rae Ryan.

18

JAKE

She's doing her deep breathing thing and I'm a nervous wreck. Of course, I can't let her know. But the last thing I need is to have to help her give birth to a baby. I have no idea how to even begin that scenario.

What I do know is that her boyfriend is the biggest prick I've ever met. He hasn't called her back. Maybe he's doing something important, but if my girl was about to give birth to my kid, I'd never let her leave my sight.

It's hard to miss the fear and anxiety all over her face. Her features are scrunched up and her eyes are tired but wide. Driving is becoming a challenge. All I really want to do is keep watching her to reassure myself she's really all right.

"Ahh... Jake, can you hold my hand? I just really need to distract myself and maybe squeeze the pain away from me."

I nod, finding her hand already close to mine. I probably didn't have a chance of saying no. Of course, I regret it immediately. Not just because she's squeezing the shit out of it because it's so right. Like her hand is the only one I ever want to touch again. The elation knowing I've got her and no one else does right now is something I've never felt before. Is it for being the only person available right now?

Parents—not answering. Declan—not answering or ignoring her. Our friends, busy but on their way. I'm the only one who's here for her, and there is nowhere else I'd rather be.

"Sorry," she grits through her teeth.

"No. It's no problem. Just wasn't expecting your superhuman strength. It's really kicking in." Accelerating at least fifteen miles over the speed limit is all I can do right now. I'd rather run over the car in front of me.

She reaches for her phone on the console. Check it and groans in frustration. "Why is no one answering me? They know I'm at a wedding, but you'd think someone might check to see how I'm doing?"

It is strange that no one has checked in on her. I get her parents are on a little trip, but Declan just confuses the hell out of me. He seems to have no interest in Harlow's day-to-day life. Does he even know she went to a wedding today? Was she lying to make it look like he's a decent person?

Pushing down the words that want to explode from my lips, instead I reassure her it's just a coincidence and everyone will be here soon. Then add, "Everyone's excited to meet this kid."

"Are you?"

"Me?" Her question takes me by surprise that my eyes leave the road for a moment too long but return them to the road.

"I know you probably aren't into kids, but do you want to meet my baby?" she asks, her voice is quieter than it has been. Christ, does everyone that's supposed to care about her treat her like shit?" She sounds so small and unsure.

"Of course. And I love kids. Annabella and I hang out all the time. I babysat for Callie and Ben last week. They had stuff to do for the wedding. Anna and I colored, played race cars, and maybe even had a tea party or two."

"Are you serious? You? A tea party?"

"I'll have you know, I'm an excellent guest at a tea party."

She laughs. It's so nice to hear instead of her groaning in pain.

"Looks like right now, you're the only one ready for this baby to make its entrance into the world." Sniffling starts after her words.

"Don't cry. You got this." I hate for anyone to cry, let alone her tears that are cutting me like a knife. They hit somewhere deep inside me.

"No. I'm not ready. For pushing this baby out of me or raising a tiny human. None of it. I'm already a horrible mother. None of my family is here. The father is partying instead of being here by my side and I keep calling the baby "it." What mother does that?" She sniffles, wiping her nose with the back of her hand.

"You're being way too hard on yourself. Everything is okay." A moment later, the sign for the hospital comes into view. It's like a beacon in the sky; the Emergency Room sign lights up, guiding us.

"Thank the Lord!" she cries. Echoing my thoughts.

Once the car is parked, we only have a few steps up to the door. I've found a rock star parking spot. Reaching around to the back seat, I grab her bag noticing she hasn't moved an inch, making no motion to get out of the car. Is she refusing to get out of the car?

"Do you need help to get out of the car?"

"I'm scared, Jake." her voice shakes.

I let out a sigh. "I'm scared too. Not like I'm doing anything, but I want to help you through this. I'm not sure I'm the right person so I'm nervous. So, let's do this together."

"Will you hold my hand again?"

Without answering her, I get out of the car and reach the passenger side. Opening the door, holding out my hand and promising myself, I'm not letting go.

***

We get Harlow checked in and they take her to a room. I text Callie and Ems that everything is going okay. Emerson and Van are on their way; they just stopped at home to change first.

Speaking of which, I ditched the tie somewhere in my car and finally took off the jacket. The nurse shows me to the waiting room while they get her changed and ready to go. The nurse told me first time births take a while. Hopefully, her parents have at least answered her by now.

After about ten minutes of pacing, worrying, and trying to find a comfortable spot to sit, the nurse comes over to me.

"You can follow me to her room. She's nice and comfortable." The short-haired middle-aged nurse says. "Are you excited?"

"Who? Me?... I mean, yeah. But I'm just a friend. The father is... well, he's not here." Fuck him, I'm not going to make him look good to a stranger.

"Oh, I see. You are a good friend then. This is going to be tough on her. So, give her encouragement and listen to the instructions the other nurses and doctor give you and you'll do great." She smiles, guiding me into the room.

Harlow does look pretty comfortable in the bed. I feel bad she doesn't have her hospital bag, only the bag with the clothes she wore this morning.

"Hey. How are you doing?" I ask, taking a seat beside her in a chair that looks like a recliner. The fake pink leather is anything but comfortable.

"I'm feeling fine, but they are a little worried about my blood pressure. It's high."

"Of course it is, you've got yourself all worked up over your parents and Declan." trying to reassure her so her blood pressure will decline.

"Mom and Dad finally texted me back. They'll be here as soon as they can. Declan still hasn't answered me." Her head drops, as she looks at her hands.

Oh no, I'm not having her sad over that jackass.

I shoot up out of my seat and stand beside her. "Since I'm here, I'll stand in until your parents get here. Got any idea what I should be doing?"

"Since I thought I'd have more time to prepare, I have no idea. Maybe just keep my ice chips filled and maybe let me squeeze your hand when I need to?" She shrugs.

"Consider it done."

After handing her ice chips, it becomes clearer that they did absolutely nothing to cool her down. Sweat rolls down her forehead. Taking a cool washcloth, I trail it along her face, wiping as much away as I can. I wish I could do more, alleviate her pain in some way. Harlow lets out a deep breath. "That feels amazing. Thank you. What else can I do for you?" I ask, helplessly. "Don't leave me, okay?" I don't know if it's the right thing to do but I can't help myself. Leaning down, my lips find her forehead and I promise, "I'm not going anywhere."

Emerson and Van came into the room twenty minutes later. I'd be lying if I said it wasn't a huge relief to see them. At least now Emerson, her friend, can give her the support she needs. I'm clueless about what to do. She's being tough as hell, but she seems to be getting worse every passing minute.

"Harlow, I know you're in labor, but are you doing all right? Your face is really red," Emerson asks.

"They said my blood pressure is high. I'm not feeling well." she says and miserably groans. This groan is different, laced with more discomfort than pain.

"I'll grab the nurse." I don't give anyone time to argue. Lunging at the first nurse I see by the arm, I tell her, "You need to get in here."

The dark-haired nurse in purple flower scrubs checks Harlow's vitals. Her eyes widen at the numbers on the screen. I don't know anything about blood pressure, but if those numbers get that kind of reaction from a medical professional, it can't be good.

"I'm going to grab a doctor. There is only one person allowed to stay now. We need the space."

"Why? What's going on?" Emerson asks.

"The father can stay, everyone else must go." Her stern voice echoes throughout the room.

"The father isn't here." Harlow says, and I can hear the fear in her voice.

"No, but I'll stay" I offer, only to realize what the fuck am I doing? I'm not the baby's father, but obviously I'm having trouble following through with the information. But I do add, "Only if you want me to stay?"

"If you want to, I don't really want to be by myself in there. I'm kind of terrified right now." That's all she needed to tell me. Her voice is small and shaky, rocking me to the core. "I'll stay. Emerson, can you call her parents and as soon as her mom is here, I'll trade places with her."

"Okay." She turns but then stops, facing me again.

"Are you sure you're up for this?" she asks, placing a hand on my shoulder.

"I'm going to have to be. I'm not letting her go through this alone. I know you would stay, but I think she needs me right now."

I'm not even sure why I said that. I'm not what she needs. But I know I want to be the person she needs. Somewhere between being her employer and now, something has changed, and I can't force myself to leave.

Back in the room, two new nurses and a doctor join us. I'm off in the corner of the room. Trying to stay out of the way. They've changed her positions and keep checking her vitals. I can't understand what's really going on. Until finally, the doctor says. "Harlow, you're going to have this baby now. Okay?" His voice is calm and controlled. "We need to do a C-section. Your blood pressure is way too high. We need to deliver this baby as soon as possible. The father can come in once we have you situated."

I don't argue with the doctor. At this point, who cares? It's been about ten minutes since the two nurses wheeled Harlow out of the room, shoved a pair of blue hospital scrubs in my face and told me to suit up. Without question, I'm pacing back and forth with my scrubs on, a mask around my face ready to stand by her side and be whatever she needs.

Another nurse who I haven't seen approaches me. "Harlow Layne?"

"Yes, I'm with her."

"You must be the right guy. You're wearing holes in my floor with your pacing."

Following her down the hall, the bleach mixed with blood reaches my nose and I'm instantly nauseated. Am I the best person for this, or should I have let Emerson be with her? God, I hope I don't pass out on her.

"Once we're inside things can get pretty gnarly. Don't look over the curtain unless you can stand the sight of blood and bodily fluids?" The new nurse who casually walks as if she's going to the beach and talking about waves instead of slicing through a woman's stomach.

"I'm good," I say. I have no idea how I am, but it doesn't matter. I'm here and so is she, lying on the gurney, with just her arms exposed to IV's and tubes everywhere. She's got a cap on her head; an oxygen tube is wrapped around her face feeding into her nose.

"Is she all, right?" I whisper over to the nurse.

"Yes, we gave her a little oxygen, and she can't feel anything from the chest down. All you need to do is talk her through. Try to keep her calm." She smiles and pats me on the back. "Go ahead and take the seat beside her. You'll do great."

Harlow's big green eyes widen as she notices me. "Jake."

My body moves as if I'm floating to her just because she summoned me.

"Hey. How are you feeling?"

"Scared. My blood pressure is too high and I'm minutes from being a mom and my boss is going to see me give birth. Nothing says coworkers like this, huh?" she says, trying to lighten the situation.

"I'm glad I can be here for you. All you have to do is lie there and the doc will do the rest, okay?"

She nods but the fear in her eyes speaks volumes. Taking her hand just to let her know I'm here for her; she turns her head to look up at the ceiling. I brush the stray strands of hair from her face. With each movement of my hand, I hope to wipe away her worries.

It all goes by so fast; the doctors have the baby out in moments and for a heart wrenching second there's silence. My heart stops at the loss of noise for a moment. We can't see anything over the curtain they have placed on her chest. Focusing only on her eyes filled with fear. After what seems like an eternity, my ears fill with the screams of a newborn baby. Above the curtain, the doctor hoists the baby up for us to see.

"It's a boy." He's covered in blood and some sort of fluid. He has a pair of pipes on him. He has a temper like his mother.

Then he's out of our view and with the nurses. I brush the strands of hair off her forehead. I lean down and do something that is only because of the miracle we just witnessed. I kiss her forehead. "You did amazing. You're incredible." I whisper against her skin.

She's crying and smiling all at the same time. "I have a baby. A boy. He's beautiful."

The nurse brings the baby over to us. Laying him on Harlow's chest so she can get a closer look. She kisses his forehead. "She can't hold him yet, but would you like to?"

"Me?" I ask, but nod yes.

He's placed in my arms, and his little face is scrunched up.

"Look at how beautiful he is," says the nurse.

"He is, isn't he?"

19

HARLOW

J ake is holding my son like it's the most natural thing in the world. His smile is as calming to me as it is to my son. My son? I can't believe he's here and he's mine.

I'm starting to get some sensation back to my limbs. I'm exhausted but can't stop looking at my baby in Jake's arms. There were a few seconds after he was delivered, I wasn't sure he was okay but then he cried and I've never been so happy. Even though he's almost a month early, he's breathing fine and passed all the doctors' tests with flying colors. After being settled in my hospital bed, I can finally relax and take in the miracle before me.

"I've got to give him a name. Do you have any ideas?" I ask.

"I don't think I'm qualified to give an answer. Besides, you should ask your parents. Emerson said they should be here in an hour."

"I was thinking of Luca."

The corners of his mouth quirk up. "I think he looks like a Luca, yes... I like it."

"You do?"

"Yeah, but you shouldn't care what anyone thinks about the name as long as you like it and think it fits him. It's all that matters."

Luca starts to fuss. Jake rearranges him and he settles. "Look at you, a natural."

He smiles while looking down at my baby. He's held him more than I have and no part of me is mad about it because I know he's safe and sound in his arms. For a second, I wonder what he would be like as a father.

An hour later my room's filled with family and friends except Jake slipped out when they took the baby for his feeding. I'm still a bit weak from the anesthesia and pain medicine, but I did get to hold him for a bit.

Jake didn't say goodbye before he left, but I understand. If I was him, I'd be uncomfortable too. At least he showed up for me when it mattered. I will be forever grateful to him.

Mom is in her glory, cooing at her new grandson. "He is just beautiful. I can't believe we missed it. And you didn't have anyone with you. I told your father trying to go to the cabin so close to you giving birth was a bad idea." She narrows her eyes, almost as if she could throw daggers at him.

"He is a month early. And I wasn't alone. I had a friend with me."

My father straightens up. "Who?"

I adjust my posture while trying to find a comfortable spot in bed or maybe I'm just trying to delay the inevitable. My father's eyes are laser focused, and arms are crossed, ready to protect me from whoever's name I'm about to confess.

It is silly for me to be so nervous. No one was there. He drove me here and stayed. Sure, Emerson would have been the more likely choice, but Jake felt like the right choice, and I still cannot explain why.

"Harlow?" My dad's stern voice echoes throughout the quiet room.

"It is funny in a way. He brought me here and things went fast. He just was there, and he helped me through."

"Who, dear?" Mom calmly yet cautiously asks.

"Jake Rae," I say, cringing not because I don't want to mention his name, but not wanting to hear any judgment from my parents.

Mom places her hand on my father's arm, assuming she's politely keeping him in check.

"That boss of yours?" He can't hide his less than pleased tone.

I nodded. "We were dancing, and my water broke. He offered to take me." I know I shouldn't use the fact that no one was there to my advantage, but I do it anyway. "It's not like I had many options."

"I'm glad… then." Mom answers first, then Dad adds, "Declan is on his way."

Seriously, they've talked to him, and I haven't heard a single word from him yet? And Jake left his own sister's wedding to take me safely to the hospital, so I didn't have to give birth on the dance floor.

"So, he called you?" I don't bother to hide the annoyance in my voice.

"He was worried about you but didn't know how to get a hold of you."

"How about my phone? It was on me most of the time, and Emerson had it to keep everyone updated. You should know because you're here right now." I'm getting angrier by the second. I know she called him, and he never answered. He didn't know it was her calling him. "It doesn't matter anyway, I needed him, and he wasn't here."

"Honey, he has obligations. He's on his way now. He couldn't control how fast the baby came," she says, while cooing at the baby. It seems to be all she's good at right now. Hovering over Luca and taking Declan's side. How can my parents be so blind? There is a big surprise for Declan when he gets here because I'm not letting him off easily.

"Give me Luca," I order my mom. If it's not the hormones that make me brave, then it's the anger welling up inside me. I've had enough of everyone. "I'd like to be alone with him. You can go grab something to eat."

Mom nods and gently places a kiss on Luca's forehead.

For some reason they don't argue, which is a huge relief to me. The drugs and sleep deprivation mixed together aren't making me perform at my best, but what is the best medicine lands in my arms as my mom hands him to me.

He wrapped like a burrito in a thin white hospital blanket with blue and pink stripes. The nurse showed me how to swaddle him earlier. I'm scared to death to try it on my own without her walking me through the steps.

He isn't what I expected; his face is scrunched up, and he yawns more than he cries. He seems to be trying to move around in his burrito which makes sense because it felt like he was doing back flips in my stomach. His little whimpers are so adorable but at the same time they're frightening. Is he wrapped too tight? Should I loosen it? The call button for the nurse is mocking me, saying "you can't call the nurse when you're at home."

Just as I'm arguing with myself, Jake stands just inside the door. As always, I find his presence a relief. As if the weight of the world has lifted from my shoulders.

"How's the little guy?"

"He's good. Noisy. Not crying but making noises like grunts and groans."

"And you? Are you better or worse? I expected you to be sleeping and your parents to be getting in as many hugs and kisses as they can." He shrugs while looking at the ground. "At least, that's what Gran would be doing. Poor Callie and Ben when they decide to add to their family. She's going to drive Callie nuts, and I can't wait." He chuckles.

His smile is infectious. I don't know if it's because he's so serious all the time or he has the cutest dimple on the right side of his cheek, his hair is long in front brushing over his eyes, and I can't help but notice he's still wearing his white shirt and dark suit pants.

Hasn't he gone home and changed? It's eight in the morning. Luca was born just after midnight. It was a very hectic night, and he stayed with me most of it, but has he not been home? "Have you been in the waiting room all this time?"

"Nah, I grabbed something to eat and checked on the bar. Didn't really get to changing yet," he says, glancing down at his clothes.

"You didn't need to come back here. My parents are here, and Declan is on his way."

Jake purses his lips, and nods, "I was just checking in and now I'll let you rest."

Why does he seem to be hurt by my remark? The disappointment on his face is vivid.

"You can stay if you want? I think you earned a visitor's pass whenever you want."

That makes his smile return just a little.

"I guess I did. I didn't really look at the blood and stuff. Just when they lifted the baby over the curtain for you to see him. I'm okay with blood. I didn't want to be the loser who passed out on you."

I laugh. "That would not have been helpful at all."

He stands beside me, with his hands in his pocket looking down at Luca and me. He swallows as if he's going to say something but then walks toward the door and disappears.

What? No see you later or bye.

The anger I felt before he walked into my room returns. Why does everyone think it's okay just to leave me?

He walks back in, and his eyes widen when he glances at my face. "Did I miss something? You look like you're ready to stab me?"

"I thought you left."

"No, I forgot I left these out in the hall." From behind him he has a bouquet of red roses in a vase and a teddy bear balloon sticking out of the top. From his other hand, he pulls out a small teddy bear.

"I couldn't decide on a bear, so I just went with one wearing a blue outfit. Seems like the obvious choice now, I probably should have gone with something unique."

"It's perfect." Because it is, all of it. I know Declan hasn't been here but even when Declan is sitting beside me, it's as if I'm invisible and lonely, yet there hasn't been a single moment when Jake has been here that I've felt alone.

"I'm glad you approve of it. I'll just put them on the stand over here." Jake sets them in place and peaks over at Luca. "May I?" he asks, as he holds out his hand for Luca.

"Yes."

Jake gently puts his hand under Luca's head and lifts him into his arms. Luca fusses a bit but quickly settles back into sleep. Jake sways with Luca as if he's got a special song playing in his mind.

As he looks at my son, I take the moment to take in his rolled up white shirt sleeves, revealing muscular forearms and a tattoo of what looks like a gear inside a motor or maybe a clock? Either way, it looks hot. Heat rushes to my face.

A commotion at the door brings my attention away from Jake and his super sexy forearm. It's the exact opposite of what I was just admiring. Declan stands in the doorway with yellow carnations, and a tie-dyed teddy bear similar to what Jake just gifted to me, only I don't seem to like Declan's gifts at all.

20

JAKE

Declan stands in the doorway with the same damn flowers and bear I just handed over to Harlow. Stupid bastard has had the whole damn pregnancy to get her and the baby something. He gets it in the hospital gift shop. Granted, I did too – but I'm at more of a disadvantage being I brought her to the hospital and all. If I didn't have Luca in my arms, I'd knock the vase right out of his hands.

He's built just like you would expect a star quarterback. Tall, blond hair looks as if he put way too much effort into making it appear perfect instead it makes him look like a douche, and yeah, he's big and muscular but the bigger they are, the harder they fall. I've been in my fair share of fights, and I've taken down some douchebags.

Dickhead finally walks into the room but doesn't even look at his girl and the baby. He's too busy eyeing me. "Who the fuck are you?" he says with a glare that might intimidate me if I gave a shit.

"This is Jake, my boss." Harlow says, politely but with a tinge of nervousness. How do I know this? She does that thing where she wrings her hands together like they're physically stopping her from doing something with them.

"Why the fuck is your boss here? This is a private room."

Glancing up from his son's innocent face, I ask, "The better question is what is more important than your son's birth?" A smile creeps on my face because I was trying to get a rise out of him, and it works because his face turns a deep shade of red.

"Listen you prick. I know all about you and don't you think for one second I'm going to let some loser like you near my family."

Harlow rolls her eyes and says, "Declan, please. I couldn't get hold of you or my parents. He drove me here and stayed with me until Luca was born."

His face twists in confusion. The prick doesn't even know his own son's name. Who's the loser now? She didn't pick the smartest player on the team, did she?

"Is that the name you picked for our son?" He seems almost annoyed when he stares up at the ceiling instead of being a proud father. Part of me knows I should leave them to this very personal moment but the majority of me doesn't trust her alone with this asshole. "We decided on Declan Jr."

"You didn't decide on anything because you would never discuss it with me?" Harlow shoots back at him, her voice full of venom. I smile with pride. *Hell yeah!*

"We may not have talked about it, but everyone knows if it's a boy, it should be named after the father."

Harlow rolls her eyes, and motions for me to give her the baby.

When she has Luca in her arms, she sits up. "I want to introduce you to your son, Luca Declan Harrison. You can have the middle name, which is all I'm willing to concede. Now, you can hold him." She lifts him up, trying to hand him over, but the plastic cord is restricting her movement.

Declan puts his hands up. "I don't know how to hold a baby." The tough guy who was here a few minutes ago has turned into a coward right before our eyes.

"It's time to learn." Harlow pushes Luca on Declan's chest, so he has no other option than to hold Luca. It's the most awkward thing I've ever witnessed. Declan has Luca's head in one hand and is holding his body with the other, and his arm is contorted in some way his fingers don't even look like they have a hold of Luca. How is this guy a quarterback?

She has this. He's not getting away with anything. I don't need to intrude on them any longer.

Turning to Harlow, I tell her, "I'm going to get going. Let me know if you need anything." This is awkward, but I suppose I should hug her or something. We have gotten to know each other much more in the last twelve hours or so. Instead, my feet take me out of the room.

Taking a deep breath, I inhale the scent of hospital bleach and whatever else permeates the air. The moment of air is clobbered by Mr. Layne. He stands taller than me in a dress shirt and dark pants. He definitely looks like a lawyer. I'm usually on the wrong side of the law when I've had to meet one.

"Jake?" He questions.

"Yes. Sir." I stammer.

"I want to thank you for bringing my daughter here. What do I owe you for your trouble?"

I'm taken aback by his question. Does this guy pay everyone who talks to his daughter?

"No thanks. I was happy to do it. She needed a ride, and I was in the right place at the right time." Drawing in a deep breath to calm my frustration with his comment, I continue, "Congratulations on your grandson."

He frowns. "Thanks. His father is here now, so she's in good hands."

Biting the inside of my cheek, I nod. "Yeah, well." I say and turn away from him and down the hallway leading to the hospital exit.

There is no way I can stay and discuss Declan with her father in a calm and polite way because I have nothing good to say about him. Right now, it seems I can say the same thing about her father.

***

Back at my apartment, I shower and change into normal clothes. It's a typical slow Sunday night. Callie is off on her honeymoon. They went on a family cruise. They took Anna with them. It's not something I would do. Callie said she couldn't bear to be away from Anna for even a night, let alone seven nights.

Whatever. Not my business. It seems like people are bugging me more than normal. I like to keep to myself and concentrate on my bar and racing. Van and Ben have the next few weeks off. It's the off season for them but for me it's just starting.

My race car is ready to go. I've supercharged and tuned the car into a piece of race car art. It's going to drive faster than anybody else's ride. Ben and Van aren't in this group of racers. This is more on the dangerous side of the law. Real street cars with real stakes. Money, titles, fights, and occasional illegal activity.

If I lose a race, it costs me much more than the loss on my racing record. Depending on the terms, to get my car back I either have to fight for it or pay a high cost, usually something the other driver wants. Sometimes the price could be stealing, drugs, or taking care of someone else's problems. Part of the thrill is what the win is worth to the other person.

My price is their car. Whatever they think is better than mine because nothing is better than my car. My boys and I are partial to Mustangs, and I've got a beauty. A 1976 Ford Mustang. I restored it from scratch. Van is the mechanic, but he only helped out a little with the mechanical stuff. I'm more into body work. She's painted electric blue with white stripes down the middle and some black hand painted pinstriping on the side, all done by me.

The last guy that lost to me, the price we agreed on, was beating up his coworker who slept with his girlfriend. I agreed because I knew I'd win. I got his 1970 Chevelle instead. It's beat up with rust and dents, but I'll be restoring the beauty back to life.

After work, I'll be meeting up with a few guys to organize the Friday race.

Mindy distracts me with the rattling of a box of empty beer bottles. "It fucking slow tonight."

"Yep. You can take off if you want?"

"No, I'll take the hours. How was the wedding? I heard through the Lake Haven grapevine; Harlow had her kid." Mindy explains, as if I wasn't there.

"Yep."

"I also heard you had a front row seat to it all."

"You could say that and more." Can no one keep shit to themselves?

She laughs. "I'm sure it was more than you thought. You're a good guy Jake, no matter how bad you try not to be." She winks and steps away to the kitchen.

The night is the same as always. I serve drinks, chat with the regulars, and close up for the night excited about planning the next race.

When I get to Wes's garage, there are four other guys I don't recognize. They're part of a street team from two states over. Two of the
guys are scrawny and look like they've done their fair share of drugs.
I'm sure if one of them is the team captain, they'll be wanting drugs.
The other two are muscular, but I think they'll be easy to take on if
they're looking for a fight.

Before agreeing to a race, we have to size up the competition. Can
we kick their ass on the track and off? Are their demands too far from
reach or is it going to cost us everything?

Wes starts off by telling them our rules. When the flashlight goes
off, you go. First one to the finish line wins. It doesn't matter if you
bump into the other car or cross the line. "What are you racing for?"

The dark-haired guy with a teardrop tattoo under his eyes demands,
"When I win, I want your bar."

"No. Absolutely not." Wes answers for me.

"That's the deal. Are you afraid of losing to me?"

"No, I'm not going to lose. It's not up for debate. Either you pick
something else, or we fight on the streets, or we can just get it over with
now."

His eyes widen, fear flashes in them. He's afraid to fight. All talk, no
follow through.

He looks over at his buddy in the oversized flannel, "Ok then. We'll
take your car."

"No, you won't but I'll let you try."

21

HARLOW

How could a father not want to hold their own child? He literally threw Luca at me when Jake left. He only held him for obvious possessive reasons. Jake isn't a threat to him because he's not the reason my feelings for Declan are changing. And they're changing fast.

It's like a light bulb that was slowly coming on, has fully reached the pinnacle of its brightness, it's almost blinding. Declan may be Luca's father, but he isn't sticking around, and I know it.

Declan has planted his large frame in the reclining chair next to the bed. He's fixated on his phone and whatever social media site has a replay of his plays. The man will watch himself all day.

Luca is now in his bed with plastic sides so I can see him. He's sleeping soundly and still balled up. The nurse has been in to change him, so I chose to watch her for the first time. Plus, my incision is angry. I don't have the energy to pick a fight with Declan right now, but as soon as Luca and I get home and settled, Declan needs to make a choice if he wants to be in this with me.

Maybe I'm exhausted or maybe I'm seeing everything more clearly, either way, I'm done letting him get away with being the absentee parent.

***

The days were long and the nights were even longer. Luca is a good baby, but he does love to eat. I tried to breastfeed for about three days and decided it wasn't for me. I'm not meant to whip out my boobs on command. I've opted to bottle feed, and it suits me just fine. Of course, Mom has had her opinions on the subject, but they aren't her boobs.

I shouldn't complain though, she's been wonderful during my recovery. When I'm too tired or uncomfortable, she has taken care of Luca's needs.

We've been home from the hospital for two days and Declan has been here once. Just one time. I haven't had the energy or the ambition to deal with him. But tonight, I have a little fight in me. He's coming over for dinner. It's time to have a little chat with him.

Declan walks through the front door and straight into the living area. He doesn't knock or say hello. He just takes a seat on the couch next to me. As he sits, the weight of his body makes the cushion cave, causing me and Luca, who is my arms, to fall against his shoulder.

"Hey." I snap.

"What?"

"Didn't you see I was sitting here with your very small newborn son in my arms?"

He sighs in response. "I saw you. I can't help it; you fell into me."

Narrowing my eyes, I say, "What is it going to take for you to pay attention to your son?"

"I'm clearly sitting right next to you. I'm paying a lot of attention to both of you. I stayed at my parents' place instead of going to the fraternity house. I can't be here every day."

"You have only been here one other day; don't you want to get to know your son or experience the joys of being a father?" I ask, wondering if his answer will relieve the weight on my chest.

He turns to face us. "Harlow, I'm just freaked out, okay?" He runs his hand through his short, blond hair. "This wasn't supposed to happen yet. Baby Declan was supposed to be here in another month. I thought I'd have time to party and get it out of my system."

I let the Baby Declan slide. This is the first time in months he seems genuine and honest with me. He looks down at his hands, wringing them together.

I place my hand on his shoulder. "I know it's scary. I'm scared out of my mind. I worry about every little thing. What if I forget to feed him? Or what if I drop him? Or what if I forget I even have a kid and leave the house? What..."

Declan grabs my arm. "Okay, calm down. You're making me even more scared than I already am." He clears his throat. "Look, I know I've been a real prick. I have to work on a few things, but I'm excited to have a son. If it was a girl..." He cocks his head to the side.

"Don't finish that thought. You're doing so good, don't ruin it." I am half joking.

"Anyway, if you could just be patient with me, I'll fix this." He takes my empty hand in his, rubbing his thumb along my skin. "Will you be patient with me?" His tone is soft and sincere.

I bit the inside of my lip, and nod. "Okay, I can do that. But can we come up with more of a plan? I'd like to know when we're going to see you."

"I'll stay here when I can. My parents would like to see him as much as possible too, so maybe we can stay there for a few nights too. I have a few more games coming up. Thanksgiving is next week, I have a game on that day, so you need to decide whether you're coming up with him to support me. We can stay at my parent's vacation house."

I really don't want to spend my first Thanksgiving together as a family at a football game. There are certain things if this is going to work between Declan and I, then I need to change my attitude. However, the only reason I'm even considering giving this a shot is Luca.

"Okay. We can do that."

He smiles a genuine smile; one I haven't seen for a long time. It's the smile I fell for when we first met. Declan isn't a bad guy; he's just young and has a lot on his plate. I understand that. Now I have the baby, I've been doing my classes online. It hasn't been easy studying then feeding and changing Luca, but I knew it wasn't going to be the moment I found out I was pregnant.

My parents enter the room, completely unaware we're having the most serious conversation of our relationship.

"Declan, we just realized you were here. How are you doing, my boy?"

Sometimes I'm certain my father likes him more than he likes me. The way his face lights up when Declan stands to greet him with a hug and a hand on his shoulder is almost too much. Maybe even a little nauseating.

An unwanted thought pops into my head. Would he treat Jake the same way? My father would never be proud of Jake. He's a bar owner, a street racer, a fighter, and many other things I don't even know of yet. However, he's done nothing but take care of me. He's been there for me when no one else has. When I think of my future, for some reason his face pops into my mind.

"Harlow, did you hear me?"

"I'm sorry, I missed what you said."

"Declan is staying the night. You two can stay in your room with the baby. If you need anything let us know." My dad says cheerfully. There really isn't anything now inappropriate going on between us since I gave birth to his child. I'm unable to do anything now anyway.

Later that night, it doesn't stop his hand from creeping up my shirt as we lay in bed together. "Declan. I'm not allowed to do anything like that. I'm still healing."

He groans and rolls over onto his back, slapping his hands on the mattress in frustration. "Harlow, it's been forever. If I have to get something out of this whole mess, it should be having you anytime I want."

"What mess are you talking about?" I roll over to face him. The anger is welling up inside me ready to explode.

"I don't want to fight. If you need me to pick him up let me know."

"Are you serious right now?" What do I have to do to get you to be a decent human being?" If Luca wasn't lying beside the bed in his bassinet, I'd be screaming at the top of my lungs instead it comes out a strained whisper.

Declan sits up. "Harlow, I love you. I'm trying here, okay? We haven't had sex in weeks. What am I supposed to do when you're lying beside me in a skimpy tank top and underwear? And then I found out your boss was there when my son was born. I need to be with you," he pleads, leaning over as his lips come to my neck. At one time, I loved it when he kissed me but now, I just want him off me.

"Declan, we need to talk about this. There's nothing to be jealous of, he's just a friend."

Declan's nose flares. "I don't want him near you. I don't like the way he looks at you."

"He doesn't look at me in a certain way. He's just my boss."

"He wants my girl, and he can't have her."

Here we go, I'm not a possession. This isn't a game where I'm the prize.

He lets go of my hands and supports his weight on his elbows, but his face is inches from mine. I swipe my hands through his short hair. "Declan, we need to make a plan for our future. I need you around and willing to take care of your family. I'm not saying we need to get married or anything. But I want to know if I can count on you as a father. That you want to be in Luca's life."

"Of course, I do. It will get better once the season is over. My future, our future, depends on how I play. The NFL is the next step. So, if it means I have to be away for practice and games to get us to the next level, I need your support too. You can always stay with me at my apartment. My roommates don't care."

"I can't stay at your apartment. There are four guys living there. They like to throw parties. Luca needs quiet and to be honest, so do I. We can try to find a place. I can finish some of my classes online, but I have a few I need to take in person. Maybe I can transfer to your school?"

As I say it, my stomach knots. I don't want to transfer to his college. I like mine and I don't want to move, but if it's to make things better, it might be what I need to do.

Declan sighs. "We'll figure something out. Let's get some sleep. Luca will be getting up soon and you need your rest."

The next morning, Declan holds Luca while I get dressed and even feeds him a bottle. He's getting more comfortable, but I wouldn't let him take care of Luca by himself yet. Heck, I barely trust myself.

"What are your plans for today?" I ask Declan.

"I've got to get to practice today. It's Sunday so I'll see you on Thursday. You'll drive up that morning, right?"

I can't believe I'm giving this another chance. I'm doing it for my son and giving Declan the opportunity to prove he wants to be a father. I don't want to regret not doing everything I can to give Luca the family he deserves. But something tells me I'm about to regret giving him a second chance.

"Yeah. We'll be there."

22

HARLOW

The car is packed, and Luca is secure in his little car seat. He looks adorable in his team jersey and matching shoes. I got them online months ago and I'm surprised they actually fit. He has a little hat on too. This is our first road trip together. My parents offered to drive but I need to do more on my own.

It's only an hour's drive. Hopefully, he sleeps, and I won't need to stop and feed him. On my way, I call Callie.

"Hey. What are you up to?"

"Just helping Gran with dinner. Anna and I are making a cake. How is the cutest baby in the world doing on your trip?" I told her about my plans last night.

"Good. He's sleeping," I tell her as I look in my rearview mirror showing his reflection from another mirror aimed so I can see him perfectly.

"I'm glad things with you and Declan are working out. Hold on a sec?" She says something I can't make out and then comes back on the line. "Sorry, Jake was rambling on about something. I couldn't hear you over his loudmouth."

"How is he doing?" I say. I want to slap my mouth shut. I'm trying to figure out my situation with Declan, not worry about Jake.

"He's...fine." I can almost hear the question in her voice. Why do you want to know? And it's a very valid question. One thing I don't want to answer. "Just thank him again for bringing me to the hospital and all." Trying to seem casual about the whole birth situation.

"Ok, I'll do that. Anyway, what are the plans for today? Game, dinner, and then what?"

"His parents have a house for us all to stay at, so we'll just spend some time together. I'm sure it's going to be great."

"Yes, it is." We spent a few more minutes chatting. When I hear Jake's voice in the background. He's joking around about something. My favorite version of Jake. When he's carefree and not so serious.

My mind drifts to his face. His smile. His hair. His everything. Deciding I need to pay attention to the road, I tell her to have a great day with her family and try to concentrate on the road ahead of me.

Parking is a nightmare. And don't get me started on the trek over to our seats. Finally, we make it to the front row, seats A6 and A7. At first the idea of a newborn baby having its own seat seemed ridiculous, now we're here, I'm thankful. It gives us more room for his car seat, diaper bag and in general more room for me to move. We're seated next to his parents, and Luca cries, letting me know it's time to eat.

After ten minutes of filling his belly, he decides a nap is in order. Luca's not a football fan yet, but I'm sure he will be the way Mercer's are. Declan's family pays minimal attention to their grandson. They are too busy schmoozing with their college fundraising buddies.

Staring off onto the field, Declan has a great game. By halftime they're up by twenty-one points. The phone in my pocket pings with a text. It's from Callie.

Callie

Jake is SOOO jealous btw.

The three little dots appear... waiting along with me.

Callie

> Gran won't let him have a piece until he apologizes for not helping me with the dishes.

Jake's face pops up on my phone. He's wearing a childish pout with squinting eyes. His arms crossed. Why do I think this is adorable?

I'm SOOO jealous too! And snapped a photo of the football field in front of me. I'd rather be there than here. The thought makes me uncomfortable. Ugh... I'm stuck here with people who care less. There was minimal holding and cooing from his grandparents.

After half time the game seems to drag, and Luca is now cuddled in my arms. They are now winning thirty-two to seven.

The clock is at the two-minute mark. I'm thrilled. It's almost over. I started to pack a few little things I have out of Luca's bag. When I catch Declan celebrating on the sideline with his teammates.

Becker is his teammate, who happens to be over three hundred pounds and the biggest teddy bear of a guy I've ever met. They slap each other on the back. He continues to give other teammates fist bumps, and even a guy hugged a few.

As the game ends, a bouncy blond cheerleader with the team's uniform and bright red bow in her ponytail comes rushing over from the sideline and right into the arms of my boyfriend.

Her short skirt rides up, as she jumps up, wrapping her arms and legs around his tall frame. He wraps one arm around her waist and hikes her a little further up his body. Not unlike what he used to do to me after a big win. He spins her around in celebration, lowering her to the ground but not before she kisses him on the cheek.

His eyes flash up to me almost as if he's making sure, I didn't see. He waves up to me and mouths something to her. She turns and wiggles her fingers up to me then trots away. Before I can even react, Mrs. Mercer interrupts. "Dear, isn't that lovely? Those kids are all a team and celebrating, even the cheerleaders feel free to celebrate with them."

My stomach sinks. They seemed to be a little friendlier than cheering for the same team. Maybe I'm just overreacting or maybe it's jealousy because those days of me running onto the field are over.

I nod, telling her I'm going to take the baby to the car, and I'll see them at their house for Thanksgiving dinner.

Normally, I'd like to stay and congratulate him on the big win. After seeing him with his cheerleader friend, I want to get out here as fast as I can.

After juggling Luca's things, making my way up the stands to the exit, and getting him settled in the car, I'm exhausted. If I didn't have an hour to drive and wasn't planning on staying at the Mercer's, we'd be headed back home.

The traffic out of this parking lot is atrocious. To distract myself while we're wall to wall cars and not moving anytime soon, I pull up the picture of Jake, enlarging his facial features. His pouty lips and sad eyes are cute as hell. I'd give him anything he wanted with that face.

I shake my head. I'm going crazy. One moment I'm crying over my child's father hugging another girl to the dreamy eyes of Jake—my boss. I'm not even sure why I pulled up this particular picture. Maybe I was looking for something to make me less miserable. For some reason, it worked.

***

Once the car seat is off the base, I toss the diaper bag over my shoulder, Luca and I head inside the massive house his grandparents have purchased just for football games. They call it their vacation house.

We walk up the flight of steps to the large yellow front door. The house's siding is white with yellow shutters framing the windows. There are perfectly manicured bushes trimming the perimeter of the house. It looks straight out of a magazine.

Mrs. Mercer opens the door with her perfectly ironed white blouse, tailored red pants, and matching red shoes. Her brown hair is styled into a pixie cut. Her makeup is applied so perfectly it's as if it's painted on. She's so sophisticated, making me feel like a mess in my jeans and a plain light brown sweater.

"There is my baby. Why don't you have him covered with a blanket?" She opens the door wider for me. "Come in here. It's cold."

I haven't had many conversations with her in the years Declan and I have dated. It's been basic conversations, and this is the first time she's sounded unhappy with me. The weather is chilly, but he has a jacket on.

"Just set the car seat on the bench there." She points to the wooden bench. "Get him out of the seat. It looks so uncomfortable."

The next twenty minutes go on like that. Questions and why did you dress him like that? Do you have another outfit for him? Are you using cloth diapers because the disposable kind will give him diaper rash? The questioning seems never ending.

We've finally settled into the living area. I would never call it a living room or family room. It's the most pristine white furniture I've ever seen. Declan's mom prides herself on her home decor. This is her showroom, not somewhere to relax and enjoy each other's company. I wonder what she would do if I changed Luca's diaper on her sofa?

"Would you like help with setting the table or making dinner?" I ask, hoping it will melt the iceberg in the room, but she responds with, "Now, honey, we have staff to do that."

We sit for at least twenty more minutes while she recounts her path to decorating this living area. I nod and say, "How lovely." when prompted. My patience is wearing thin with Declan. Mrs. Mercer directs us to the dining room as she concludes her tour.

Me

> Are you at least on your way?

No response.

Five minutes later...

Me

> You need to get here ASAP! Dinner is being served in five minutes with or without you!

Still no response. At this point, I'm holding Luca who has taken a bottle and is looking as if he's in a happy little food coma.

Declan's mom announces it's time to eat. "Have you been able to reach Declan?" I ask her, probably for the fifth time this evening.

"No. But we can start without him. He knows when dinner time is." She nods as if he pays any attention to her demands. Declan only does what Declan wants to do.

The annoyance level is approaching catastrophic. I'm ready to get up from the table when Gretchen, the server for this evening, plops a scoop of mashed potatoes on the porcelain China plate with a flower pattern. Secretly, I wonder what the plate would look like to shattering off of Declan's head.

Declan's father carries on stuffing his face and not once has spoken. It's been his mother's show the whole time. No other family members or friends of theirs are here. My parents always told me you can tell a lot about a family by who attends their dinner table. Today I gave up Thanksgiving dinner with my parents, not to mention Luca is spending his first holiday with two obnoxious jerks. Although I don't have any siblings, we have several family friends, aunts, uncles, and cousins attending and I'm missing it all.

After a quiet meal, and I mean you can only hear the clinking of utensils off the China, Luca is starting to get restless in his infant chair. I've had it on a rocking motion through dinner. He's as over it as I am.

As I pick up Luca from his seat, his father finally texts me.

Declan

> Sorry, I can't make it. Coach makes the team celebrate together.

"Are you freaking kidding me?"

"Excuse me?" Mrs. Mercer questions, her tone appalled as she places a hand over her chest.

"Your son is celebrating with his team and won't be coming to dinner." If she's appalled, then I'm pissed. Instead, I keep my tone steady and curt, not wanting to express my true emotions. If I did what I really wanted, I'd be flipping tables over.

In a dramatic fashion, I stand and toss the delicate napkin on my half-eaten dinner. "We won't be staying for the rest of the night like we planned. Your son has better things to do than stay with his family, so I'll spend what's left of Thanksgiving with mine."

"Oh dear, you can still stay here. We'd love to spend the day with Luca tomorrow."

"That would be nice; however, Declan's priority is football and mine is our son."

Mrs. Mercer doesn't argue further. Thankful for the moment of silence, I gather our things. Of course, instead of seeing us in the car, Gretchen gets stuck with the duty. Again, I'm thankful.

"Good night, ma'am."

I nod at Gretchen. I'm not much older than her.

When we hit the interstate, I'm going to call Callie to tell her about my so-called trip. Normally I'd think she wouldn't believe it, but in this case, she might expect nothing less.

23

JAKE

After dinner, I should be in a turkey coma laying on the couch but instead, I'm at my bar drowning in some whiskey all by myself like some loser.

There are a few receipts scattered throughout this week's schedule. Harlow's name is still on some, blinking at me like a neon sign. I should remove her name; she may not be coming back to work for a while. I'm going to need to find a replacement, but I can't make myself do it.

Tonight, she and Declan are celebrating their baby's first Thanksgiving together. They are reveling in the joys of being new parents. Enjoying their own little family, living the perfect life. Here I am wishing she'd come back to work just so I could see her smile.

Ugh... this isn't right. She's with him and they have a kid. I'm not a homewrecker. I'm not my mother or my father. She cheated on him, and he cheated on her. My father skipped out of town years ago when I was five years old. My memories of him are foggy. Most of my childhood was spent with stepfathers who were nothing like a father to me.

My father hasn't attempted to contact me. Even if I wanted to contact him – which I don't, I'd have no idea where to start.

Out of the corner of my eye, I catch movement at the door. This would be the third person who's tried to come in for a drink. I should have stayed open tonight, but Gran wouldn't allow it.

Approaching the door, loudly I say, "Sorry we're closed." But the closer I get; the familiar long strawberry blond hair and wide greenish gray eyes stare back at me.

"Harlow?"

She gives me a shy smile along with a sheepish wave through the glass door. My hand moves on its own. She steps through. It's as if a gust of wind and peace walks in with her.

"What are you doing here?" I can't hide the awe in my voice.

She looks around and must notice no customers are here. "I didn't even stop to think you wouldn't be open on a holiday. I'm sorry. I'll go." She shakes her head.

"No." Clearing my voice so she can't hear the panic, "I mean, do you want a drink or something to eat?"

"Yeah, sure. What are you drinking?"

"Whiskey."

"I'll have that too. It's been a day." I pause, wondering if it's okay for her to drink because she just had a baby a few weeks ago but then think better of it. She knows what she's doing. She walks past me and takes a seat next to the one I vacated. She looks beautiful, wearing slim dress pants that hug her body perfectly and a plain light brown sweater matching her eyes.

"Shouldn't you be at home with Luca?" As soon as I ask, I know I sound like a dick, regretting my words, and the fall of her smile tells me I'm right. "Being Thanksgiving... I figured you would be home with him and Declan."

Moving behind the bar, she says, "I was hoping Callie was here. My parents offered to put Luca to bed. She didn't answer my texts, but I thought she might be here working. It never occurred to me she wouldn't." She swipes her hand through her hair. "But now I realize how silly it was for me to come here. You don't need some whiney girl telling you her problems."

I smile. "You know that's in my job description as a bartender. It's practically written across my forehead." I slide my finger across it and say, "Tell this guy all your worries and he'll get you drunk."

Harlow chuckles at my stupid joke.

"At least I got you to laugh." I fill her glass with whiskey, sliding it over to her. She picks it up and waves it toward me. "Cheers."

She swallows and scrunches her face. "Wow, that was stronger than expected."

"You probably haven't drank in a while."

"Or barely ever. I'm not a big drinker, but tonight it's a good idea."

"Can I ask what happened?" My instincts tell me, the football star screwed up.

"Have you ever been so tired, you know, of not being someone's priority? I don't need him to be with me twenty-four seven, but some attention would be good. First, there was the cheerleader wrapped in his arms practically dry humping him. Then I was stuck with his asshole parents who ignored Luca and I for their stuck-up friends. To top it all off, Declan never showed up for dinner. He celebrated with his team instead."

She brings the glass up to her plump lips. As if needing a break to compose herself.

"Anyway, it doesn't matter. I kind of got myself into this situation."

"What situation?"

She scoffs, "Having a baby."

"I know it's a lot to handle, but you got this. I've never met anyone more responsible than you. Plus, I've also seen you with Luca, you're an amazing mother."

She's silent – staring off in the direction of the empty stage then she drains her drink without an expression. Granted, I didn't put much in there, but I can't recall the last time I saw her drink.

Harlow sets down her glass, then lowers her head into her hands and moans. "I'm so sorry, I should go. I'm so depressing."

Setting my hand on her arm, "Stay with me. We both have had a shitty day."

Her head rises and those damn beautiful eyes full of unshed tears stare back at me. "I'm a complete and utter mess. My life is a complete cluster fuck."

Unable to hold back my laugh, "I had no idea you had it in you."

"What?" she asks, completely unaware of how she holds herself together. This is the first time I've seen her falter.

"I didn't think you would get worked up. I mean, I've seen you snap at a customer or two, when they've gotten out of line, but never full of piss and vinegar."

Turning to face me, she narrows her eyes, quietly assessing me. It isn't sending me warm and fuzzy feelings. I probably should stop while I'm ahead.

"What are you eighty years old?" she snaps, clearly annoyed with me.

"Have you met my Gran? It's unavoidable."

"Yes, I have and love her to pieces, but I don't love that I'm a hot mess." She lifts her arms in the air in frustration. "I'm a single mom who's waiting for the father of her child to decide to actually be a father. I'm not sure if we should stay together. I have to finish college online instead of in person, still live with my parents, and can't go back to work until her incision and vagina heals!" Her voice rises on the last part.

I spit the sip of whiskey I stupidly took during her speech.

Her arms fall to her side with a loud sigh. "See, icing on the cake. Now my boss thinks I'm a lunatic. Are you trying to be an ass to me tonight because I've had about all I can take?"

Wiping the liquid with the back of my hand. I say, "Listen. I just mean you always seem so put together and to see you upset and flustered it makes you seem so... maybe more relatable than I ever thought possible." Harlow's left eyebrow raises, "What do you mean, am I like a bitch or a spoiled brat because everyone seems to think I'm this rich girl whose parents pay and do everything for her. And yes, they help but not in the way people think. They make my life harder some days." She lowers her head and crosses her arms.

Stepping closer to her, I do what I've dreamed of doing since the moment I met her. My finger reaches up, tipping her chin, so I can see her eyes. I want her to know I mean every word.

I'm just going to jump, especially since she confirmed she's having doubts about Declan.

"Stop. You don't have to show me how perfect you are or put together or independent, because you don't need to prove a damn thing to me or anyone else. You are who you are and damn it if I don't already think you're perfect." The words spill out in a rush. I've never been more honest with someone in my life.

Our eyes lock, studying her glistening emerald globes; she's anything but imperfect. We're transfixed at this moment. I don't think anything could pull me away from her beautiful, freckled nose, soft pink plush lips, and long dark lashes. An amusing smile tugs at my lips. *Have I ever noticed a woman's lashes before?* No... I know I haven't because there has never been anyone who I've been so attracted to.

Unable to stop myself, my thumb brushes across her bottom lip.

She inhales and I stop breathing all together. "You think I'm perfect?" she asks in a quiet voice.

"Yes, just the way you are. I wouldn't change anything. If I had the chance, I'd tell you every day."

My hand finds its way to her hair and threads through the silky strands. My eyes fall to her lips, glistening, making me want to taste them. The electricity between us is undeniable, the pull is almost unworldly. There is nothing I wouldn't do at this moment to have her be mine, but I'm not worthy of her. Not like this. Somewhere in my brain, a voice I've heard a million times speaks up, whispering, "You aren't good enough for her."

That voice stops me from moving any further with her, with every inch of my body protesting. Closing my eyes, my hands fall away. I step back.

"Umm...we should get out of here."

She turns around and clears her throat, "Yeah, yeah. I should go home and check on Luca."

Unable to let her go, I blurt it out. "Do you want to check out a race with me?"

"Yes." She exhales. Relief evident in her smile. "But it's late. Where do you want to go at this hour on Thanksgiving? I mean..." She pauses, gesturing toward the empty bar. "You're not even open. And you are always open."

"You think you're so funny, don't you?" I wag my finger at her, sparking a knowing expression on her beautiful face. "I think you need something fun and different. Are you up for the challenge?"

She puts her finger up to her chin, thinking for a moment. Damn, can she be any cuter?

"Yeah, I think I am."

I tug her hand, and we head out the door. Looking as fast as I can behind me, she doesn't change her mind. I'm going to give her some adventure.

We reach my car; I open the passenger side door for her and without hesitation she gets in. We head out of Lake Haven. She doesn't ask where we're going or what we're doing. She sits quietly while listening to the radio. I'm a wreck on the inside. She's got my nerves on edge.

What will she think of me racing? I'm nothing like her jock boyfriend. Which I'm pretty fucking proud of, but her family probably feels different from what she's told me. They think he's inventing a cure for a disease. I got news for them, nothing cures a dickhead.

Minutes later we reach Echo Valley. It's the next town over. We race here on a regular basis and have yet to get caught by the police. Ryder, my friend who drives a blue Thunderbird, has a cousin who usually covers for us.

We aren't racing any other team, so we'll be fine.

I make a right turn down a narrow gravel road with trees lining both sides.

"Okay, I trust you and all, but this is super creepy. I'd like to make it home to my son tonight."

Without thinking, I place my hand on her knee. She doesn't react so I leave it there. I'm not sure what I'm doing. I just know I want her anyway she'll let me have her. So, if a friendly hand on her thigh is okay with her then it's definitely okay with me.

"If you trust me; then relax. I've got you."

"Okay," she says quietly.

Turning one more time, we reach our destination where my buddies; Ryder, Cooper, and Wes have their cars lined up, ready to test their cars.

Turning to face her, I ask, "Have you ever raced before?"

"What?" Her eyes widened. "No. Are you crazy?"

"Yep, and you're going to love it! I know you've been to Ben's races, but to a very different version. It's more organized and the drivers are well known around the country. This is small town racing. Where Ben, Van, and I really grew up. They've outgrown it but not me."

She looks like a deer in the headlights while I try to explain this to her. "See I love racing with Ben and Van, but there's something so different about this. It's the adrenaline. It's the new guys who come out of nowhere thinking they're the best and I like to show them how wrong they are."

"I guess I don't get it. Racing is racing. Isn't it?" She questions, crinkling her nose. Damn, she's cute. It's refreshing.

"The stakes make it different. It's not for points or money. It's about being the best at racing. Our races are much more personal, and the stakes are much higher." I don't really want to tell her more. I've had to beat guys up because of the outcomes of bets. I'm not proud of it but when you make a bet, you better keep up your end of it. I just got her to come to me on her own; I don't want to scare her away yet. "Don't worry, tonight we're just going to practice against each other."

Cooper knocks on my window. "Hey, bro." His grin widens. "Who's the lovely lady in your passenger seat?"

"No. Don't even try it. She's just here to watch. Don't look and don't fucking go near her."

He puts his hand up. "All right. Jeez. We're waiting for Cam and his guys."

"Cam? No... I'm not racing. I thought it was just going to be us testing."

"He put up a thousand bucks." he says gritting through his teeth, so maybe Harlow can't hear.

"Fuck. Fine."

Harlow shifts in her seat. Damn it! I can't race with her in the car, but I don't want to leave her alone with any of the guys either. I don't want Cam and his guys to think if they see a pretty girl standing on the sidelines; they can try and hit on her. No... I can keep her safe.

"What's wrong?" she asks.

"I'm racing, but I don't want you in the car with me, and I don't want you out of it either. What do you want to do?"

She pauses for a moment then says, "Let's do it. I trust you. Besides, I need a little adventure."

We wait another ten minutes until Cam shows up. I take Harlow's hand as we walk up to the circle where all the racers are standing. She doesn't pull away. We're standing so close to each other that our shoulders are touching. She distracts me which never happens when it comes to race details. Thankfully, Ryder calls my name bringing me back to the conversation.

"One thousand bucks. Ryder flags. We race down to the stop sign. No scraping each other and crossing the lane is acceptable." Cam rattles off his terms.

Cam is a big guy. He must use the gym every day. His arms are crossed like he's about to bounce someone in this circle. I know his game though. He's just trying to intimidate us; good fucking luck.

"No crossing the line. I don't need anyone smacking into my car." I say back.

Cam looks at some other guy in a sweatshirt and ball cap I don't recognize. He nods to Cam and extends his hand to me.

"Deal." We shake hands on it. I tighten my grip on Harlow.

Harlow's eyes are glimmering in the lights. "That was exciting. I see what you say about adrenaline."

"You haven't seen anything yet."

24

HARLOW

I can't believe I'm doing this stupid thing. Jake has asked me at least six times if I want to get out of this race and sit in Ryder's car. In all honesty, I want to stay with Jake. He's such a mystery to me and that almost kiss? I literally have never felt the heat along with a rush before. Certainly, never with Declan.

For the most bizarre reason, there isn't an ounce of me that doesn't trust Jake. My alarm bells should be blaring at street drag racing.

Me?

Nothing.

I want to do this. I trust he wouldn't put me in any kind of danger.

Jakes glances over at me. "I'm sorry about this. I wasn't taking you to a race tonight. We were supposed to just test our cars. Like making sure everything's working correctly and making sure the car are tuned correctly to meet the speeds that we want."

"It's exciting. I've obviously seen the other kind of races, but it's more fun to have a literal front row seat to the action."

Once we're back in the car, I ask him, "So how does this work?"

"The fastest wins."

"I know that, ass." I say, swatting his chest. "What do I do?"

"Just enjoy the ride, baby."

The way he held my hand earlier, like he was protecting me and letting all of those guys know I'm with him. Guilt creeps in as I smile at the thought of being his. Pushing it down, I concentrate on getting ready to race. I'm going to have some fun on this ride.

I buckle up my five-point harness seat belt. Jake leans over from his side and tugs at the straps to tighten them up. He looks up at me. Our eyes lock for just a moment. Glancing back down, he clears his throat.

"So, we're going to get up to one hundred twenty or so; you'll feel it by getting forced into your seat when I accelerate." His warning amps up the butterflies in my stomach.

"Is that the fastest we'll go?"

"Hard to tell. Maybe a little faster. We don't have a long stretch of road, so it'll depend on how fast his car can go. Regardless, I'll go however fast I need to in order to win. And Harlow..." He looks directly at me. "We will win."

I don't doubt him, not for one second.

The engine revs to life, and my seat vibrates underneath me.

"Loud, huh?" he yells.

"Yes, it really is." I yell back.

He shifts the car into gear, drifting up to the starting line that the group agreed on earlier.

Ryder's voice drifts over the sound system in the car. "Is that a CB radio?"

"Yeah." He chuckles, "I'm impressed you even know what that is. We need a decent way to communicate, and we run on a channel the cops don't check. Ever."

"Cam is ready to go." A voice comes over the CB.

"Let's go." Jake's deep voice fills the car.

Ryder walks by the passenger window while another car pulls up on the other side of us. It seems it could be louder than Jakes. I have no idea what kind of car it is, but it looks like it could have been from the 1980s.

"He's a fast son of a bitch. But we'll get him," Jake tells me.

Ryder stands in front of us, motioning with his hand for us to pull up and then makes a fist and we stop.

He leans over to the other car, making the same motion at them. I can't see our opponent. So much is going on at the same time. Jake pushes on the pedal, revving the engine.

Ryder takes a few steps back. A flash of light shines brightly with the rise of his arm. My body catapults back into my seat and in moments it feels as if I'm flying through space. Never have I felt like this in a car or anywhere else. My eyes are closed yet I can tell we're straight as an arrow, instinctively I can't help but keep them closed. The adrenaline rushes through me unlike anything I've ever felt. Both fear and excitement rip through my body. I want to stop and never stop at the same time.

Jake's voice floats through, "Woo-hoo!"

My eyes fly open as I'm slammed forward and then whipped back. The car does some type of fishtail or slide until we come to a stop. Before I can scream in either excitement or terror, Ryder calls over the radio. "Red wins by three cars."

"We won?" I ask, excitement and confusion, battling in the haze of this moment.

Jake's eyes dance with excitement. "Yep, you're good luck. You okay over there?"

"Yes. No. I don't know." Clearly, I can't form words right now. "I have never done anything that wild. Crazy. Irrational yet so fun!" I answer, pushing the loose hair off my face.

He unbuckles, opening up the car door. My breathing starts to come back to some type of normalcy. Jake opens my door and pokes his head through. Then I lean and start undoing my harness. His scent envelops me. The leather and cologne mixed with the car fumes all seem familiar in an odd way.

His smile is radiating. A big grin on his usually serious lips.

He slips an arm underneath my bottom and hoists me up in his arms. Once out of the car, he spins me around in celebration. My grasp tightens around his neck. The excitement isn't just because we won, it's because I'm in his arms celebrating with him. I ignore the guilt. This isn't the time, pushing it down deeper where it belongs.

Ryder, Cooper, Wes, and some other people come running up beside us. Hoots and hollers break out all around us.

Jake glances at me as we come to a halt. His eyes roam to my mouth then slowly close. He places his lips against my forehead, then sets me down to my feet.

"That was awesome, man. Cam is so pissed. He'll hate to give you a grand. It was a clean race, too. Nothing for him to bitch about."

The blue car is nowhere in sight. A stalky stranger walks over wearing a flat expression and frowns coming over to us. He doesn't say a word, puts his hands in this pocket, and yanks out a stack of bills. Slaps the stack into Ryder's hands and walks in the other direction.

Just as Ryder starts to count the money, a loud siren fills the chilly night air. And then someone yells, "Run!" and then "Fuck!"

Like something out of a movie, two cop cars surround Ryder, Jake, and me. Where did everyone else go?

"Ryder Jones I've warned you."

"Officer Milton, how are you on this fine evening?" Ryder asks casually, as if we're out for a stroll and happens upon two friends, not law enforcement officers with guns.

I'm overcome with how calm Ryder and Jake are at the moment. Fear mixed with adrenaline comes over me. I have to be overreacting, right? Maybe this always happens after a race. The races I've been to with Callie, all the cops knew about the race. Most of the time, there are officers there for crowd control.

Jake leans over, quietly says, "Don't worry. I'll get you out of this. You won't go to jail."

Jail? Why would I be going to jail? I've never seen anyone go to jail after a race. Panic spreads like a wildfire through my pores.

"You might, it's up to your boyfriend over here," the officer in uniform responds.

"They've been warned before. It's so much better for me when your cousin is on vacation, isn't it, Ryder?"

"Officer Milton. We've been over this. There wasn't any racing going on. See, it's just us." He motions toward his and Jake's cars. I literally have no idea where the hell everyone else disappeared to. Clearly, my brain isn't working as fast as theirs.

"You've been warned. This isn't my first rodeo with you boys." Office Milton reminds me of an old southern cop. Burly, obnoxious, overweight, and cocky as hell. He grates on my nerves. "I told you boys the next time I caught you we were taking your cars and then tucking you nicely in the back of our patrol cars. I'm just sorry you got such a pretty young lady in the mix." He nods in my direction.

"We were not racing. She's innocently caught up in this mix-up. We were just coming out here to catch up and look at the stars." Jake lies, his voice never betraying him.

"Your name and address?" directing his question to me.

"Harlow Layne, Halfacre Road, Lake Haven..."

"Layne as in Attorney Harold Layne?" He stops writing, glancing up at me.

I want to roll my eyes but suppress the urge. Everyone seems to know who he is. "Yes, he's, my father."

"Christ, he'd kill me if I took his daughter to jail." Officer Milton says to himself then places his cuffs I didn't see before back into its holder. "I tell you what, I'll give him a call, and he can come get you." He turns to Jake and Ryder. "You two are not free to go. So, stay put."

"Your father has helped many people with his legal knowledge. He's a very important person in the community. He's also helped me out a time or two. I'm sure he's worried about you." The officer walks away from me while pulling out his phone.

"If you'll just let us go, Jake can give me a ride home. I really don't want to wake my father up at this time of night," I plead, hoping he won't add to the long list of problems I've already accumulated.

The officer faces me. "He's probably pacing the floors right now wondering why you're out so late."

I groan. "I'll call him."

Taking my phone out of my pocket, I pretend to dial his number only Mr. Outstanding Police Office or wherever – is quicker on the drawl and dials my dad's number. How did he get his number so quickly and why is so familiar with my dad? We live a whole town away from this place?

"Mr. Layne, this is Officer Milton." I stop listening, wanting to crawl into a hole and hide for a few years.

My father is the last person I want to talk to about this let alone have him come and pick me up.

I glance to find Jake and Ryder already in handcuffs, standing beside the other police officer seems to be answering questions. Jake, as if he can feel me, looks up and nods. His eyes staring straight into my soul. The remorse on his face is unlike anything I've seen before. He seems worried and sad and mad all in the same crinkle on his forehead.

We were racing and we shouldn't have been, but this seems excessive. We didn't hurt anyone. It's a vacant road. We weren't drinking or doing drugs. Just a little harmless racing. People do it all the time. Hopefully, my father will see the injustice in this, right?

The officers are walking around Jake's car, looking inside and I can't really make out what they're saying. Officer Milton still has his phone up to his ear. What on earth could he still be talking to my father about?

He hangs up after another few moments. My stomach is in knots. My parents were supposed to put Luca to bed and relax for the night, not picking up their adult daughter who was street racing. The last thing I need is more disappointed looks from him and my mother. I'm not an irresponsible person but my one and only oops resulted in a beautiful baby boy and many kinks in my perfect plans.

The officer gets my attention with the crunching gravel under his boots. "I have a few questions to ask you?"

The officer rambles on about how wonderful my father is and asks a ton more questions. Then he walks over to Jake. The officer is keeping us separate for some reason.

My father's car comes into view. He must have gone double the speed limit to get here so fast.

"Do you know if any money exchanged hands?" he continues.

My father slams his car door. "Don't you answer any questions, Harlow!"

"Mr. Layne, good to see you, sir."

"I'd hoped the next time I'd see you would be at the fundraiser, not my daughter's arrest," Dad deadpans with no hint of amusement.

"I was just asking her if money exchanged hands or if this race was planned ahead of time?" Officer Milton directs his attention to me and seems a little less pleasant now that my father has arrived.

"From what little information you gave me over the phone, I assume she is not under arrest?"

"No, she is not. But I'd like her to answer some questions."

My father nods, prompting me to continue.

I swallow because the answer is of course yes – we were racing for money. If I answer yes, everyone is going to jail. I'm not a liar. But I don't see the benefit of telling the truth in this case. On the other hand, if I would have been thinking straight, and not been distracted by those lustful dark eyes, I wouldn't have to lie.

The less I pretend to know, the better. I'm not going to fully lie, but I'm not going to tell them anything they don't need to know.

"We went for a ride. I had a bad day. I stopped by work and saw it was closed. Jake offered to take a ride here to get my mind off my problems. His buddy, who I don't know, had a great spot picked out to see the meteor shower. That's it. We were looking up at the sky when you folks came barreling in like you were from the Dukes of Hazzard."

"Huh? He cocks his head to the side. "I had no clue kids still knew what that show was," Officer Milton chuckles, distracted by his own ridiculous thoughts.

"Focus, Milton. My daughter and her friends are not going to jail for stargazing. I think you're making a mountain out of nothing. Let's call it a night and go home. Clearly you're needed for much more important incidents."

Jake and Ryder are still in handcuffs, watching and listening to my father.

"Okay. You're right. I just need your daughter to confirm no money exchanged hands, and no one raced tonight."

Both men glare at me, trying to see if I'm lying.

"Of course not, Daddy." I swallow and lie but kind of want to laugh. I've never lied to him before in my life. I can't tell if he believes me or not. I keep going. "It was all just a stupid misunderstanding. My boss just wanted to help get my mind off the crappy day I had." My dad frowns. Frowns might be too mellow of a word for the contortion of rage that's dancing on his face right now.

"This is your *boss*... from Rae's *Bar*?" he asks, emphasizing the words as if they taste bad in his mouth. "And he was not street racing, correct?" He drops his head, and glares into my eyes as if looking like I'm five years old and stole a cookie out of his special cookie hiding spot.

"Correct. He wasn't street racing. I don't even know what street racing is." I add emphasis. Of course, he can see through the lie. He knows I've been to races and my best friend is Callie Rae. Her husband's job is street racing only on a bigger scale.

My father faces the officers. "There you have it. Let the boys go."

"Mr. Layne. I'm happy to let your daughter go, but I can't let them go without more questioning. We received a phone call. We can't just ignore it."

"Do you have any proof they were racing, or did you see them racing with your own eyes?"

"Well..." he says, looking around like he's going to find some proof out of thin air. The only evidence is the parked cars on the desolate road could look like they got done racing, or they brought people here to stargaze. Hopefully, these officers aren't able to see the skid marks. "We didn't see them race and their cars weren't even running when we pulled up."

"There you have it. No arrests tonight, Milton." My dad places a hand on his shoulder and ushers him over to the side of a police car where I can't make out what they're saying. I don't really care as long as Jake, Ryder, and I can leave.

Speaking of Jake, he's getting his handcuffs taken off by the other officer. Jake rubs his wrist at the freedom.

All of my instincts are pleading to go check on Jake. But if I know my father as well as I think I do, it won't help the situation at all. This will be a blemish on him if my little escapade gets out to the community or worse, his friends. To him and my mother, their reputation is everything.

When it was finally made "public," my pregnancy wasn't as big of a deal as they originally thought. Because it was all-star quarterback Declan Mercer who knocked me up. He'll be in the NFL soon, and his parents are among the elite in our community.

So, tonight's escapade isn't socially acceptable. Lawyer Layne's daughter caught street racing with the owner of Rae's Bar; all while leaving her new baby at home. It's absolutely scandalous.

Jake grabs my attention by clearing his throat. He mouths, "Are you okay?"

I nod. Why does just a simple gesture make me giddy? Smiling back at him. I'm glad it's dark. Hopefully he can't see my face, I'm sure it's as red as a stop sign.

"Harlow!" My father's eyes narrow, then he follows the direction of who's occupying my attention. "Let's go."

"What about Jake? Ryder?"

My father starts walking briskly toward his car. "They're allowed to go. I got them off, too. I'm not sure why your bartender friend happens to be around so much, but I'm sure Declan wouldn't appreciate it. And I don't want you around this nonsense anymore. Do you understand me? You need to quit your job and stay home with Luca."

"He's not just a bartender. He owns the bar." My dad huffs at me, but I continue. "I'm not quitting. I make good money, and it fits my schedule with school and Luca." Picking up my pace, I walk faster. "I need this job."

"No. You do not. Declan and the Mercers are fully capable of helping you out and you know we're going to help you as well so there is no need for this whole working woman martyr thing you're trying to do."

I scoff, completely offended by his remarks, but ignore them to keep the fight alive. "I can't rely on Declan for anything. Football comes before his son. And definitely before me. Do you really think I can count on him financially and emotionally?"

"He has a career to think about. We can help out until he's established. Give him some time to provide the right type of life for you and Luca."

My father and I grow silent. Staring each other down when Jake comes up from beside us. "Harlow? Mr. Layne?" He rubs his wrist; I'm assuming he's happy to be free of the handcuffs.

That's really not the impression I want him to make on my father.

"Not now. I don't want to hear your lies. I've got to get my daughter home."

"Dad!" I scold.

"It's okay. I just wanted to apologize for the misunderstanding and to thank you for your help with the officers tonight." Jakes shoves his hands in his jean pockets.

My father scowls at him and guides me away from Jake. I give him a small smile. I'll talk to him later. I need to figure out some things first.

25

JAKE

I don't blame Mr. Layne. If she was my daughter, I'd lock her in her room and never let her out. I can't believe this happened tonight. Someone had to have ratted us out. There is no way in hell those cops knew where we'd be tonight.

We're from two different worlds. Her father only sees me as a dive bar owner with no future who plays with cars and gets arrested.

Back at the bar, Harlow's car is still in the parking lot. Her dad must have driven her straight home. I can't be pissed. She has a boyfriend and a baby. But there is no light in her eyes when she talks about Declan. I need to find out how she really feels about him. I can't believe I'm even entertaining the idea of the two of us but tonight, when we were alone and I almost kissed her, it was the most whole I've ever felt in my life. I know she belongs with me. But I have no idea how to make it a reality.

I decide I'm not staying at the apartment tonight. I need a decent shower and a meal.

"What are you doing stumbling through the door so late?"

"I'm not stumbling. I haven't had a drink tonight." I tell Gran who's currently scraping the chocolate icing off her plate and into her mouth. We all know she needs to watch her sugar; but she's allowed to do whatever she wants in my book.

"You know it's after three in the morning?"

"Do you?" I counter.

She purses her lips at me. "I know exactly what time it is, smartass."

"It's been a rough night. I'll let you eat your cake then get to bed."

"Nonsense. You sit down. I'll get you a piece of cake. I'm an old lady. I get too much sleep anyway. It seems like all I get done is napping." She shuffles over to the sink, opens up the cupboard, pulls out a glass, and sets it on the table. This means it's going to be a long conversation.

Gran is feisty as ever at three in the morning. "You get more done in a day than most twenty-year-olds." It's true; she keeps herself busy all day with housework, gardening, and watching Anna for Ben and Callie.

Callie worries about her since she had a stroke, but there really hasn't been any effects. She's as tough as nails.

"I'm assuming you had a bad night?"

"Do you really have to ask?"

Gran pours two glasses of milk, taking a seat across from me. Here we go, the Betty Rae inquisition.

"I'm simply asking how your night was, not tying you to the chair. I'm giving you the option to tell me or not. Whatever." She waves her hand like she couldn't care less which only means she wants to hear it all.

"I came this close," pinching my fingers together but not quite touching them, "to getting Harlow and myself arrested."

She gasps. "Oh dear. Harlow?"

"We went for a drive." Her mouth forms a straight line. "But it turned into a race. The cops got called. It wasn't supposed to turn out like that."

"Don't keep me in suspense any longer; you obviously sweet talked your way out of it."

"It wasn't me who did the sweet talking. Harlow did the talking and then her dad showed up. Her dad saved all of us from a night in jail."

"Oh my...that must have been a sight to see. Mr. Layne in his pajamas picking up his daughter." She laughs a deep, chuckle. I'm waiting for her to slap the table with emphasis.

"Gran. It's not funny." I growl.

"You really do like her, don't you?"

"Okay. Yes, I do. I feel like shit she was there tonight."

"Did someone rat you out or did they catch your keester?"

I chuckle and tell her the rest of the sorted details, especially Mr. Layne's reaction and what color his pajamas were.

"That is quite a night. Tell me the rest of it."

Scrunching up my face in confusion. "What do you mean? I just told you everything."

"I'm talking about the rest of the night. The part where you tell Harlow how much you care about her and have feelings for her."

"Gran. What are you talking about? I didn't say any of that."

I push around the frosting on my plate, hoping she'll stop this interrogation.

"You never worry about the consequences of your racing or who's involved. You also never bring a girl to your races unless she's part of the gang and races herself. What makes Harlow so special that you're here in the early morning spilling your guts out to your Gran?"

"Nothing. Can we just drop it? I feel awful she almost got arrested and her dad had to come and save us."

She purses her lips and leans closer.

She's giving me the look that says I'm going to kick your butt if you don't spill it now.

I let out a breath. "Ok, fine." I've been caught. Maybe if I tell her, I'll get this out of my system.

Dropping my fork, I lay it all out for Gran and maybe me too.

Releasing a breath, I say, "She drives me crazy. She's all I think about. Worry about. Hell- I even worry about her kid. When her blood pressure dropped and had to have emergency surgery." I pause, the words getting caught in my throat. "I was scared. Really fucking scared."

It's a relief to tell someone. I've been holding on to the words for what seems like forever. I've held on to that secret trying to keep it from myself even, denying myself reality. I'm crazy over Harlow Layne.

Gran reaches her hand across the table, patting hers over mine. "I knew you'd find someone who would reach you. She does belong to someone else and has a child with them. You need to wait until that part of her life is resolved. But you can be there for her as a friend until she's ready."

"When we're together, there's something there I can't explain. Like I'm a magnet being pulled to her no matter where I am or what I'm doing. I'm trying to find her. Declan, he's going to shoot himself in the foot eventually. My problem is with her parents. They hate me. We're from two different worlds."

"Nonsense, the Layne's are nice people. Sure, they live on the hill in the fancy house, but it doesn't make them any better than us."

"I'm not good enough for her, Gran. Declan is the football star, the one with the powerful father running for Senator. I'm a small-town bar owner. He sees me as nothing but trouble especially after tonight. I ruined any chance of gaining his respect. I was reckless. Stupidly by showing her that part of my life I wrecked my chance with Harlow."

"It was reckless, but you can't beat yourself up over it. Apologize and learn your lesson. Now, if I were you, I'd go see her first thing in the morning and show them respect by admitting you were wrong and explaining how you'll never do that to Harlow again."

"Do you really think it will help and not make it worse?"

"You've already shown your worst quality. Stupidity. Now show them who you really are."

***

Callie and Anna stop over for breakfast. Thankfully, they only live across the street so I can see them any time I want. Anna has quickly become part of our family. Anna jumps on my lap. "Uncle Jake." Her little dark curls brush across my face.

"What do you have there?" I ask, hoping she'll stop swinging her ponytail in my face, so I don't inhale it.

"My blue car." She frowns.

"You don't like your blue car?" I ask.

"I lost your car. The red one." She tucks her head into my chest. "I'm sorry Uncle Jake."

I kiss the top of her head. "Don't you worry. I'll buy you a new one. Matter of fact, I know I have another one around here. I'll give you that one."

Callie pipes up. "We looked everywhere for it. She wanted to tell you herself. She thought you'd be upset because she lost the car that looks like yours. Anna was worried you might lose a race if she lost it. But I told her you could never be mad at her."

My sister glares at me with her hand on her hip. I better say the right thing here or I'll be getting my ass handed to me by my five-foot one little sister.

"Anna, I could never be upset or mad at you. Let me go get another red car." I feel like a piece of shit thinking she would ever think I'd be mad at her. The thought kills me. Knowing it's trauma her mother caused her, just like my parents caused me. I shake the thought away. I can't go there. Not now. "Please dry those tears. Let's go get some pancakes and chocolate milk, while I go and grab a new red car for you."

"Ok." she swipes at her eyes. Another girl who wrecks my heart.

"Did you go outside yet?" Callie interrupts. "It's freezing. They're calling for a huge ice storm to hit in the next few days."

"In Lake Haven? Sounds a bit far-fetched to me." I add.

"Remember years ago, when we had that big ice storm and lost power for almost two weeks?"

The memory of being stuck inside with my mom and one of the meanest stepdad's in the world tries to break through my memories, but thankfully it's kept at bay.

"Longest weeks of my life." It is all I have the energy to reply with.

"The Buck era. He was a lazy son of a bitch." Callie tells me like I don't already know. Thankfully, she doesn't know half of it. Buck didn't bother Callie like he did me. He used to use me as a punching bag. That was okay, as long as he didn't take whatever it was out on my sister. But he was so drunk during the literal blackout it was one of the few times he wasn't beating me.

"Remember we had to carry in all the firewood because he couldn't stand long enough. He even fell over the back of the couch trying to stand up." I let out the smallest chuckle because it was funny as shit to see that big fucker fly over the couch and land on his ass.

Our childhood barely had any good memories when it came to my mom and her many boyfriends, but old Buck wasn't the worst, a vague

vision of Frank Miller with a cigarette dangling from his lips pops into
my mind and I shake it away.

"Harlow told me about last night. I can't believe someone ratted.
Any clue who it was?"

"None. It was supposed to be just me and Ryder then it became a
money race with some guy from a county over. Let's just say, I hate that
she got caught up in the middle of everything. It wasn't my intention.
I just wanted to show her a good time. Something new and exciting.
She's been dealing with a lot lately."

"She told me she had fun, but her dad wasn't convinced. You
should probably apologize."

"Already on it."

***

On my way to Harlow's parents' house, I've thought of every way
imaginable to apologize for putting his daughter in harm's way. It's the
one thing I would never want to do. It was supposed to be fun. I can't
figure out who would have called it in. Everyone who knows us would
have never done it, so it had to be an outsider. Maybe from another
county or team.

When I pull up to Harlow's house, there are no cars in the driveway,
but it doesn't mean anything because her father has several garage
doors to choose from.

Just as I'm about to leave my car, her father comes out of the front
door.

He looks much more put together than he did last night. He's
wearing a suit, and his hair is jelled back. He's wearing his glasses and
clearly headed to work. Mr. Layne glares when he sees me and instead

of walking over to his garage door, he heads in my direction. If he could kill me with his eyes, I bet he would.

I get out of my car, close the door, and lean against the passenger side waiting for him to reach me.

"What are you doing here? I thought I made it perfectly clear I didn't want you anywhere near my daughter."

I straighten, knowing I look like a fool, not showing him more respect.

"I wanted to apologize for last night. I would have never put Harlow in harm's way. Things just got out of hand and..."

Mr. Layne puts up his hand. "Enough. There is absolutely nothing you could explain your way out of. I want you to stay away from my daughter. She has enough problems right now. You don't need to add to them."

He takes a step closer. "Here is what you are going to do. You are going to take Harlow off the work schedule and never look at her again. You are not worthy of my daughter. She deserves someone better than you. You're an adult and you're still playing with those cars. She's a mother and trying to take care of her son. What would he have done if she went to jail? It would have been your fault if she lost her freedom and her son."

What can I say to that? "You're right, sir. But I won't let anything like that happen again. I'll always protect your daughter."

"No. No, you won't because I won't allow it. Not while she's in my house. And since she's here for the foreseeable future, you won't be. If I find out she's working in that bar, I'll shut it down."

"Sir."

"Go!" he says, in a low growl.

Then walks away from me.

26

HARLOW

L uca is two months old today. My doctor gave me clearance to go back to work. Of course, I still can't lift anything too heavy, but it won't be a problem. Especially not with overprotective Jake.

I'm on holiday break from school and Christmas will be here soon. Luca's first Christmas. I did some shopping for him, and I can't wait to see him with his new toys. Every day seems like something new; a smile, a look, a cry, I'm loving every minute of it with him.

I sent Jake a text letting him know I'd like to be added back to the schedule, but he hasn't texted me back. In fact, he hasn't really been in contact with me since the night of the race and it's been several days since that night. He apologized by text the next day but nothing more than that.

I'm a little disappointed in his message. I thought we shared a moment, many moments, and then going through something like that, well, I thought he'd have a little more to say than just, "I'm sorry for almost getting you arrested."

Annoyed, I remember Callie told me he feels awful. I know he feels awful, but I wish he wouldn't shut me out like this. There are things I want to talk to him about. Mainly, how I can't shake these feelings that are building up inside of me? How he is all I think about, but I'm technically still with Declan. I need to figure it out before I can give my full attention to Jake.

Luca coo's from the floor reminding me he's more important than either of them. "Yes, you are, little man. My silly love life is on the back burner." I kiss his chubby cheeks, loving his little personality is starting to shine through. The smiles and bubbles he greets me with are all I need.

However, Declan is coming this evening to ruin all of our fun. We've had this dinner planned for a few days. He hasn't seen Luca much since his birth. He has commitments with school. How much longer does he think it's a practical excuse? It isn't acceptable to treat Luca or me this way.

Our feelings have changed for one another. We're both too cowardly to face them. But how can I throw away a relationship with him when we have a child together? I'm so up and down. I don't see Declan in my future, but I want him to be a part of Luca's. I can't bear the thought of him not having a father in his life.

My mind wanders to Jake. It seems whenever chaos intrudes my thoughts, his face appears, sending a quiet calmness that somehow grounds me and flushes out all the intrusive thoughts.

Jake's dark hair and eyes are always on my mind. The way the stray hairs fall seems to accentuate his features. The way he wears his black leather jacket that was made for him and only him. The moment at the bar when I felt like he could see me. We almost kissed. We were so close, yet he pulled away.

The last thing I wanted was for him to pull away. Touching my lips at the memory, my phone pings with a text.

I'm going to talk to Declan tonight about how things are changing between us. Maybe he feels the same way. But am I failing Luca by giving up so easily? Am I hurting Luca by developing feelings for Jake?

I growl at myself for thinking all of these crazy thoughts. Causing Luca to cry.

Picking him up, I shush him by patting his bottom. "I'm sorry, Mommy is a lunatic who clearly can't make up her mind or pick a man. I'm trying to get it together for you. I promise. Give me a little time, I'll figure it out for you."

"Who are you talking to?" Mom asks, as she starts picking up Luca's blanket and straightening up a bit. Glancing up at her, I can't help but wonder if she's ever felt this way. Her hair is perfectly in place, and she's wearing a light pink button up blouse and tan slacks with matching tan loafers. She's so put together. How does she do it?

Knowing she's waiting for an answer, "Just talking to myself. And Luca of course. He likes my rambling."

Mom reaches out her hands. "Hand him over."

When he's in her arms, she squishes him to her cheek. "He just loves his grandma." She coos. Then in a more adult voice adds, "Declan will be here soon. You should clean up this mess."

"It's not really a mess. Just his toys."

"You don't want Declan to think you did nothing all day. He'll appreciate knowing you can keep a clean house and take good care of his son."

"Why do you say things like that? You sound like you're straight out of 1950."

"I do not. I'm just trying to make things easier for you. Declan hasn't been able to see Luca much. I'm sure he'd enjoy a clean area to connect with him. So, they can bond."

I literally don't understand this woman. How have I not noticed how robotic she is? She leaves the room with Luca. I head up the stairs to my room, when my phone pings again. Any excitement is washed away when Declan's name appears.

Declan

> **Sorry. Can't make it. The coach has us running drills tonight. Only a few more weeks of this. Miss you and the kid.**

The KID? I throw my phone. Literally throw it across the room and it bounces off my bed. I wish I could throw it at his head. How can he justify missing his son?

I'm done. I'm going to confront him and ask if football is more important than his son?

***

An hour later we are loaded up in the car. I packed everything we need for at least two overnight trips. I told my parents Declan changed plans and wanted us to visit him. They asked me to wait out the weather, but the local weatherman said it wouldn't start until the middle of the night and be gone by tomorrow. I should be there and back before then. I'm not planning to stay, honestly, I'm not expecting him to be there.

With Luca snug and cozy in his car seat, I start the hour-long drive. Putting on a lighthearted first time mom podcast. Maybe I'll get some tips for this whole motherhood thing.

The drive is uneventful and relaxing. I'm not even anxious, determined to speak my mind. The weather has held off. It's a little dreary, but nothing worth giving a second thought about.

When I pull up to the fraternity house, nothing looks any different than the last time I was here. The house is huge. I know there are at least ten rooms. The house is filled with random couches and recliners. Nothing matches. It smells like a locker room. After a party, it smells even worse. I've spent a few nights here with him, but I couldn't stand hanging out and talking about football all day and night. Declan has made it his whole identity.

Looking at the wrap around porch, I see so much potential, but it looks like a rundown southern home that once held so much beauty. There are even a few recliners arranged haphazardly along with a glass patio table filled with cans and beer bottles.

Taking Luca's car seat from the base as fast as I can manage. I want to get this over with as soon as possible. Before I reach the door to knock, there's a girl in a bra and panties hanging out from the door smoking a cigarette. "That's attractive. Luca, don't ever date a girl like that, please." I whisper to him so whoever's one-night stand she belongs to doesn't hear me. She's probably a nice person, but in this scenario, she's somebody's mistake.

The skinny blond with smudged lipstick and dark circles under her eyes, glances up at me. Her black mascara has seen better days.

"What do you want?" Her voice is rough and raspy.

"Is Declan here?" This girl takes another puff of her cigarette, blowing the remnants toward me. This girl is almost naked, which is no surprise. She looks like the typical frat girl and one of the reasons why I don't hang out with Declan at these parties. I just don't fit in with this crowd.

Apparently, my type is dive bar owning street racer.

"Yeah. I think so. Who are you and why do you have a baby with you?" Her eyes roam up and down, judging me.

"This is Declan's son."

She drops her cigarette to the ground and smooshes it with her bright pink flip flop.

Classy.

"No shit. Declan's got a kid. Wow."

Snapping because I'm tired of her crap, "Can you just go get him for me?"

She puts up her hands, "Okay. Geez," she murmurs, retreating inside the house.

"Dec! There's some chick here to see you. She's got your kid with her!" She's almost singing it like she's got some big secret to spread.

Adjusting the carrier on the crook of my arm, I brace myself to see what type of shape Declan is in.

"What are you talking about, Amber?" Declan scrubs a hand down his head, as he tries to adjust his eyes to the light. He's shirtless and wearing gray boxer briefs. At least he's dressed. Miss no pants goes into the room across from the one he just exited.

His eyes widen as he takes in the sight in front of him.

"Harlow?" His face contorts into a look of horror.

"Yep. It's me in the flesh."

He tries to shut the door behind him, but I already catch a glimpse of a girl with long red hair in his bed, and her large bare chest is on full display.

"Dec?" she calls, as he shuts the door.

Is this why he likes to be called, Dec. How am I not surprised I'd find him like this? I'm unfazed by her sudden appearance. Part of me knew I'd find this exact scene if I surprised him, which is probably why I never did.

"What are you doing here?"

Trying to keep my voice even and not full of hate, I say, "I thought I'd come see you since you couldn't see us. But I guess you surprised me."

"Are you talking about Carrie? She was just hanging out in my room. I was sleeping on the couch."

My blood pressure must be at an all-time high. My heart is racing and not in a good way.

"She's naked in your bed. Seriously, Dec?" I emphasize the c sound.

"She's just a friend," he lies.

"Can you just stop? Don't lie in front of your son and please stop lying to me."

He drops his head, then peeks up at me. "I didn't want you to see this."

I think this is the first honest thing he's said to me. I can't even be furious with him. I knew this was what I'd find, and I was right. Part of me is even happy that I found him this way. It really is over.

"Look…" He takes my empty hand. "I would never want to hurt you this way. It was a weak moment. It'll never happen again."

"No, it won't. We are over, Declan."

"Please don't end us. I have a lot going on and I just need to relieve stress and have fun. I can't do that with you and the kid."

"Would you stop calling him the kid? He has a name and it's Luca, your son. Which you seem to have forgotten."

"I love you, Harlow. Please don't give up on us." He takes Luca from my hand and sets the carrier on the ground beside me.

"You can't say that with another girl in your bed."

He creeps closer, both hands on my arms now, "Please, we can work through this. We have a son." He looks down at Luca for emphasis. "She doesn't mean anything. I love you."

"Are you serious right now, there is nothing about this moment that makes me trust you. I can't even believe you think we can work through this, because it's so much more than some side chick in your bed. You've ignored me the whole pregnancy, you were too busy for the birth of your child that my boss had to be in the delivery room with me holding my hand and most of all you wanted me to get rid of this precious life."

"That was a mistake."

I take a deep breath. "I can't. I don't want to do this anymore." A slight chuckle escapes. "I'm actually relieved." I admit. "We both knew this wasn't going to work. If you really wanted it to, you would have been around more, and I would have made a bigger effort. Neither of us did."

"You need to stop talking. Football will be over soon. Then I'll be able to spend more time with you and Luca."

"I'm not waiting for you to make time for me and your son. To find a small spot where we can fit in your life."

"No! You can't do this." He tugs me and I try to pull away, but his grasp is too firm. He pulls me closer to his chest. I can't fight against him.

His face comes close to mine. "If you leave me, I'm going to fight to get custody. No one leaves a Mercer. Especially not someone like you," he spits. "Do you know how bad this will look for my family? I already knocked you up. I don't need a girl like you fucking with my legacy. As far as the world knows, I'm the best quarterback in my division and I'm headed to the NFL. I'm the best fucking father there is."

Declan lets go of me. The force of his release makes me stumble back, catching myself against the wall.

Everything happened so fast; I could hear it all through an echoing tunnel. He's going to take Luca from me. As my hearing clears, a few voices fill the hallway from behind me.

"Dec... hey man. Who's this hottie?"

It's a guy's voice. I don't even turn around to look at him. This is my chance to leave. Picking up Luca while Declan is distracted and I make my escape.

It doesn't take me long to secure Luca in his car base. My only goal is to get the hell out of here.

As I turn the key, I notice the icy rain falling on my windshield.

27

HARLOW

C allie answers immediately. "Where are you? Please tell me you aren't driving in this weather." Callie's sassy and stern voice is not a good combination.

"I went to see Declan. We broke up. He was with another girl." I say as fast as I can and explain in detail my encounter with Declan, leaving out the part of his aggressive behavior. I'm still shaking over it.

"That piece of donkey shit! I'm cutting off his balls!"

"I'm not surprised at all. It doesn't even hurt. It's just disappointing it didn't work out for Luca."

"Aw... I'm sorry to tell you this, honey. No one is." She pauses as if she's choosing her next words carefully. "Are you okay, really? I know you're upset, but you're going to be fine. You don't need him to help you raise Luca."

I consider her question. It doesn't take long for me to know the true answer. "It will be hard, don't get me wrong but I've already been doing it on my own. Of course, my parents help, but I have you and Ben and Jake. Jake has spent more time with Luca than Declan has."

"I'm so relieved to hear you say that. I thought I'd have to nurse you back to life from a breakup." I laugh at her until a bright light blinds me. My car slides and spins. I fight against the wheel. It all happens so fast. My heart launches in my throat. All I can think about is whether my baby is safe.

The car comes to a stop. Callie is screaming my name over the car speaker.

Trying to focus, my car is facing the opposite direction, and no other car is in sight. I don't remember hitting the brakes, but we aren't moving. We somehow slid off the side of the road.

"Luca!" My heart fills with dread. Unbuckling my seatbelt, I twist my body until I'm on my knees on the center console checking Luca. His eyes are closed, still asleep, but I shake his little feet to wake up and make sure he's okay. He opens his eyes and moans obviously upset, I woke him up.

"Harlow!"

"Yes. We're fine." I yell, aware of Callie calling me.

"Thank God! You scared the shit out of me. All that screaming."

"I didn't even realize I screamed. It's so icy. Someone crossed into my lane. The car slid and spun."

"Don't you dare move the car. I'm coming to get you."

"You can't. I don't want you out in this weather either."

Glancing around, I notice a small diner with their lights on. "I'm going to park at this diner for a little while until the road clears."

I hear another call coming through; I don't look to see who it is. I ignore it until it starts again. I tell Callie to hold on and I answer it.

"I'm coming to get you. Don't move the fucking car an inch." Jake's voice roars through the air.

"Jake." I can feel the relief in my bones.

"Send me a ping with your location. I'll be there as fast as I can."

"There is a diner across the road. I'll go wait in there."

"What's it called?"

Reading the sign, I say, "Pam's Diner. It's a metal building. Kind of like an old diner you might see on TV." I don't realize how nervous I am until I hear my voice shake. "I'll take Luca inside and wait for you."

The ice balls are now dancing off my windshield. The noise is pounding in my ears. I can't stand it. It's like they're yelling at me, warning me to get off the road.

As if Luca's reading my mind, he starts to cry. No, cry isn't the right word. Wailing is more like it.

"Is he okay? Did something happen?" Jake's voice is audibly worried.

A smile comes from nowhere in this chaos. "Yes. He's fine. He's ready to get out of this car like I am."

"I'll stay with you until you get into the parking lot."

"Why is it you're always there when I get myself into these situations?" I ask him.

"I have no idea why you seem to find yourself in these situations. I have never met somebody who has worse luck than you. The last time I was with you, you almost got yourself arrested."

"Me?" I gasp. "I recall someone else illegally racing their car."

As we talk, I drive over to the diner. When the car is safely parked, I continue to talk. I don't want to get off the phone with him.

"It wasn't supposed to happen that way." His voice turns serious. "I would never let anything happen to you."

"Jake. I know. It was just bad timing."

He clears his throat. "Are you there yet?"

"Um...yes."

"Okay, I'll be there as soon as I can."

"Please be careful."

"I will."

"And I appreciate you coming to my rescue again."

"Anything for my damsel in distress." I want to argue, but unfortunately, it's true.

Once Luca and I are safe in a booth, my whole body exhales in relief. The booths are set up against the windows. I have a great view for when Jake gets here. On the other side of the aisle is a counter with stools.

An older waitress comes over to our table. Her hair is up in a bun, and glasses hang from the tip of her nose. She's wearing a Pam's Diner T-shirt with a cute dancing burger logo. "Here's a menu. You might be stuck here for a while with the weather."

"I have a friend who is coming to get me."

"Oh, you're not from around here?"

I shake my head no.

"I hope he can drive in this weather. Not many can now adays." I don't miss the hint of sarcasm in her voice. She adds, "I'll be back to take your order."

I already feeling guilty about making him come and get me in this weather, so her attitude isn't helping.

Luca's wide awake, not fussing, but I have an overwhelming urge to pick him up and cuddle him as close as I can. He snuggles close to my chest.

I text Callie to let her know Jake is on his way, which she probably already knows since she's the one who texted him while she was on the phone with me. Part of me was a little annoyed when she called him. It seems like he's always saving me. The damsel in distress. I smiled at the way he called me that. It's ridiculous but true. I'm so grateful that he's my life and I can always count on him. I'm worried about him but if there's one thing I know, he knows how to drive.

I fix Luca a bottle. He has been an exceptional participant in his mamma's shenanigans. I'm just thankful that he won't remember any of it. Especially the part where his father was threatening me. He's never acted aggressively toward me before. I don't know what he would have done if we were alone. The memory of his eyes is enough to send chills down my spine.

Luca fusses, maybe feeling my tension. Taking the bottle out of his mouth, I sling him over my shoulder, so he can get out a burp. I take in the scenery.

An older man in the booth in front of me is eating a hamburger bigger than my head but it looks absolutely delicious. Sitting at the counter is a cute young couple sipping on their milkshakes completely unbothered by the weather.

"Isn't he precious? How old is he?" the waitress asks.

"Two months."

"He's just a new little thing. I'm glad you decided to stop here. It doesn't seem to be getting any better out there, only worse." By the look of it outside, she's right. The ice is dripping from the railing and thick on the tree branches.

"Well, I didn't have a choice. My car slid, thankfully your diner was across the street."

"I don't recommend you drive any more tonight. My sister has a little motel a few blocks from here. I can call her and see if she has a room for you. She probably has one of those Pack 'n Play things for the baby to sleep in."

"That would be great, thanks!"

"Let's get you some food so you can get into a nice cozy bed." She waits for me while holding a little notepad and pencil. Jake usually orders a bacon cheeseburger for his after-work dinner. So, I order it for us but tell her to give it a bit before she actually puts in the order. It'll probably take a little longer for him to get here.

The waitress, who finally lets me see her name tag, Penny, thanks us and tells me she'll be back soon.

Luca starts to settle in my arms. His mouth forms an "o" and his eyes open and shut repeatedly until they finally remain closed. We settle into our own quiet world. While I'm fixated on Luca, Jake slides in the seat across from me.

"Hey."

I thought I was calm; however, the anxiety returns in full force, but in the form of a swarm of butterflies.

Jake shakes the snow and ice from his wet hair. "It's really bad out there. I slid like three times getting here. I'm glad you stopped at this place. It's not safe for you to drive home."

Taking in his wet, inky black hair, his signature strand falls in his eye. The leather jacket is wet and shiny. His forehead crinkles, his jaw ticks. He's literally the most handsome man I've ever seen. I want to reach out and push the strand away from his face.

Instead, I say, "Um...I ordered a bacon cheeseburger for you."

"Great. Thanks." He shrugs off his jacket, revealing a black Carmichael Racing T-shirt. "How's the little man?" A hint of his cologne mixed with cigarette smoke graces the air.

"He's doing great considering his mom is stupid to drive in this weather. Although in my defense, I thought it wasn't supposed to start until the middle of the night. I guess the news was wrong."

"Luca is fast asleep. He doesn't seem bothered by anything." Jake watches his peaceful face. "You weren't stupid, just misinformed." He teases me.

I love when Jake teases. And the smile that goes along with it is mesmerizing. It occurs to me that I need to make him smile more.

I twist in my seat, so Jake can see. "Yep, definitely a milk coma going on over there."

"Yep, he's pretty tuckered out. The waitress offered us a place to stay tonight. Just a few blocks over. She was going to call and let me know if they have an empty room. I think it's a good idea if we stay here, just until the weather clears."

He gets that intense look on his face, the one where he's picking his words closely. "I'm not sure I like the idea of you two staying alone in a motel. It could have bed bugs or a creepy manager…"

I reach out for his hand hoping to stop his crazy thoughts. "You can stay with us or get your own room. I'm not making you drive back in this crap."

Penny clears her throat, setting down two plates filled with food in front of us. "There are no bed bugs or creepy people around my sister's motel for your information." She obviously overheard our conversation. "There's a room available if you want it. I suggest taking it."

She looks at me with raised eyebrows, obviously waiting for an answer.

"Does she have two rooms?" Jake asks.

"Just one. Do you want it or not?" She doesn't seem to like Jake.

"We'll take it." Penny nods and heads back to the cute couple.

Jake doesn't seem comfortable with the idea, but I've had a long day. I'm not waiting around for this weather to pass. Jake frowns but then asks Penny as she stands at the counter. "Where's the motel?"

She tells us it's a few blocks over and rattles off the street address. "I told my sister you'd need the crib play pen thing. We didn't have those around for my kids. You women are spoiled nowadays." Even though she's trying to be helpful, it comes with a bit of an attitude.

"Thanks." Jake tells her.

"I'm sorry you had to come out here and get us. Now I'm making you stay in a small motel room. I hope it won't be too uncomfortable for you." I say.

"What? I'm not uncomfortable. I thought you might feel awkward with me around. I'm sure Declan won't appreciate me staying with his girl." Now he looks like the awkward one while saying his name.

"Nothing could be more awkward than almost getting arrested and then having the cops call your dad." I tease, but he doesn't smile.

"I'm really sorry about that. I'm sure your father hates the idea of you being here with me."

"It's not really his concern. He'd probably want me to call Declan, but that's what got me into this in the first place."

"I was going to ask what's going on there but..." Jake takes a bit of his burger and doesn't finish his sentence. Penny picks this moment to ask about how we like our food.

"It's delicious. I think I might need to get the recipe, and these fries are absolutely perfect." Penny nods at his approval.

We chew in silence for a few minutes. Concentrating on our food but I'm really waiting for him to ask me about Declan.

A few more moments go by, and he finally asks, "Is he not at his place or something? Callie said you went up here to see him. Is that why you'd be heading back so soon?" He stuffs a fry into his mouth. Maybe to stop himself from asking any more questions.

I exhale, a little ashamed to tell him about the mess I'm in. "He was supposed to spend the day with Luca and me. Then he said he had practice. I wanted to surprise him. When I got there another girl was in his bed."

"So, you were the one surprised. Can't say I didn't see that coming." He adds, "sorry."

"A surprise in the form of a naked girl. It may have been a cheerleader I saw hanging on him when I visited him for the Thanksgiving game."

Jake extends his hand out, taking mine in his. I can't help but examine the intricate tattoo snaking down his arm. Engine parts and skulls. Nothing I'd ever place on myself but somehow, they seem perfect for him. I notice a snake from his wrist to his knuckles. "Is that new?" I ask, gliding my fingers over the design. I hear him inhale, but he doesn't pull away.

"I got it last week."

"I thought it looked new. It suits you."

"Please stop trying to change the subject and tell me how you really feel about Declan, not what you think you should say."

He knows me so well.

"I hate him. I'd like to punch him in the face but most of all I'm relieved. I should have dumped him a long time ago."

"Did you dump him?"

"Yes. I'm not regretting one second of it. It was the easiest decision I ever had to make. Although it took me forever to come to that conclusion. We haven't been a couple for a long time. We just stayed in, whatever this was for Luca. I never really loved Declan." I pause, looking down at Luca. "Do you think he'll hate me?"

"No. Coming from a kid who had a ton of guys who were wrong for his mom, he'll be proud you wanted better for yourself. I know I'm proud of you. It takes a lot of guts to walk away from a future you want."

I lean closer. "I'm not brave because I never really saw a future with him. Just a facade of what I thought a family should look like. He isn't my family." I confess. Jake's eyes narrow and at the same time are alive with an emotion I haven't seen since we almost kissed that night.

Unable to look away, my eyes flash to his lips that are framed by dark stubble. His tongue darts out, licking his bottom lip, sending a shiver in places I haven't felt before.

Jake is becoming everything I want. I didn't think I'd ever want someone like him. But as I stare into his intense eyes that are fixed on mine, a light in them is calling me home.

"He never deserved you. You shouldn't ever settle for anyone."

"We need to close up, and you should probably get going to the hotel."

the annoying waitress interrupts,

"Yeah, I'll take the check."

28

JAKE

The few side roads we take to the motel are somehow worse than the roads I took on the way up here. I'm never nervous behind the wheel, but tonight it's different. I have precious cargo. An innocent little boy and his mother, who both have quickly become the two most important people in my life. I will literally do anything to keep them safe.

When Callie texted me, Harlow was stuck and driving in this storm. It was if someone knocked every particle of air from my lungs.

Callie said she spun out and almost wrecked. I couldn't get to my car fast enough. I didn't even know where I was headed, I just got in the car and started driving.

That prick not only cheated on her; but he also didn't bother to make sure she got home safe in this weather. Not any inch of him deserves her. Even though Luca is his blood and wouldn't be on this earth without him, Declan isn't worthy of being his father.

We slide three more times before we finally get to the motel. I've never seen an ice storm like this before.

Once we get all of the baby's things and get inside the motel lobby, an elderly couple greets us. Lobby is a stretch; it's just a small desk.

"Penny said you were a nice little family and she was right. Aren't you all the cutest," she practically squeals. "I've got everything you are going to need. I hope we don't lose electricity but if we do, there's a backup generator in the shed out back."

Trying not to pay attention to the way I like when she says little family, I pay for the room. There is no way in hell Harlow is paying for anything.

The older gentleman is gray-haired and balding. His wife is wearing a pink robe, obviously ready for bed. She says with a smile, "I'm sure you can't wait to get into a comfortable bed." She hands us a key for our room. It's an actual metal key, not some plastic card.

The husband says, "We are renovating the other three rooms, but this is the first one to be finished. The other rooms don't have heat. Don't worry because I made sure your room is nice and toasty." He pauses, then adds, "I almost slipped on my way to the room, so I put extra salt on the sidewalk. We don't need the little lady slipping with the baby."

We follow him outside where the ice pellets along with wind assault us on the short trek to the motel room. The older man battles with the key for a moment, dropping it once. I'm fighting the urge to rip it from his hand.

He finally gets the door open; the room is fairly plain. The one and only queen bed in the middle of the room is like a big flashing sign we're finally alone. He tells us goodnight. A little concerned about his safety, I peek out the door making sure he doesn't slip on his way back to the lobby. Once he's inside, I examine the room more thoroughly.

The queen bed has a large fluffy blue comforter, nice pillows with matching flowers, and minimal furniture. The room exceeds my expectations. I'm glad we landed here tonight. Although, it would have been much better with two queen beds.

It's not like anything is going to happen between us, it's just now there's no one in between us. Don't get me wrong, there isn't anything more I want than to pull her in my arms and kiss her. But she just broke up with her boyfriend, the father of her child, a couple hours ago. She's too important to me to ruin our relationship, whatever it might be. They both are.

Harlow spots the Pack n' Play, inspecting every inch of it. She takes a blanket out and situates it to where she wants it.

"How do you know what to bring?" I ask, amazed she always seems to know what he needs. When I think back to my childhood, the only thing my mom was good at was heating up a frozen pizza. It's the only childhood memory involving her, not the revolving door of potential stepfathers or the abusive drunk that stuck around too long until Gran came to my rescue.

Harlow brushes a strand of hair from her face. "I have no idea what I'm doing most of the time. Every day is a learning experience." She shrugs.

"Trust me, you've got this whole new mom thing figured out."

"I wish I felt as sure as you seem. But thank you for saying that." She gives me a small smile and looks down at Luca, who is now sucking on his pacifier with his eyes closed.

"Do you feel comfortable watching him while I grab a shower? I'm freezing and my nerves are shot. I just need to feel some warm water over my body."

"Yeah, sure. Take your time." I try to shake away the image of hot water all over her body and steam surrounding her. To help, I take a peek over at Luca. Focus on him. He wouldn't want me to think of his mother that way.

"Thanks." Harlow scurries to the bathroom, leaving me alone with her son. He's so peaceful. Everyone complains about what a pain in the ass kids are, but I can't wait for him to wake up. I head over to the bag and pull out a few diapers in case she needs to change him through the night. My phone is close to being dead. I sent Callie a text letting her know we'll be staying at a local motel.

Callie replies with a smiley face. It could mean anything, knowing the way her mind works.

I must admit; I was against the motel thing, but I'm glad to not be driving in the weather. These roads are too awful to travel with my precious cargo. But now I'm alone with her it's more nerve-racking yet peaceful at the same time.

There's a desk, cheap black leather desk chair, and bed. Nothing but essentials. I don't even see a coffee pot on the desk. I turn on the tv, making sure to turn the volume down as soon as the picture comes on.

I flip through the three channels then shut it off. My gaze makes its way over to the bed. Maybe if we put a pillow between us, I can sleep on the bed without touching her. We're adults, I can sleep next to an insanely hot, attractive, beautiful woman who I haven't been able to get out of my head since I met her.

Ever since the first moment my sister introduced her to me, I haven't had feelings for anyone but her. The universe keeps finding ways to push us together. Just because it chose tonight for me to be stuck in a motel room in a freak ice storm doesn't mean anything, does it?

I run my hands through my hair unsure of what to do next. Sitting on the bed, I take off my boots and shrug off my leather jacket. It's kind of stifling in here. They weren't kidding when they said they turned up the heat. I might as well get comfortable before I spend the night wide awake or on the cold hard floor.

Luca grunts from where he's napping, worrying if he needs his mom, I peek over at him. His little face is scrunched up making noises. He seems perfectly content with the world.

"Hey, little man," I whisper to him. "That was a crazy night, huh?"

Luca coos back at me. Fisting his mouth with his hand.

I grab a hold of his other hand, and he holds on tight.

How could Declan not want to be a part of his son's life?

"Don't worry, I'll be here for you whenever you need me." I intend to keep my word whether his father is in the picture or not.

Luca's heavy eyelids started to close. He hasn't let go of my hand, but his fist falls from his mouth. Peace and calm are all I see in his serene face.

The water turns off, breaking my attention away from him. I can hear her shuffling around in there. I'm staring at the door as if I can suddenly see through it. Getting my shit together, I head back to the bed. I need to stomp down these...nerves. Is she really making me nervous?

I turn the TV back on, picking the show about antiques. Anything to distract myself from the beautiful woman who I'm falling for. She doesn't even know how amazing she is or how much strength she possesses.

The door opens, and Harlow steps quietly out from the door frame in what seems like slow motion. Her bare legs are what I notice first, followed by her hot pink toes. The fact she's wearing a long white Carmichael Racing T-shirt has me weak in the knees and I'm laying down.

Yeah – the floor is where I'm sleeping. I don't trust myself to sleep next to her.

Harlow gives me a small smile. "Thanks for keeping an eye on him. I'm human again," she says while towel drying her hair.

Human and driving me crazy.

"He's so peaceful. He has no idea what a crazy day he's been a part of. I wish I could be in the dark too."

"I'm sorry about Declan." I'm sorry she's upset, but not for that piece of shit who doesn't deserve a second of her time.

"No, it's not about him. We should have broken up a long time ago. I feel like I failed Luca. I never wanted to do that to him. I'm a failure as a mother."

I pat the bed beside me. "You aren't a failure. If anything, you've been strong for him and not settling for someone who doesn't treat him right."

She sighs and takes a seat beside me while her fresh scent assaults my nose. "He still wants to make it work. He's texted and even called once." Lifting up her phone, showing me a string of texts from Declan. I can't see what they say because she sets her phone down too fast, but there's a seriously long list of texts from him.

"You don't, do you?" I ask, knowing she has said many times she doesn't. I shouldn't keep asking but it's like I need her to keep confirming it for me she doesn't want a future with him.

She shakes her head, "No, it's over, for sure. He's treating us so poorly."

"He doesn't deserve you or Luca. He can't just ignore you for months and now wants you back because it's convenient for him. Life doesn't work that way. He's not worthy of you."

"I used to think I should put in all the effort I could, but...you showed me differently." She shrugs and her cheeks redden.

"Me?" I hold my breath. What did I show her? I'm the last person who knows about relationships. I've never even been in one.

She shifts to face me, her knees hitting mine.

"I know we've had our fair share of disagreements." She smiles. I can't help but smile back. "You showed me that it doesn't have to be money, status, and who's the best, which was the way I was raised. It's the little things. Like somehow when I need something, you're there. Willing to help." She lowers her head into her hands. "God, that sounded so stupid. I guess what I'm trying to say is that no one really cares about what I want, only about what looks good on the surface. But you don't make me feel anything other than important."

I can't help but reach for her cheek, brushing my thumb across her soft skin.

"They care about you, maybe it just comes across in a different way. But I'm glad I can be there when you need it." My thumb moves slowly on its own, and brushes over her lips. Her bright green eyes close then open.

"It's not just when I'm playing the damsel in distress." I let out a little chuckle. "It's when I'm busy, there's a drink waiting, or you somehow find a way to give me exactly what I didn't know I needed. You have a big heart. You are the least selfish person I know. I hope you see that about yourself."

I'm taken aback, no one has ever said those words to me.

Her eyes glisten as she waits for me to respond. "I seem to be in the right place at the right time. But it's because I care about you and I can't seem to *not* want to be near you. You're all I think about. Worry about. I know I shouldn't. You just broke up with Declan."

She leans close. The scent of vanilla and coconut from her hair invades the air around me. "I can't help but want you with me too. Today I felt absolutely nothing for Declan and haven't in a long time. I know it's too soon; I should take my time and make sure it's the right time. To concentrate on being a mom and finishing school, not starting a new relationship, but I can't seem to stop thinking about us being together. I can't even begin to describe how I felt tonight when you called and said you were coming to get me."

"I can tell you how I feel right now. I've completely fallen for you. I don't care you're a single mom. In fact, I'm amazed at how strong and incredible you are. I had a mother who put a man or a bunch of men ahead of her kids. Then here you are, putting your son's needs above all else. I admire you for that."

A tear falls from her eyes, and I brush it away with my thumb.

"I'm falling for you too. I don't know how it happened. At first, I thought you hated me. You barely talked to me but then there you were, making me feel whole. Like I can do anything. No one has ever supported me the way you do."

"I'm so fucking happy to hear you say that."

In what seems like an eternity, our lips touch. Her soft lips move with mine. She tastes like home. This is where I belong. My hands move down her neck, moving slowly down her bare arms, inching their way down to the skin on her legs. I savor the touch of her smooth body.

I lower her onto the bed, moving over top of her. As my hand brushes up on her thighs, the lights blink then we're encompassed in darkness. Is the universe telling me to end this now?

I break the kiss, "do you want to stop?"

"No." she pulls me back to her lips. A spark of something so intense and powerful comes over me. I can't get close enough. My hands travel up her thighs, coming to rest at the feel of the silky fabric.

She sighs. We continue to kiss. Her hands find my shirt, and she yanks at it, trying to pull it over my head. Grabbing at the fabric, I helped her take it off. The cold air cools my heated skin.

She's fucking gorgeous laying there in the moonlight illuminating her features. She's in a Carmichael shirt; her strawberry blond hair splayed out like she's on the cover of a magazine. I move over top of her, supporting my weight on my elbows, hovering above her lips. Gently I lay a trail of kisses from her mouth following down her silky-smooth neck. Tugging at the hem of her shirt, I push it above her breast.

Even in the dark, I can see her beautiful breasts. All my senses are alive with her nearness. All I want to do is feast on every inch of her. So, I taste them, licking and pulling with my teeth until she moans with pleasure.

She bucks against me as I wander down to her panty line. Savoring every inch of her with my tongue until I reach her sweet, wet, delicious spot. My tongue laps at her.

Tasting. Licking. Exploring her in every way until her hands thrust through my hair. Her sweet little moans confirm I've hit the right spot.

As I continue my journey, my tongue never stopping, my hand roaming, she writhes against my fingers until finally she lets go and her release is the most beautiful sight I've ever seen.

Unable to look away, I watch as she falls apart. Her eyes roll, she sighs in relief, then opens her eyes and smiles.

"Oh my God," she breathes, trying to regain her breath. "Thank you," she mouths.

"It was my pleasure."

Harlow chuckles.

I cover her body with a blanket, moving to lay beside her.

"Wait, I'd like to..." I place a finger over her lips. "Not tonight. I just want to lie naked in these sheets, here in this bed with you."

As we lay here, in the dark, naked and side by side, I know there's nowhere in the world I'd rather be. I have her at my side, Luca safe in his crib. He hasn't even cried. Catching myself, I imagine a world where we get a house, one with a yard for Luca to run around. She gets her dream job as a teacher. The bar turns into a real Lake Haven staple and the place where everyone wants to be. Her parents may even accept me someday.

29

HARLOW

As we lay side by side this morning, our hands threaded together, I've never felt more loved and cared for by anyone.

He rolls onto his side, gently brushing the hair from my face. "You have no idea how much this feels like a dream."

"Do you want me to pinch you?" I tease.

"I want to kiss you." He rises to his elbow, his lips meeting mine. The kiss is slow. He takes his time like he's savoring every second, tasting me for the first time.

When he pulls away, he lands one last kiss on my forehead. "As much as I want to lie here with you all day. We need to get Luca home. We only have formula for a few more bottles."

As if he understands, Luca fusses from the crib.

The lights also take that moment to turn back on. I guess our little dream world has come to an end.

Jake jumps in the shower while I change and feed Luca. Once Jake gets out of the bathroom, we move in synchrony getting dressed, catching his eyes on me as I put on my clothes for the day and I can't help watching his muscular, slim body move and his abs ripple as he pulls a shirt over his body.

I smile as he catches me checking him out. He really is a beautiful man inside and out.

Once we're dressed and packed up, we pay our bill and thank the motel owners for their hospitality. The rain has stopped. The sidewalk is still icy, but the roads seem clear.

Since the weather is much better, Jake is following me home. "If the roads seem bad at any point, pull over and I'll drive."

"What about your car?"

"I'll come back later with Wes or Ryder and get it."

Thankfully, we make it home without any issues.

He follows me all the way to my parents' house but doesn't get out to walk me to the door. A part of me is disappointed, but I try not to make a thing of it. I'd love for him to walk into the house, and I introduce him as my new... is he my boyfriend?

We didn't put a label on it. We didn't even talk about the future. A sense of panic sets in, but I push it aside, hoping it doesn't creep back up. We have some things to discuss, but for the first time, I'm not terrified of the future.

As I enter the house, I call out, letting my parents know we're home.

My dad comes toward me from the living room. He's wearing a scowl on his face. "What have you done?"

"Excuse me?"

"Declan called. He said you broke up with him. He couldn't reach you and wanted to make sure you made it home. Thankfully, you texted us to let us know where you were and you were fine. I can't believe you let him worry like that."

"Are you kidding me?" If I could shake my father, I would.

"Don't take that tone with me. He was concerned for you and his son."

He's being ridiculous. "Believe me, he wasn't worried about me. He had other things on his mind." Or in his bed.

Setting the car seat on the ground, mom comes into the room.

"Stop all the yelling. I'm so glad you made it home in this weather. Let me have the precious little angel." She ignores me, which is normal, and grabs Luca from his carrier.

"You need to fix this with Declan. He loves you and wants you back."

"Dad, I don't want him back. He had another girl in his bed. That's the situation I walked in on when I visited him. Then he didn't care if I left upset in an ice storm with his son. He only thinks of himself."

"He explained that it was a misunderstanding. I'm sure he has a reasonable explanation. You can't give up on him. He's got major opportunities, law school, maybe the NFL. And most importantly, he's the father of your child."

"Dad, I don't love him. Please just stop this," I snap at him.

"You got yourself in trouble. You can't just walk away from your responsibilities. Your son needs a father."

"Declan hasn't acted like a father since the moment I found out I was pregnant. He was sleeping with a cheerleader. I'm not going to live my life like that. Don't you want me to be with someone who loves me, and I love them back? I don't love him."

"He said you misunderstood. I'm sure he has a reasonable explanation." He stands waiting with his hand on his hips.

"You know what? I'm finished with this conversation."

Mom comes down the steps. "What is all this yelling about?"

"I'm done talking about Declan. We broke up and that's it. We're not getting back together. We'll figure out custody and how to coparent. Now, I'm going to check on Luca and take a nap. I have a shift tonight." At least, I think I do.

I really wanted to tell my parents about Jake. He's who I want my future with, not Declan. It's too soon to drop the bomb on them. Clearly, they're in a different headspace.

"You need to quit that job too. It was a bad idea to begin with. Now you forced Declan out of the picture, your mother can help out with Luca, and you can concentrate on school."

He's not listening to a word I've said.

"I'm not going to quit. I like working there and I do have to support Luca."

"Then we aren't going to help you, anymore." He raises his voice.

"Harold!" she scolds. "We..." She cocks her head, giving my dad a 'shut up Harold' look. "We are done talking about this."

I can't remember the last time she raised her voice to him like this.

"We understand you do not want to quit, but we just want you to reach your potential. Just don't make this your career. Finish your last semester and do your student teaching then get a great job."

"Mom, that is exactly what I plan on doing."

"Good. I'll be in the kitchen. You two take a break from fighting."

My father doesn't say anything else, but he nods at me in a quiet understanding. But this is far from over.

The last thing I'm going to do is quit. Especially now since Jake and I are together. I think?

30

— · —

JAKE

The bar is busy tonight. Mindy and Mark are busting their asses, but I'm on cloud nine. Harlow is finally my girl. We can finally be together. There is so much more I need to know about her.

Now I've had a taste of her, she's all I can think about.

"Hey, bossman, we need another keg from the back," Mark yells over to me.

"I'm on it." Making my way to the storage room, Van and Ben stop me.

"We heard you almost got arrested. How'd that happen? I thought you were smarter than that." Van teases.

"I felt like such an ass. I'm sure you heard the best part, Mr. Layne?"

Callie comes up beside Ben. "Hey guys, what's up?"

"Just giving Jake a hard time about his big race against the cops." Ben chuckles.

They love giving me a hard time. I'm still kicking myself over that night. It was stupid of me to even bring her there. It wasn't supposed to be dangerous. I was just supposed to show her a small part of my life. For her to see something I enjoy and to see if she might fit into part of it. Never did I think we'd get caught by the cops and her father would be saving my ass from going to jail.

"Thank you for going to get her in the ice storm. She sounded so scared when her car spun..." Callie shivers. "Almost wrecking to see that asshole."

"We actually ended up staying in a motel room together. Luca was tired and the roads were still unsafe."

Van's eyes widened. "Seriously?"

"You heard me." I push the cloth over the bar, wiping up the non-existent liquid. Doing anything from having to look at their judgmental faces.

"So did anything happen?" Van asks, just as nosy as Callie, maybe even worse.

"No." I lied. I want to scream that we are together and I'm falling for her. I'll let her make the call about when she wants to share the news with them. She's become my whole world, yet she can wreck it too. I'm going to take this at her pace.

"Guys, why don't you go hit the pool table. I need to speak with my brother for a minute."

They nod like the good boys they are. It's funny how Ems and Callie can control them with a word or two. If I think about Harlow, she does the same to me.

"Tell me what really happened." Callie demands, pursing her mouth.

"We got a motel room. Put Luca to bed and watched a movie before the power went out, then talked a little." Or a lot.

"I know that dumbass. Did you talk about maybe going out on a date or something?"

"No." We skipped the whole first date thing and went right for the main event.

She narrows her eyes at me. "Jake Ryan Rae spill it? I know you're hiding something from me."

"Fine. We kissed. I told her I had feelings for her. She said she been feeling something for me too." Her eyebrows rise while she covers her mouth in excitement. "But don't say anything yet. It's still too early and she just got rid of Declan."

"Yes!" She grits through her teeth and gives her fist a pump. "I knew it."

"Thanks for being discreet." I roll my eyes.

"You two are so perfect for each other."

"That I'm not so sure of. Sure, I've been lucky to be around when she needed me, but I almost got her arrested. Plus, she had plans to end up with an NFL star and have a fairytale life. Not with a small-town dive bar owner moonlighting as a street drag racer. I'm not exactly the kind of guy you bring home to your father."

Callie reaches for my hand. "Yes. You. Are. I know mom wasn't a good role model and you had a hard time with Freddie and all the other fake dads, but you are nothing like them."

Just the mention of his name makes me want to punch something. She doesn't know half of what that man did to me. I endured so much through the revolving door of men my mom brought into our lives, but Freddie was an evil son of a bitch. Scrubbing at the counter with the cloth, I give myself something to do in order to get rid of the rage this conversation is generating.

"Anyway, I'm relieved she came to her senses about Declan."

I love my sister; she knows when I'm over a conversation. I'm sure Freddie's name doesn't bring up fond memories. I tried to protect her from him.

"Me too."

"I just hope he sticks around for Luca. He deserves to have his father in his life."

"Yeah." That's all I can say, because I do want that for him, but I'd be lying if I didn't want to be his father too.

Callie and Mindy take care of the remaining customers while I finish up some of the paperwork in my office.

A quick knock comes at the door.

The door creaks open a few seconds later. Wes is at the door.

"Got a minute?" he asks.

"Sure." I've never been so relieved to see him.

"What's up?" He takes a breath, like he's going to ask me something I won't want to answer.

"I have some news. It's a little out of the ordinary, but I think it's a great opportunity."

"Oh yeah?"

"How does twenty-five thousand dollars sound to you?"

"Like a fucking wet dream. So, what's the deal or should I ask who I have to rob, there has to be a catch in there?"

"The catch is we don't know what the bet is until the night of the race."

"No. It's too risky. It could be anything. The last time I was offered ten grand, I was supposed to kidnap some fraternity kid from a football game, then beat the crap out of him, and finally drop him off in the middle of the frat house yard. At least, I knew what I was going to do, and I turned it down. This could be worse."

Wes moves to sit in the chair opposite me. He's got his band T-shirt on and his leather wristbands. The telltale sign he's got a gig after he tries to convince me to race. "We won't know until we meet up with them for the race."

"Who's them?"

"Mickey from Belvedere. He hasn't raced in a few months because he's had football. His uncle helped him get a car ready. He wants to get back into it."

"Can I back out when we get there and find out what the deal is?"

"No. We automatically forfeit the money. How bad can it be?"

"Twenty-five thousand dollars bad. I don't have a good feeling about this."

"You can handle anyone or anything. We'll have more information about his car and the exact location. Once we know that, we can prepare. Come on, think of what you can do with the money?" Wes pleads, knowing I could use the money.

"When do they need to know?"

"Tonight. I'll leave here and meet up with Mickey."

Nothing about this sounds like a good idea. Every bone in my body is yelling at me to ignore him. I can do so much with twenty-five thousand dollars. Really make this bar into something special. A place I can be proud of. Put some money down on a house for Harlow and Luca. Give them a real future.

One last risky race. I can always go back to racing with Ben and Van. After almost getting Harlow arrested, I don't want to put either one of us in that position again. But one last time, one last adrenaline rush and I'll be the man Harlow and Luca deserve.

"Okay. I'm in."

31

HARLOW

I passed Wes leaving Jake's office. He gives me a big smile. "Good evening, beautiful. Did I ever tell you how much I love the effect you have on Jake."

He pecks me on the cheek, practically skipping away.

Well. Then. That was weird.

Letting myself into Jake's office without knocking, he's got his face buried in paperwork.

"I already said yes." Jake says, not looking up.

"You did. To what?"

He brushes his hair from his face, stands up and wraps me up in his arms. "God, I'm so glad to see you, beautiful."

"What was all that about? Wes was really happy with whatever happened."

"Don't worry about it. What are you doing here?"

"Mom wanted some baby time, and I wanted to see you. Also, to discuss my return to Rae's."

"I love discussing anything involving you."

"I'm serious, I want to come back. In fact," I lean in and kiss him. "I'll help you clean up and maybe stay for a bit, if it's okay with you?"

"Damn, baby. Everything you do is okay with me. Let's kick these fuckers out and head up to my room."

It takes about thirty minutes before the customers and all the other employees leave for the night.

I'm at the sink, washing dirty glasses, when Jake comes up behind me. Swiping my hair from my neck, he gently kisses my skin. Chills rush up my spine. "I love that you're here," he tells me, leaving a trail of kisses that leave me weak.

"I love it here. With you," I breathe.

His hands find my waist, pulling me close to him, I feel his length against me. He continues to nip and suck at my neck.

"You keep that up and I'll take advantage of you, Mr. Rae."

"Promise?" I can feel him smile against my skin.

His hand moves from my waist and finds the edge of my skirt. I don't usually wear skirts, but I wanted to be sexy for him. Most of the day was spent in my yoga pants changing diapers and cleaning spit up from my shirt.

Jake slides his hand along my legs. I can't help the little moan that escapes my lips.

My hands remain motionless in the water. He moves behind me, gently lowering himself as he glides his fingers down my legs, moving back up and under my skirt until he reaches in between my legs, finding my panties.

"You're so soft." His hands leave my skin. "Turn around, beautiful."

I do as he asks. I'm met with his dark eyes filled with his intense glare but it's igniting passion between us. His lips meet mine.

The passion takes over; his hands find my bottom, lifting me up. My legs automatically wrap around his waist. Jake moves us away from the sink, taking us to the other side of the counter, setting me on top of the bar.

Bottles clang as he rearranges, so we're not breaking anything.

I'm leaning back while he stands in between my legs. "You're making my fantasy come true." He says, his voice low and husky.

"What is that?" Excitement courses through me.

"Making love to you, right here. Licking every inch of you." He pushes up my skirt, tugging me toward him. "Starting here."

Jake pushes my panties aside, sliding a finger ignites a spark I've never felt.

My eyes close at the sensation of pure pleasure. I'm lost in the motion of his fingers when a flick of his tongue follows. My eyes fly open; my hands tug in his silky dark hair.

My body moves to meet his motions, to bring me closer to the release I'm seeking. Something I've never felt, something I didn't think I was capable of feeling.

A flash of heat explodes from within, and I'm brought to the brink of the most incredible feeling in my life.

Jake moves and picks me up as my faculties return. "I'm making love to you in my bed."

"Yes." I breathe. "Make me feel that again. And again." He smiles against my lips. Our tongues mesh together. He tastes like mint and a splash of liquor.

Carrying us to his bed, he gently lays me down. Removing his shirt. I can't look away as it falls off his shoulders to reveal his lean, hard muscles which ripple as he moves. Running my fingers down his strong chest and chiseled abs sends heat down my body.

Following the trail to his belt, I unbuckle with fumbling fingers eager and nervous for what's next. Not because he makes me unsure but because I want it to be perfect for him.

His hand stops mine. "Wait. Let me look at you." Jake removes my shirt along with my black and white polka dot bra, lifting up my skirt he moves to my panties. "God, you are the most beautiful woman I've ever seen." He brushes a finger over my tender scar that isn't fully healed.

"It doesn't hurt." I reassure him by answering his unasked question. "It's been well over six weeks."

Gently resting his forehead against mine, he caresses a hand just below the scar, moving his hand between my legs returning to the very spot that brought me over the edge a few moments ago. We touch every inch of each other with tenderness, appreciation, and love.

He moves to fit inside me.

It's nothing I've ever felt. It's more than I could have ever imagined I'd experience. Excitement, pleasure, and above all... love. I love this man. He is who I want to be with.

***

Lying in bed with Jake after making love, has become my new favorite activity. I'm at peace when he's near me. I'm at home.

I've got my head on his chest, the sheet is down around his waist, exposing his muscular chest, running my hands along his body as his six pack ripples. I must have touched a sensitive spot.

"Careful, I'm going to kidnap you if you keep that up."

"I won't fight back, I promise."

"There was a time you fought me on everything. Including working here. I've never seen anyone want to work at a bar so much." He chuckles while running his hands up my back before circling my shoulders.

"I thought you hated me. You would be stuck with me because of Callie, but you wouldn't say more than two words to me."

He kisses the top of my head. "I'm sorry if I made you feel that way. It's just that from the minute I met you; you've had some type of hold over me. You were taken and I'm not into taking what isn't mine."

"I'm not taken now."

Jake playfully rolls on top of me. "You are a taken woman. You're mine." He growls, then kisses me, emphasizing his point.

A rush of nerves catapult through my body. Am I ready for another relationship? Is he ready for all the baggage that comes with me? My mind starts to go off the deep end: my parents don't approve of him or my job or his business or his racing.

"What's that face for?"

"Huh?"

"Like you're unsure."

"I am."

Jake frowns, clearly not believing me.

"Don't hide from me now." he says, rubbing his nose against my cheek in a sweet gesture.

"I don't know how to tell my parents about us...you. They don't like I broke up with Declan."

"What do you think they'll say?" He watches me closely.

"That it's too soon. I can't blame them for it. It is too soon."

"Only for everyone else who doesn't know the situation. From the outside it looks like we just met but from where I'm sitting, it's been forever."

"It almost feels too good to be true."

"It's the realest thing I've ever felt. I've never had this with anyone. I'm always ready to rush them out the door; head to the bar or go to the garage to help Ben and Van prepare for a race."

"Them?"

"I've had a few ladies in my bed. My point is I've never ever felt this close to someone."

"What way is that?"

"Like I never want this to end. I don't have anywhere else in the world I would rather be."

"With a single mom who is a hot mess and has no idea what she is doing?"

"No, with a single mom who is strong, genuine, beautiful, and in the short time she has been a mom is the most amazing mother to her son."

The thickening of my throat chokes any response. I don't know what to say, so I change the topic.

"Speaking of Luca, I need to get back to him. My mom is generous with babysitting. I can't rely on her all the time. It seems the more they watch him, the more they treat me like a child."

"They are just being overprotective."

"I wish they'd be a little more protective about Declan." I sit up covering myself with the sheet. Taking a moment to breathe, I add, "I'm not going to tell them about us yet. And I need you to support me on this."

"Of course I support you."

"They still want me to forgive Declan. They aren't objective. Only thinking of their reputation. I don't want them to hate you before they even get to know you."

Kissing my forehead, he ignores my comment. "Let's get you back home to your son."

We dress in silence. An awkwardness is in the air. Looking at the clock, it's late. Is this what our time together will be like? A few stolen minutes in secret?

32

HARLOW

Luca's up every hour on the hour. I'm exhausted.

I've got to study for the final in childhood education. I start my first shift back at the bar in a few hours. I'm both excited and a nervous wreck. It's been over a week since Jake and I made love. We text every day, nothing of importance. He hasn't mentioned seeing me. Not that I've had time to see him, I'm uneasy about the way we left each other.

Jake was so quiet, lost in his thoughts. Maybe it was because I wanted to keep our relationship a secret from my parents.

I wanted to ask him what he was thinking about. I'm too afraid of what his answer will be.

Now, Declan has started to text and check up on Luca. He hasn't cared in months, all of a sudden, he's interested in how many bottles a day Luca has.

Callie is at the bar when I arrive. Luca is with my parents. This last week, I made sure I didn't use them once to babysit. They agreed to watch him until I graduate and then they expect me to get a real job.

"Damn, am I glad to see your face. Everyone is such a party pooper around here." Callie greets me with a broad smile and hug.

"Look at you, did you even have a baby? You look amazing in that outfit." I glance down, forgetting what I put on—oh yeah—jeans and a cropped Rae's Bar shirt. Nothing out of the ordinary.

"Are you sure I don't look like a zombie? Because I sure do feel like one."

She gives me a side hug; we catch up while getting the bar stocked for the night. I have yet to see Jake. It's killing me not knowing where he is. I'd love to ask Callie. I don't want her to know the extent of our relationship. Of course, I don't even know the status. He didn't put me on the schedule until tonight, and his texts were short but caring.

Declan is the only boyfriend experience I've had. If I compare his texts with Jakes – Jakes are far more attentive and appreciative of me.

***

"Harlow! Order up!" Mark calls from the kitchen. I forgot how busy it can be now that we have food on the menu. Thankfully, it makes the night go faster.

Grabbing my order from under the heat light, I take it to table three. Placing the plates in front of an older couple. Turning around to refill their drink, I'm greeted by Declan standing in my way.

"Hey," he says in almost an over joyous greeting.

Stepping around him, ignoring him, I manage to make it over to the bar.

"Do you have a minute to talk about Luca?"

"I'm working. I've been home all week. You decide to stop by my place of work in the middle of my shift? No...I don't have time."

"It'll just take a minute."

"Fine. Wait here. Let me drop off these drinks." Filling them up, and taking them back to the table, I catch Callie watching me. She mouths, "You okay?"

I nod, untying my apron, but she heads me off. "Do you want me to come with you? I don't think you should talk to him alone."

"It'll be fine. I'll talk to him in Jake's office."

I lead Declan away from Callie, knocking on the door of Jake's office, hoping he isn't hiding in there. Where the hell is he?

Knocking three times, and getting no response, I let us in. Being in his office with Declan doesn't seem right. It's like I'm doing something wrong.

Instead, I slam the door, lead him out to the hallway and then to the parking lot back exit.

"Why did you come here? You could have just texted me. There is no reason for us to see each other than when it's your turn to have Luca. Which you have yet to do," I emphasize, because he's annoying me by the crooked smile on his face.

He huffs. "I wanted to see you in person. I need to plead my case. Apologize for the way I've treated you and Luca." The sincerity in his voice takes me by surprise.

"Let's just focus on Luca. Not us. There is no us."

Taking a step closer, he says, "You can't believe that. We spent years together. Football is my career. I stupidly chose it over you and Luca. I want to change all of that. I want us to have another shot and be a family."

I want to laugh in his face. Is he serious right now? What happened between the last time I saw him and now? Did he get amnesia?

"While I appreciate what you are saying, I'm sorry. I really wanted this to work. We've been through this; we can't be together."

His eyes darken, and an expression washes over his features that sends chills up my spine. "You loved me once, right?" he says, in a deep guttural voice. "It couldn't have just disappeared." He pauses, "is there someone else?"

"No." I lie because it's none of his business. I want to be with Jake but since I haven't seen him in a week, am I really with him?

"I'm sorry." Declan's expression softens. "I really would like a second chance with you and Luca." He reaches for my hand. "I'll change. I promise."

Part of my heart cracks at the sincerity in his words not because I want to be with him but because where was this Declan when I actually wanted to be with him? He cups my face with his hand. There is no excitement, no butterflies, no tingles, nothing like when Jake touches me.

"It's over, Declan." Declan's grip tightens to the point he's squishing my cheeks together, causing a jolt of pain to my jaw.

"Declan. Let go." I say, the words are mumbled because of the grip he has on me.

In a low voice, he says, "I told you no one leaves a Mercer. From this point forward. I left you. You are an unfit mother. Look at you," he sneers. "Selling yourself in that shirt and your tits hanging out, so the local drunks can drool over you."

Declan finally loosens his grasp, but not before shoving my face away from him, causing me to stumble backward.

"Declan!" Someone says off in the distance. I briefly notice a car in the distance.

He gives me a disgusted scowl, "You'll be hearing from my lawyer. I'm taking Luca away from you."

I'm left holding my cheek, trying to digest how horribly wrong the conversation went and how I've never seen Declan react this way.

A voice calls my name.

My vision clears. Callie is holding my shoulders. Telling me to breathe.

"Come on, Harlow. Focus on the counting. One. Two. Three." Callie's voice filters through. "That son of a bitch. What did he do?"

"He. He. He's going to take Luca away from me."

33

— • —

JAKE

I'm an hour away from Lake Haven, waiting for this Mickey to show up with twenty-five thousand dollars. Wes says he just texted him. He's ten minutes away.

I've raced more opponents than I can remember, but this one feels off. Something isn't right. I feel it in my bones.

Wes has assured me he took care of the cop situation. He called in a favor with his cousin who is also a cop. That it will only be me and Mickey on this vacant back road.

"Do you have any idea how much twenty-five thousand dollars is? So, what if we don't know who we're racing? We'll still spend the money. You can beat anyone," Wes pleads.

"Don't you think we're being set up for something. I'm waiting for SWAT to show up and arrest us," I tell Wes.

He tosses his long, straight dark hair over his shoulder. He plays the part of a rock star even at a race.

It's dark and foggy tonight. An eerie haze has settled over the road. It's unsettling, almost confirming this is a horrible idea.

My car was hooked up to the computer to give it the perfect tune, new tires, and a few odds and ends to bring it up to the best possible shape for tonight's race. On a night like tonight where the weather conditions can affect the road minute by minute; whether it be from temperature to the moisture of the road, the driver is the key to success.

The road we're racing on was once part of a major highway. A new highway was built with a more direct path to the city; this road has been forgotten.

My red Mustang is fired up. I even have a helmet for tonight. Not that I don't wear them, but my gut is telling me I need some extra protection.

Wes and Ryder are here with their cars. Ready to back me up if needed, or if this bet turns into something more.

We're well over ten minutes from when they said they'd be here.

"I think we got played," I tell Wes, hoping it's true so I can get to the bar.

Harlow's first night back is tonight. We haven't spoken much. I wanted to give her some space after the last time we were together. I'd be lying if I said her not wanting to tell her parents about me didn't wreck my soul. It just confirmed what I've always known, I'm not good enough for her. The peace that surrounded us when she was in my arms withered away. I wanted to ask her more and convince her to tell them about us but part of me knows she's right; they won't ever approve of me. Hearing the words from her lips was rough.

She wants to keep me a secret and that kills me. I want to let everyone know she's mine.

"I knew this was too good of a fucking deal. Shit!" Wes slaps his hand on my open-door frame while I sit behind the wheel lost in thoughts of all things Harlow Layne.

"Let's get out of here before we get arrested or something." Ryder adds while he lights up a cigarette.

Agreeing with Ryder, I start my car, anxious to get Harlow in my arms.

Just as Wes starts to walk away, a line of cars come into view. Not just any cars, Porches, Mercedes, and even a Bentley. Fuck me, these guys came to race. Probably with daddy's money, but I guess it spends the same too.

A knot forms in my gut. What am I going to have to give up if I lose this race? My car, my bar, or who will I have to beat up? What are the stakes?

Wes comes back over. "Fuck, this is going to be good. Right? Look at those cars. You're going to win some serious cash tonight."

Wes has no idea how fast this race can go wrong. He doesn't race; he just flags and sets them up.

Deciding meeting this mystery driver will make my decision final, I exit the car.

Their cars are parked on the opposite side of the road, facing ours and shining their headlights on our cars.

Six large guys exit all three of the cars. A husky and tall group of guys. I'm tall but a bit on the skinny side.

I recognize one of them, Mickey Epson. The Epson family has been racing in this county for as long as there have been cars on the road. We are insignificant for them to race. They usually set their sights on Carmichael Racing and Ben, not a small race team like mine.

"Aren't you guys a little out of your league here?" a shaved head ogre asks.

"Let's skip the bullshit. I know who you guys are. There is no sane reason why you would waste your time on me." I can't keep the frustration from my voice.

"Let's just say I was also offered a large sum of money. If I win, I get a big payday."

"Don't worry you won't win." I promise him.

"Let's get on with it then," Mickey says, turning back to his race car.

Something isn't right. Who would pay him money to race me, and what is the end goal here? I don't have time to call Ben or Van to figure out what these guys want. Who would pay them money to race me?

My mind races through all the people. Trent would be the first guess since we ran him out of town for what he did to Callie. David might be in contention just because he's rich and I helped Van and Emerson when he gave them a problem. Would Harlow's dad have something to do with this or possibly Declan?

It doesn't matter, either way; I'll beat them. I've got this. I don't have any other choice.

We're lined up, ready to start. I'm on the see-saw of adrenaline and rage. This prick comes into my territory looking to make bank and doesn't even have the balls to tell me who and why he's coming for me. It doesn't matter who's behind this, he's mine.

There is some girl standing with a flashlight between us, ready to start the race. She's dressed in an Epson Racing tee, her jeans look as if they have been painted on. She has long fake blond hair down to her ass. Before Harlow, I would have tried to take a closer look but not now.

Annoyance radiates through me. If they think she's going to distract me from racing, they're fucking crazy. I only have eyes for Harlow. They've never seen a beauty like her.

The rules are simple; don't cross lanes and don't wreck into each other. The first car to reach the stop sign at the end of the road wins.

If Declan or Mr. Layne have anything to do with this race, I'll deal with it later. I'm not going to let this asshole beat me.

My engine revs in anticipation of the blond about to flash the light. Mickey mimics my rev. His car is going to be a beast, but I've tuned mine to perfection. On a night like this, it comes down to the road conditions and the driver.

Out of the corner of my eye, I see a nod of his helmet. I don't let it distract me. Her arm is down. He could try to go before she raises her hand; jumping the light, but I don't think he'll do that. If he's strictly racing for money, he'll want to do it by the book or he'll risk losing it.

Paying close attention, I don't let my thoughts wander any longer. I'm fixated on her arm and the flashlight. In three, two, one— the flashlight blinds me. We're off. Neck and neck. My attention's fixated on the road ahead of me while watching my gauges. Everything is where it should be.

Reaching one hundred and twenty, I easily gain a few feet on him. Tunnel vision has taken over. I see the sign ahead. The finish line is in sight; I grab another gear. The steering wheel unexpectedly jerks. A loud bang rings in my ears. Before I know it, the car's out of control, spinning, and screeching. I overcorrect the wheel hoping to regain control. It doesn't work. I'm fighting against the car. Fist over fist. My head thrashes side to side as I spin, coming to a stop.

I rip the helmet from my head. I can't see shit and can't breathe. Smoke, fuel, and dust fill my lungs.

Glancing around, the car I was racing turned in the opposite direction. He stopped, too. Several engines enter the spectrum of ringing in my ears. "Fuck." I squeeze my eyes closed, trying to get the dust out of them. I need to get out of here.

My seatbelt comes unbuckled easily. I try to open the door, it protests. Shoving my shoulder against the door, it finally releases, but not before a shooting pain knocks the air from my lungs. "Argh..."

I fall onto the ground, my knees and hands catching me. The skin on my hand ripping from the pavement with little stones digging through. Suddenly, a sharp, stabbing pain pummels my head. I grip the back of it, seeing stars.

I should have kept the helmet on. What the fuck was that?

As my vision clears, several pairs of sneakers become clear. Rolling onto my back to get a closer look, there are the assholes from the race and one of them is holding a tire iron.

"Look at the tough guy now. Piece of shit! He thought he could win. Prick." The ogre from earlier snarls. "Dec is going to be happy about this. We got the idiot to race, wreck his car, and beat the shit out of him."

"Jake!" Wes screams, but they've got him pinned down on the road.

"Get the fuck off me!" Wes yells.

"So do you want to know a secret?" Epson slouches down to my level, elbow resting on his knee. "You were never going to win or get the money. This was an ass beating deal and a message from Dec Mercer. Stay away from his family or this will seem like a Disney ride compared to the torture you're going to face."

He turns to his tribe of guys, which must be five or six. "Leave them."

I lie there, unable to get up. Head throbbing, vision blurred, and heaving onto the pavement. Car doors slam and engines start. Tires squeal, all while I lay there paralyzed by pain.

Wes and Ryder look like I feel when I look over. All of us are rubbing some parts of our bodies. "We have to get out of here before the cops come. You know those fuckers called them." Wes croaks out.

He's right. That would probably get them another couple grand for doing Declan's dirty work. Trying to get up again, my stomach rolls. I've got to get out of here. I crawl on my knees over to my car. It's smashed but it might still be drivable. With the little brain power I have left, I noticed it slammed into the telephone pole.

"Do you think you can drive it?" Ryder asks, making his way over to me.

"I'm going to try. The last thing we need is the cops." Climbing back inside the death trap, which now seems caved in a bit with a little less room, I start the engine. It turns over a few times but roars back to life.

"Fuck yeah!" Wes screams over the engine. "Let's go!"

34

HARLOW

My mind replays what happened last night with Declan. Something has shifted in him. He's scary and unhinged. I don't understand. He's the one who was cheating. Now he wants me.

Callie checked up on me what seemed like every ten minutes. I left shortly after my little altercation with Declan. Mindy even was behind the idea of me going home. She was actually human to me for a few minutes. Of course, she may have wanted to have my tips.

On the way to my parents' house, I tried calling Jake, but there was no answer. To say I'm still worried at two thirty in the morning is an understatement. I've texted him several times with no response. He was supposed to come into work. Even after I left, Callie texted me, letting me know she was leaving. I asked if Jake was okay with me leaving early and she said he never showed up.

She didn't seem worried but I am. Is he avoiding me? Are we over before we even have a chance? Or did something else happen?

Peeking over into Luca's crib, he's fast asleep, cozy in his jammies and sucking on his pacifier. At least I have the cutest little man to keep me distracted.

My thoughts wander back to Declan's behavior earlier. He isn't the same person who I've known for years. I don't know this Declan, or I guess now, Dec. Thinking back through the years, I'd be lying if I said there haven't been signs. He never had time for me and now, us. He didn't even care that he missed the birth of our son. The only things that has affected him is the fact that I work at Rae's Bar or I'm spending time with Jake.

Just as my thoughts calm and my eyes shut, my phone pings with a text. Shooting up, I waste no time to see if it's Jake.

I don't recognize the number.

> **Jake needs you. Come straight to the bar. This is Wes.**

Attached to the text is a video. I hit play, and it starts out as a race line up. Jake's car catches my attention immediately. Jake takes the lead, and within seconds the other car hits the back of his spinning Jake's car out of control. After spinning multiple times, the car door opens, and Jake falls out. I can't see his face, but I know his body. He's supporting himself with his hands and knees, gasping for air. Then the video cuts off.

Shooting out of bed, I don't even think about it. I'm coming to see him. He needs me. As I pack up a bag for Luca, I almost decide to leave Luca here, but my parents already watched him all day. I leave a sticky note on my door, letting them know I'd taken Luca, and I'd be back soon.

Before I leave, I text Jake and tell him I'm on my way.

Pulling up to the bar, I see there are two cars in the parking lot, but I don't recognize who they belong to but guess they belong to Wes and Ryder.

Luca and I walk up to the door, and it opens before I get a chance to touch it. I don't see anyone. "Hello."

"Jake?"

"He's not here. Yet." Declan's unmistakable voice travels from behind me. The sound of the door locking also enters the room. Whirling around, Declan and two other guys stand like bodyguards with their arms crossed over their chest. A wall of muscles stopping me from leaving.

"What are you doing here?" I barely squeak the words out.

"I just wanted to see what a dedicated employee you are. I think you're more than a good employee. I think you're fucking him. Why else would you come running when you saw the pussy on his hands and knees like a little bitch."

I squeeze Luca's carrier tighter, reassuring myself that he's all right. His father wouldn't put him in danger; would he?

"I can tell by the expression on your face, maybe I freaked you out a bit, huh?" I nod, still unable to form words. "I shouldn't have said those things to you or made you feel uncomfortable." He extends flowers for me to take.

"Declan, this is... why are you here of all places?" My voice cracks and damn it, I don't want to show him how much he affects me. There's no reasonable explanation why he'd be here.

"I'm sorry. I lost my temper. I just wanted a chance to apologize and to see if you'd give us another shot. But then you come running for him. He was racing for you; do you know that? I bet him twenty-five thousand dollars to stay away from you. He raced to prove he was a tough guy. But he isn't though. I'm sure you saw the video."

I don't respond to him. My whole body is shaking.

He continues to ramble on. "It's just that you working in this shit hole bar is hard for me to deal with. It's beneath you. You're a Layne not a bar waitress. I never could figure out why you wanted to work here. It's because you're fucking Rae." He narrows his eyes, as if he's trying to read my mind.

"That's none of your business. We broke up. You were cheating on me." I spit back at him. His arm jets out to grab mine, clasping my elbow instead. "It is my business. You have my son. I'm not having his mother prancing around for all the fucking losers in this town to stare at you."

His grasp tightens. His eyes darken, jaw ticks, and I swear he's grinding his teeth. He pauses, and his grasp loosens, and his features soften, but his eyes still remain trained only on me.

"I'm sorry. Please. Look, I just want to start over. My temper is getting the best of me. I just don't want you to fall for Jake's lies. He's a nobody; he's going to take you down with him."

He's scaring me. His flip flopping of emotions is freaking me out and not to mention there are still two of his friends standing guard by the door. Even though I'm a nervous wreck and don't trust Declan's next move; I try to be a little nicer, but I still want to come across sternly.

"Declan, you can't tell me where to work and who to be friends with. Besides, if you cared about me, you wouldn't have cheated on me – you did. I can't forgive that, nor do I want to. There just isn't a future for us. You know it, or you wouldn't have cheated on me." Trying to soften the conversation, I touch his arm. "We will be friends so we can coparent Luca."

He yanks his arm away. "Coparent. You're fucking crazy if you think I'll let you take my son away from me." He grits through his teeth. "And let me tell you something else, that fucking loser just raced for money. I set him up. He raced for twenty-five thousand dollars, and he agreed to leave you alone."

"What are you talking about?"

"He only cares about money. You mean nothing to him. He gave you up." Snapping his fingers, he says, "Like that."

"He wouldn't do that."

"So, you are seeing him, or you wouldn't be so upset?" He seems to be talking to himself. His face darkens; the same intense jaw ticking returns. His arms jet out, shoving me up against the wall.

"Declan. Don't!" In a swift motion, he grasps my free forearm.

"He isn't going to win you. Do you understand? He isn't going to take you away from me. I won't lose to him."

He's unraveling before my eyes. A strength -- more like rage, deep inside of me rises. I somehow manage to push him away. I won't let him treat me like this anymore. He isn't going to intimidate me ever again.

"Get off me." I shove him again. I don't budge him, but at least he releases me.

"No one leaves me. Do you understand that?" The venom in his voice sends chills all the way to my core, chilling me from the inside.

"Declan. Let her go!" Jake's voice booms from behind me.

Whirling around, Jake moves toward me, but one of Declan's goons stops him. Throwing him up against the wall; restraining him. The guy is twice the size of Jake and has his forearm against Jake's throat. His face is red. He's trying to push the guy away.

"Declan. Stop this."

"Nah. He thinks he's tough. Let's see how tough he is." Declan struts past me and the other friend of Declan stands beside me. I try to get to Jake, but the guy grabs my arm, stopping me in place. I grasp Luca's car seat tighter and closer to my chest. I have to protect him.

Luca fusses in his seat. I shush him as Declan punches Jake in the stomach. "Stop!" I yell.

"Harlow. It's okay." Jake says, from across the room. "Stay put and do what he says."

The asshole holding me, pulls me back. "Listen to your lover boy. Stay put. We aren't going to hurt you or the kid."

What seems like slow motion, Declan unleashes a few more punches as his friend holds Jake in place. Jake spits blood from his mouth. I want to run to him, but I can't move from my spot. I have to shield Luca from his monster of a father.

"Declan. Please stop. I'll quit. Okay?" He gives Jake a final punch to the face. Jake's eyes roll to the back of the head. Declan's goon lets go of him as Jake drops to the ground.

Unconscious.

"No one leaves me. Do you understand? Especially not a whore like you. I'm taking Luca from you. You'll never see him again. He's mine." Spit hits my cheek as I struggle to hold on to Luca's carrier.

I can't fight him. He's too strong and his friend yanks me in the opposite direction, loosening my grasp on Luca's carrier.

Before I can stop them. They have Luca.

The door slams behind them and Luca is gone.

35

JAKE

My head is screaming. I'm trying to open my eyes but it's so blurry. Her scream cuts through the fog.

Harlow.

"He's gone!"

Harlow. She's frantic.

Feeling around, the hard tile under my fingers register. The memory of the beating I received pushes through. I need to get up. Who's gone?

My eyes open, and Harlow's long strawberry blond comes into view as she sits on the bar floor. Her face supported in her hands. She's shaking and crying. I slide on the floor over to her. "Harlow."

She launches herself into my arms. "They took him," she cries. "He's gone."

My mind clears at her words. Those fuckers took Luca. I couldn't protect them. My worst fear. I couldn't protect my mother or sister and now I let Harlow and Luca down.

Ben and Van come barging through the door. "What the hell?" Van asks.

"Declan took Luca." I say and part of me dies. I don't think I've ever felt this type of paralyzing fear.

***

Mrs. Layne rubs Harlow's back as she explains to the police officer what happened. She can barely say the words without choking up. Tears haven't stopped streaming down her face. My heart is shredded for her. I failed her. I failed him.

I want to be the one to comfort her, but I can't bring myself to be the one to console her. I should have fought harder. I shouldn't have raced.

"Jake?" Mr. Layne comes up from behind me.

I nod.

"You need to explain to me your side of this. How do you fit into this?"

I fucked up, that's how. But I love his daughter more than anything.

"I failed her." Is all that comes to the surface.

"We all did. I wanted her to try and stick it out with Declan and that bastard..." he doesn't finish the sentence.

"No, sir. I couldn't stop him. It's my fault. He had it all planned. I fell right into his trap. One last race."

"From what my daughter told me, you tried. You can't fight off three linebackers, son. No matter how tough you think you are, but an offensive line is another thing."

Harlow comes over and wraps her arms around me. Holding her tight, I run my hands down her silky hair. I try to hush her cries.

"How do I get him back? He's his father."

The police officer comes over to us. I've never seen this officer before. He's a bit on the hefty side. I'm not sure he could run me down if he needed to. He's got a cup of coffee in his hand, casually sipping as he talks. "He's listed on the birth certificate so at this point without a custody order we cannot deem this as a kidnapping situation."

"He took him from my arms, trapped me here, and assaulted him. He has to face some repercussions." She wipes away her tears. Her voice is laced with confusion.

"You can't let him get away with this. Since when is what he did legal?" I add.

"Mr. Mercer has an impeccable reputation, and this is all just hearsay at the moment. Until we question him, I'm afraid there's nothing more I can do. You'll have to go to a lawyer and make custody arrangements." He takes another sip of his drink as if he's talking about the weather, not about a child being ripped from his mother's arms.

"The fuck he does. Didn't you hear a word we said, or can't you see the bruises all over my face or on her wrist? Can't we press charges for assault?"

"I don't see any evidence. You don't have security cameras to prove your claims. For all I know, you got in an altercation with someone else. You do have a reputation for getting in fights over those race cars. By the way, there was a report of an accident in the neighboring county and it's the description of your race car."

This prick has to be under Mercer's payroll. Nothing coming out of his mouth makes logical sense.

"You're a dick," I tell him.

He smirks. "You keep that up and you'll be leaving here in handcuffs."

Mr. Layne places a hand on my shoulder. "Calm down. Harlow needs your help."

As the police cleared the bar and left us with no help.

Luca isn't my son, but I've been with him more than Declan, and my heart is breaking. I put him in danger. I was too weak from my own injuries to stop him from being ripped from his mother's arms. I chased the cash, risking all I love.

I'm going to get Luca back and make this right. I have no idea how I'm going to make it happen.

We are all at a loss. The cops have been of zero help. Mr. Layne was on the phone with a lawyer who specializes in child custody cases. There is nothing we can do at the moment because he is listed on the birth certificate, and she hasn't filed any custody paperwork. So, it's her word against his. Which seems one hundred percent ridiculous.

"I miss my baby." Harlow murmurs into her hands, wrecking me into a million pieces. How could Declan just rip Luca from her arms?

We can't just sit here and do nothing. I texted Ben and Van to bring the girls and get over to the bar ASAP. I have no idea what we're going to do but sitting here doing nothing isn't it either.

We fill in Callie, Ems, Ben, and Van on all the information we have. We're sitting around the table going back and forth on how to get into the Mercers house and get Luca back.

"We can't just go steal him back. That will never be held up in court. We need to do this legally, or it won't stick," Emerson says.

"What the hell are we supposed to do, just let him have Luca? No, the fuck we are not!" Callie practically shoots out of her chair.

"We do need a plan. Short of waiting to petition the court, what can we do?" Emerson tells her and places a hand on her shoulder. Probably trying to calm her down. I glance over at Harlow who is staring out the window, lost in her own thoughts.

"What about Declan's parents? They can't be supporting this kind of behavior?" Van asks, while his hand rubs Emerson's back.

"My father tried calling them. No answer. Besides, they aren't going to side with me." Harlow tells us, in a low, shaky voice.

Mr. Layne is still on the phone. We have no idea who he's talking to.

"Do you want to go home?" I ask her, she needs to lie down and get some rest.

"No, but I don't know what else to do."

The tears in her eyes along with the way she's hugging herself has me on edge. I'm worried about her. I take her in my arms, rubbing my hand up and down her back. Peeking over her shoulder, I see Callie on the phone.

She's waving her arms, animated as ever. I wonder who she's talking to.

After another half an hour, we decide to leave the bar. Just as Callie goes to open the door for everyone, Gran and a man in his pajamas walk through the door.

"Gran? What are you doing here?"

She has her walker, gingerly taking a step while the mystery guy helps her by the shoulder.

"Thank you, Russ. You've always been such a good kid."

Kid? He's like fifty. He's balding and what hair he has left is gray.

"Now honey, don't you cry anymore. We'll make sure Luca comes back to you tonight," Gran promises Harlow. Harlow goes straight into her arms.

"Gran, who is this guy?" I ask, not wanting to deal with her shenanigans. I wouldn't be surprised if she yanked some lawyer out of his bed while he was sleeping. Harlow let's go of Gran, stepping back into my arms.

I'm happy she's back in mine but annoyed at Gran.

"This guy is Russ Rogers, Poland University's Dean. He used to work here in the summers at this bar while he was putting himself through college. We've kept in touch over the years. His oldest just got married…"

"Poland University? He knows Declan?" Harlow's voice is a whisper.

"Yes, I do," Dean Rogers answers. "Your Grandmother called me. I knew it had to be important. I was worried that something might have happened to her. She told me about Declan, and I called his parents immediately. They will be here shortly."

"You spoke with them? We've been calling all night." I say, not understanding what the hell is happening.

"I simply explained to the Mercers what would happen to Declan's scholarship and his football career if we found out he did in fact kidnap his own son from his mother. They thought it was his night to keep your son. I explained that it wasn't the case. Now that I have a complaint about Declan, I told them I'd have to look into these allegations," Dean Rogers explains.

Harlow sighs in relief, "Oh my God. Thank you." She runs out of my arms, wrapping the Dean in a big hug.

He rubs her back, shushing her. "You're welcome. You'll have your son soon."

He's right, within ten minutes, the bell above the door jingles. A couple sharply dressed for the middle of the night walk into the bar. The woman is holding Luca's carrier. Harlow is frozen at my side.

"Dean Rogers, we had no idea he wasn't supposed to have Luca tonight. We don't want this to be held against him. Harlow, you can have Luca back," the guy says, handing Luca over to Harlow.

Harlow moves beside me, taking the carrier, unbuckling Luca from the seat. She runs her hands over him, checking him over. Next thing

I know is that he's in her arms. She's holding him close to her, cheek to cheek.

"My baby. Oh... my baby, I'm so sorry," she cries.

"Thank you for bringing him home so quickly," Gran says, in a polite manner.

"Once again, Declan thought he could have his son this evening," Mr. Mercer, I assume, lies straight to our faces.

"He knew he couldn't have him. He hasn't given a shit about him since he was born. He just doesn't want to give up his football career. Football is all that matters to him, not his son." I let everyone know what a piece of shit Declan is. "Where is he?"

Mr. Mercer answers, "Declan returned to school. Now this misunderstanding is cleared up, we can forget this little ordeal got out of hand."

"You're just going to let him get away with the way he treated Harlow and ripping the baby from her arms?" I say, taking a step forward, ready to fight if I need to.

"No. We are not." Mr. Layne says with fierceness. "He needs to face the consequences of his actions. He can't put my daughter through hell and expect us to just forget."

"Declan has agreed to give up all parental rights to Luca. He's proven he's not ready to be a father. It's better for everyone if they cut ties." He pulls a thick packet of paper from inside his jacket pocket. "But Harlow will also have to agree to not seek monetary compensation in the future. They can go their separate ways. No contact," Mr. Mercer adds, laying them on a table beside us.

Mr. Layne takes a step toward the paperwork, snatches it up, and reads it over. His eyes dart back and forth, giving nothing away. We all wait to see what the next step is. Harlow hasn't moved or said a word. Her attention is only on Luca.

After a few seconds more, Mr. Layne says, "If Harlow agrees to these terms, you will never see Luca again. He is not a Mercer and won't ever be. Ever."

Placing my arm around her shoulder, I say, "Is that okay with you?"

"Yes. I don't need or want anything from him," Harlow says with determination and a fierceness that is unmistakable. "I want to take my son home."

In awe of her, I watch as she walks toward the door.

***

When we arrive at the Laynes, I'm welcomed to their home. I never thought I'd be here, like this... greeted with a smile and a glass of water in hand. I've got a wicked headache from my injuries, but I've never mentally been better.

"Please, make yourself at home," Mr. Layne says, motioning his hand towards the fanciest couch I have ever seen. "I know you've had a rough." He points at my head.

"Yeah. I'll be all right." It hurts but once Harlow's in my arms, it won't matter.

Mrs. Layne and Harlow are upstairs, settling Luca in bed for the night.

"Thank you, sir." I say, as I take a seat. It's as if the heater has been turned on to its highest setting. My hands are clammy as I rub them down the pants covering my legs. He has a small glass of what I can tell is whiskey.

"Son, Jake, I'm sorry for my actions against you." He doesn't look up from his glass, but the expression on his face is pained. "You've done nothing but shown loyalty and responsibility when it comes to

Harlow and my grandson. I've been giving praise to the wrong person because I thought he was best for her." Mr. Layne looks up from his glass and reaches his empty hand toward mine. "I give you my blessing to date my daughter because you are who's best for the both of them."

***

Harlow

Luca's safe in his crib. I've moved it closer to my bed so I can hold his hand through the rails of the crib while I lay in my bed next to him. I won't let anything, or anyone hurt him again.

I can't describe the terror I've felt for the last few hours. Not knowing what was going to happen to Luca. Not knowing what Declan might do to him. If I'd ever see him again. What was going through his head when he ripped Luca from my arms? He's a monster.

Thank God Callie called Gran. Of course, she didn't know Gran would know the Dean of Poland University, no one could have guessed.

It amazes me how easily he gave up his rights to his son. And how his parents did the same to their grandson. Just gave up on some college football career. He'll never see him grow up, be a part of his life. After today, I am one hundred percent fine with it. I'll give him everything he needs.

My father had a lawyer friend of his that specializes in these types of custody cases read over the document to make sure it was iron clad to protect Luca and myself from any future contact from him. If he tries to contact him in the future, we will face that hurdle.

A knock at the door pulls me away from staring at the chubbiest little cheeks that are my world.

"Come in."

Jake slips the door open, peaking his head inside. "Hey."

Sitting up, I motion for him to crawl beside me by lifting the blanket and inviting him to lie in bed with me. Slipping off his leather jacket, he lets it fall to the ground while slipping off his boots. He doesn't say anything but glances over to Luca.

Jake melts my heart, giving me hope Luca will have a father figure in his life. Someone to show him how to be a man. A good man.

The bed dips. He slides in beside me, wrapping his arms around me. Peace washes over me. "Thank you," I whisper.

He kisses my hair. "I'm so sorry you had to go through this."

"Gran saved my son. I owe her everything." I swipe away the millionth tear from my eyes.

"It's crazy how life works out. She's so happy she could help in some way." He brushes his hand through my hair. "He looks so peaceful sleeping. Did you get any sleep?"

I roll over to face him. His eyebrow wrinkles, drawing together. Trying to release the tension, I brush a hand over his forehead. "I did. Probably too much. Did my dad let you up to my room?" I can't believe he's here, in my house, in my room.

"We had a little talk." He swallows. "I told him I'd do anything to protect you and Luca and... that I love you. Harlow." His eyes glance above my head. "You don't have to say it back or feel the same. I want to take care of you and Luca. I know you don't need me to, but I want us to be a family."

Reaching for his chin, I gain his attention, making him look into my eyes so that he can listen and understand what I'm going to say to him.

"I don't want you to take care of me. I want us to take care of each other. I love you too, Jake. It seems crazy I wasted all this time on Declan. But I wouldn't have Luca. He will always be my priority. You've proven that he's yours too."

His jaw ticks as he takes in my words. "I'll always make Luca and you, my priority. I hope I can make you proud. I want to give you everything you've ever dreamed of. I'm just not sure it'll be enough."

Rolling on top of him so that he'll understand. "I don't need you to be anything other than who you already are. I'm okay with whatever the future holds for us."

"What do you think that holds for us?"

"Everything and anything we want."

THE END

36

EPILOGUE

It's Harlow's Graduation. She's had some delays graduating on her
timeline but there she is standing at the podium in her cap and
gown giving the opening ceremony speech looking more beautiful
than I've ever seen her.

Her smile is infectious. Everyone's under her spell. I know the
feeling.

I never thought I'd be here with her like this. Sitting next to her
parents, holding their grandson in my arms. He's clapping for his
mama. He's almost a year old and is well on his way to taking his first
step.

Luca stands on my thighs, his hands clutching together. "Come
on, Luca. Let's clap for mommy!" I say, while guiding his hands in a
clapping motion. It takes him a few seconds, then he's off on his own,
showing his mama he's proud and excited for her even though he has
no idea why. But I do.

I couldn't be more proud of her. She's overcome so many chal-
lenges. She's finished school, found a job, makes her own money, and
above all, is the best mother I know.

This morning, we had a little talk. Luca was eating his breakfast of
scrambled eggs and pancakes while I told him about my plan of asking

his mom to move in with me. Callie and Ben have moved into a larger house a few blocks away, and I've purchased their house.

I'm going to ask her tonight.

Mr. And Mrs. Layne have been guarded but they accept us a couple. Harlow still works at the bar, but she's got a teaching position at the local elementary school next year. Kindergarten.

Her plans are all coming together, now it's time to make mine fit into hers.

***

Harlow

My graduation day has been perfect. My parents wanted to have a big party to celebrate but I just wanted a small family dinner. We've cleaned up the dishes and are sitting outside around the small firepit my dad made. He's so proud of the circle of bricks he built to hold the fire.

Luca's in bed, and I have the baby camera aimed at him so that I can see his every move. Jake sits beside me, holding my hand. My dad hands him a beer and sits down beside him.

What a difference time makes. My parents have grown to like Jake. Once Declan showed his true colors, they finally saw the wonderful person Jake was to me and Luca.

I haven't heard a peep from Declan or his parents. And that is fine with me. I'm sure as Luca gets older, he'll want to know his father, but we'll cross that bridge. I'm not opposed to Luca having a relationship with him, but I want it to be under my terms. He must understand that he can't play with my son's emotions just to suit his own motives.

As we sit around the fire, I bask in the peace of the night. Jake and my dad talk about what it takes to keep a fire burning. I laugh to myself; this wasn't on my bingo card last year.

My parents leave after a half an hour or so and it's just Jake and me.

"I've got some news." Jake pulls me from my thoughts, grabbing my hand, and placing a key in my palm.

"What is this for?" I ask, he's wearing his infamous smirk laced with excitement.

"I know you wanted to buy a house on your own but with Ben and Callie moving, they offered me to buy their house. So, I did."

"You bought a house?"

"I did and I want to know if you and Luca would want to live there with me and eventually marry me?" he asks, his voice is quiet and almost shy.

I don't even need to think about it. He is all I see in my future.

"Yes!" I practically scream.

He takes my face in his hands and presses his lips to mine then pulls away. His face turns serious, and my stomach twists. "What?" I ask cautiously.

"I have one condition..." he pauses, changing the air around us. "I would like to adopt Luca. I want to be his father in every way possible."

Tears prick my eyes. He loves me and my son. He makes us his... everything.

"Yes, a million times yes to marriage, to the house, and to being Luca's father."

Jake wraps me in his arms, and we spend the rest of the night planning our future.

37

— · —

FOLLOW TRISHA

I 'd love to hear from you! Follow Me!

To sign up for updates and my newsletter, go to https://ww
w.trishamadley.com

Website: https://www.trishamadley.com

Facebook: https://www.facebook.com/trishamadley

Facebook Group - Madley's Mob

Tiktok: https://www.tiktok.com/trishamadleybooks

Instagram: https://www.instagram.com/trishamadley

Pinterst: https://www.pinterest.com/trishamadley

38

—•—

More Books

LAKE HAVEN SERIES
BEAUTIFULLY RESTORED

Forced into a loveless marriage due to a business deal, Emerson has always done what was expected of her. Even if that means submitting to her controlling husband and his vindictive family.

Yet when she is ordered to oversee a car restoration at a shop on the other side of the country - she meets mechanic, Donovan Bradley. The chemistry between them is instant and undeniable. Beneath his rough exterior and bad boy ways; Emerson finds a kind-hearted man, full of compassion and a protective nature she's never experienced before. It doesn't take long for him to become everything she never knew she wanted.

But can their love survive the wrath of her husband? Or will his family's malicious agenda destroy their chance at happily ever after?

Fans of forbidden romances sprinkled with the spiciness of opposites attracting are sure to love Beautifully Restored by Trisha Madley!

BEAUTIFULLY BUILT

Callie Rae developed a crush on her brother's best friend, Ben Carmichael, when she was only eight. At eighteen, he broke her heart.

When she gave him another chance, it ended in a heart-wrenching goodbye.

She thought when he moved to Las Vegas to drag race cars she would finally get the chance to get over him, but now he's back in Lake Haven with a secret.

Callie sought solace in the arms of Trent Harrison, Ben's racing rival. Still, her heart refuses to move past her first love. Little does she know Ben had a reason to leave town he never revealed.

Now, as the truth comes to light and his heart longs for the one who got away. Can he convince Callie they are meant to be? Or will the pain of the past ruin their chance at a happy future?

THE WITH YOU SERIES

Safer With You- Book One –

Nora Skye must start her life over again. She notices that her boyfriend Luke has become distant and secretive, leaving her with no other choice than to spy on him.

When Luke learns of what she has done, he discards her. Forcing her back home. Upon her arrival, she attends her sister's wedding where she meets the sexy, charismatic, and outrageously out of her league Jase Madsyn.

She knows his reputation, the mystery that surrounds him, but that doesn't stop her from experiencing the best night of her life. But she soon discovers that he may be the person responsible for her pain.

FEARLESS WITH YOU - Book Two –

Nora Skye has survived the unimaginable. Now that the chaos has settled, she is free to enjoy her new life, with the man who saved her in more ways than one—Jase Madsyn.

Jase killed the man who hurt Nora, but now new obstacles arise. His career starts to wear on their relationship, but the problems don't end there when Samantha, his ex-fiancée, shows up with a surprise of her own, and his mother disappears without a trace.

Nora tries to be supportive, but too many secrets cause their fragile relationship to crumble. Can their love survive his secrets...but most of all, his pa

39

ACKNOWLEDEMENTS

I want to thank my girls, Madison and Hayley. I write so that they know whatever they want to do in life, no matter how challenging, they can accomplish it.

To my mom, no words will ever be enough to express the strength she has shown throughout her life, but I've learned so much from her. Love you, Mom, and I'm so proud of you.

To Nana, thank you for being the first person to read my books, and helping me become the person I am. May you be dancing in Heaven with Grandpa Joe.

Kathy Blinkiewicz, my second mom, who is the best Trisha Madley book promoter and one of my biggest fans! Thanks for all you do for me.

Amy Dobbs is a wonderful author, and the proofreader of *Fearless With You, Beautifully Restored, and Beautifully Built.* Thank you for the countless things you did to help make these books possible. I can't wait to see your books in print.

My beta readers: Lane Mercer, Amy Dobbs, and Rebecca Boothe.

To Jason, the love of my life, my partner and best friend. Thank you for supporting my passion.

Most of all, to you, my readers:

Thank you to all of you who have read and purchased *Safer With You* and *Fearless With You and Beautifully Restored, and Beautifully Built.* I can't tell you how much it means to hear people ask me, "When is your next book available?" Thankfully, I can finally answer, "Today!"

ABOUT THE AUTHOR

Trisha felt she had a story inside her to add to the list of self-published authors, so she put herself to the test, and Safer With You was born. She now has five published books! She loves to write, read and design teasers and other graphics for books.

She is mom, wife, and has two fur babies.

Visit Trisha at https://www.trishamadley.com